Praise for Shelli Stevens's *Savage* Series

"The author of this story has combined a smolderingly sensual love story with an action-packed suspense novel and has done a great job with both."

~ *Coffee Time Romance*

"A good read that promises more stories from this world in the future."

~ *Night Owl Reviews*

"The first book in the Savage series, *Savage Hunger*, has lots of intrigue and emotional ups and downs... I am looking forward to the next book in this series."

~ *Literary Nymphs Reviews*

"*Savage Hunger* was fast paced and exciting, with interesting plot twists and turns, good chemistry between Warrick and Sienna, and hot, steamy love scenes. I would recommend *Savage Hunger* to lovers of both romantic suspense and paranormal romance, as it was a great combination of both."

~ *Sizzling Hot Book Reviews*

Look for these titles by

Shelli Stevens

Now Available:

Trust and Dare
Theirs to Capture
Four Play
Foreign Affair

Seattle Steam
Dangerous Grounds
Tempting Adam
Seducing Allie

Chances Are
Anybody but Justin
Luck be Delanie
Protecting Phoebe

Savage
Savage Hunger
Savage Betrayal

Holding Out for a Hero
Going Down
Command and Control
Flash Point

The McLaughlins
Good Girl Gone Plaid

Print Anthologies
Chances Are
Holding Out for a Hero

Savage Betrayal

Shelli Stevens

Samhain Publishing, Ltd.
11821 Mason Montgomery Road, 4B
Cincinnati, OH 45249
www.samhainpublishing.com

Print ISBN: 978-1-61921-506-1
Digital ISBN: 978-1-61921-256-5

Editing by Tera Kleinfelter
Cover by Kanaxa

First Samhain Publishing, Ltd. electronic publication: November 2012
First Samhain Publishing, Ltd. print publication: October 2013

Acknowledgments

Thanks to my family, friends and readers for your wonderful support. To my editor, Tera, and my niece, Megan, for being the eyes on this book. And thanks to my martial arts buddy Bob Crouch for some excellent fighting advice.

Chapter One

Someone was on her property.

Despite the massive heat from the glass-blowing furnace in front of her, an icy chill swept through Grace's body. It faded into anger that coiled quickly through her limbs, tightening her muscles as disbelief pounded in her blood.

How? How had someone made it through without tripping any alarms? No average human could've done that.

Which is exactly why he'd succeeded. He wasn't average. He wasn't even fully human. Whoever was stalking her house was just like her. Their genetic abnormality meant they were part of a species that most of the world's population was oblivious to—would be incapable of comprehending. It also made them highly elusive.

But she knew exactly what he was—this person on her property, and the knowledge that he was one of her own kind offered little comfort. Maybe once it might have, but not anymore.

He made no attempts to hide what he was, or his arrival at her isolated home a half hour outside of Seattle.

The son of a bitch. Her fury expanded, growing as hot and threatening as the fire she'd been using to create her glass sculptures.

For a moment she considered using the blowpipe in her hand as a weapon, but decided it might hinder more than help. With steady hands, she laid it down and turned off the furnace before rushing back to flick off the lights in the garage.

Whoever was approaching the building might want the element of surprise—like hell would she let him have it. He should know better than to think he'd have that advantage.

Even if he'd deftly avoided all her little traps and alarms, she would never be a sitting duck.

Grace moved to the window, tugging the curtain aside just enough to peer out into the chilly autumn morning. The sunrise left streaks of pink in the sky and the fog outside curled its heavy fingers through dense evergreen trees, past the rotting wood of her fence some fifty feet away. It left patches of her property in shadow and gaping open areas where there was nowhere to hide.

And yet he did. Though she couldn't immediately spot the intruder, she knew he was there. Watching. Waiting to make his next move. She could smell the scent of his confidence and determination.

Come any closer, you bastard, and I'll shove that self-assurance so far up your ass...

How fucking *dare* he come onto her property? She would never again be a victim. Been there, done that, and had the nearly faded scars to prove it.

The dark memories, still so fresh, so raw, threatened to bubble to the front of her mind, but she ruthlessly shoved them back. They were better hidden away, not to be dwelled on or psychoanalyzed...

She almost missed the blur of movement as the person leapt stealthily above the silent alarm she had rigged at the far end of her yard.

Her heart thumped and her shoulders went rigid.

Shit. Shit. *Shit.*

Grace dropped the curtain back into place. There were several more alarms and traps set to slow someone down, but she knew he'd avoid them just as deftly as the ones he'd already passed.

Who was he? The question raced through her mind as she went to the metal garbage can in the corner and jerked off the lid. Guns, knives, and perhaps the underestimated baseball bat, were all among her choices in weapons.

Though the idea of taking her Louisville Slugger to this

shifter's head had appeal, it was along the lines of the blowpipe. Not quite what she needed. Instead, Grace pulled out the Glock and removed the safety before slipping up against the wall beside the side door to the garage.

Whoever had snuck onto her ranch wasn't looking to steal her Eclipse out front—they'd come for her. She knew it with a certainty that gave her the calm and determination to face this head-on.

The birds that had been chirping outside went ominously silent. Grace turned her head and stared at the door.

He's here.

She waited for him to break in, for some kind of dramatic entrance so that she could pull the trigger. Seconds ticked by. Slow. Menacing. Making the clouds of fear she'd kept at bay threaten to seep back in.

Her training kept her completely still and kept every one of her heightened senses on the alert. She drew in slow, deep breaths to keep calm.

But it was hard. Because with each breath drawn in came the image of what could potentially happen. Soon he'd be inside, and if she didn't successfully defend herself she'd be at his mercy.

Memories assailed her. Being grabbed. Held down.

She tried to shake the image from her head. But her throat closed up as she could almost feel the prick of the needle again. And then hell. Pure hell. The present vanished as she was completely sucked into her reality from two months ago.

You think you'll be free when you leave here? I'll find you again, Grace, and I'll make you pay.

She always wondered if the threat from a shadowed male figure had been real, or a dream. Today it seemed she'd find out.

Bile rose in her throat, and her hands—a moment ago so steady—began to shake.

If she'd learned anything, it was that she had to focus. *Had to fight.*

There was the smallest thud outside the garage and Grace pulled the trigger. Four times. The bullets splintered the wood and pierced through the door, but there was no answering sound of pain or shock from outside.

Son of a bitch, how had she missed?

The door burst open and Grace lurched forward, desperate to shove him back out. Instinct screamed at her to keep him at bay. But he pushed back harder on the door, and her sneakered feet skidded on the cement floor as she was thrust back into the garage and toward the wall.

Grace let go of the door and struggled to regain her balance. Darkness hid his features, but she lifted her gun at the silhouette of the man who filled her doorway.

Her finger just brushed the trigger before the gun was knocked fiercely from her hands and clattered across the floor.

No.

"Stop shooting," the male voice rasped.

Something registered. That the voice was familiar, but rational thought disappeared as her assailant grabbed her around the waist and dragged her against him, forcing her body against a solid wall of muscle and man. Her scream of rage started to morph into terror, and she increased her energy in fighting him.

Despite the strong fingers that manacled her wrists, she tried to use her elbows to drive into his ribs, but he quickly subdued her. He put her into a position that made her helpless to fight back.

"Stop fighting me, Masterson."

Even as realization clicked into place at what he was—exactly *who* he was, she knew she'd failed. She'd completely *choked.* And this was so much worse than if he *had* been an intruder with a sinister purpose.

"Take a deep breath." The rough, familiar voice of her fellow P.I.A. Agent confirmed his identity. Darrius Hilliard.

Oh God. Grace went limp against him and bit her lip, unable to hold back her sob of frustration. Of relief.

He held her for just a moment, his arms closing around her almost in comfort, and she instinctively melted into him and clung to him. He was safe, not some bastard who'd come to hurt her.

"You're okay." His gruff voice soothed, and the hand moving down her back reassured. "Just...hang on a moment."

And then he let her go so he could move away, and her legs could no longer support her.

Grace sank to her knees, burying her face in the palms of her hands. Her breathing was still erratic and shaky. The seconds ticked by and her pulse slowed once more, and she came fully back to reality as he turned the lights on.

Agent Hilliard's footsteps approached once more, but she resisted the urge to look up. She couldn't bear to see him staring down at her with pity and shock.

This was bad. This was really bad. Tears burned behind her closed lids and she drew in another ragged breath.

She'd always been so composed, so determined to prove herself as an agent and keep her shit together. Being new, and the only female on their team, she'd worked her ass off to earn their respect. And she'd had it, until she'd made one fateful choice.

And now Agent Hilliard had seen her like *this*. Vulnerable. Paranoid. Weak. It had been a reaction left over from the emotional trauma of the experiments. Understandable, she could rationalize that, but humiliating all the same.

Dammit, why had he come here today? Why now?

Get yourself together, Grace.

She slowed her breathing and waited until the tears that threatened finally dissolved. Then, forcing her expression into complete indifference, she lifted her head from her hands.

Agent Hilliard's expression was definitely not one of pity. He didn't even look uncomfortable. Instead there was a gleam of amusement in his dark, coffee-brown eyes, and his mouth was curved into a smirk that had her blinking in dismay.

"Hey, Masterson, while you're down there..."

"W-what?" And then she realized the suggestive position she was in—on her knees in front of him.

"Oh, go to hell." But her words held no sting, because she was too relieved he wasn't going to treat her with kid gloves. He wasn't walking on eggshells or looking at her like she was going to break. Even if they both knew she'd been dangerously close to it.

His grin widened and he let out a laugh that resonated in the small garage. She took the hand he held out to her, because having this conversation on her knees wasn't doing much for her dignity. Or what she had left of it.

There was no assisting her to her feet. He simply pulled her right up off the floor as if she weighed no more than a blow-up doll.

She stumbled to keep her balance and then gave a brisk nod of thanks. "A pity you didn't call first, Agent Hilliard. I would've skipped the part where I tried to blow your head off."

Hilliard shook his head and made a *tsking* noise. "I did call. Twelve times in the last three days."

Yes, he had. Guilt sent a flush of hot color into her cheeks and she slid her gaze away from him.

"I apologize, I've been having trouble with my phones."

"Is that so?"

No. They both knew she was lying, but he obviously wasn't going to call her out on it. Besides, it was her choice to answer or not answer the phone, and she'd chosen not to plenty of times in the last couple of months.

As the silence stretched on, she finally turned her gaze back to him. There was no judgment in his eyes, only a subdued scrutiny.

She took a moment to do a little scrutinizing of her own. Who had sent Agent Hilliard today?

Like her, Darrius was an agent who worked for the Preternatural Investigation Agency. A secret government agency that protected and enforced the law within a secret species of humans who had the ability to shift into wolves.

They were both on the same elite field op team. He'd always been the agent to crack the jokes and ease the tension. Even when they were all hungry, dirty, frozen with cold, Hilliard had a way of making it feel like it was a day at the fair.

He wasn't mated and was notorious for flirting with the female agents. And, well, most women he came into contact with. And the women flirted back, almost like they couldn't help themselves. He had a smile and laugh that put people at ease, and a tall, dark, muscled body that made women nearly trip over themselves to get his attention.

But to Grace he'd always been more like a big brother—all the men on her team had. She couldn't afford to think about them in any other way. She didn't want to be seen as the lone female in the group, but as their equal.

"What are you doing here?"

Agent Hilliard arched a brow. "Seriously? You're not taking anyone's calls, responding to any attempts at contacting you—"

"I'm on a medical leave of absence. It's common knowledge."

He took a step toward her, his expression gentling. "You've been on leave for almost two months now, Grace. When are you coming back?"

The use of her first name threw her. She'd always been Agent Masterson, or just Masterson, to them. Somehow, hearing her name on his lips and having him here in her garage added an intimacy to the situation that was far too much of a threat. It made her too damn vulnerable.

Grace folded her arms across her chest and shrugged. "So that's why you came? Why you snuck onto my property and broke into my garage? To ask when I'm coming back to the agency?"

His gaze darkened, became unreadable. No. That wasn't the only reason he'd come today. She sensed it by the slight tension that had invaded his body.

"Did the agency send you? The boys?" Boys was a loose term she gave to her fellow agents, because they were fierce, full-grown men.

"Everyone's concerned," he admitted quietly. "But I came on my own accord."

Why? The question hovered on the tip of her tongue as her stomach did some weird little flipping motion. He'd come on his own. For what purpose?

"We should talk." He gestured toward the south end of the garage. "Think we can head over to your house? Have some coffee or something?"

Invite him into her home for coffee. The whole scenario was so normal. Non-threatening. And yet the idea of it had her wanting to shake her head and bark out a refusal.

She'd do it, but on her own terms.

"Let me finish this last piece first."

Chapter Two

In the handful of months he'd worked with Agent Grace Masterson—and on every dangerous mission they'd been on together—Darrius had never seen any indication that she was capable of fear. Not even during that God-awful week...

Until tonight, when the terror had been radiating off her in nearly tangible waves.

He watched as she strode past him toward a fire burning in some type of oven that glowed red, her chin lifted and her gaze unreadable. He allowed his gaze to follow the curve of her body. Her chestnut-brown hair was fastened on top of her head in some sort of loose bun, which exposed the graceful curve of the back of her neck and a tattoo he hadn't realized she'd had. A small, blue flower that looked vaguely familiar. Probably something native to the Northwest.

His gaze slipped lower to her outfit. He wasn't used to seeing her in clothes that showed off her form so well. In work clothes it was easy enough to write her off as a scrawny white chick. But what she was wearing now...*damn.*

The purple tank top she wore hugged decent sized breasts before disappearing into the waistband of her jeans. Jeans that he had to wonder how she even got into. They were skintight, clinging to gently flaring hips, a curvy ass he hadn't seen coming, and then molding down her slim legs. The look was a little too girl-next-door slash sex-bomb, right down to the scuffed up, stained sneakers on her feet.

Uneasy that he was becoming all too aware of Agent Masterson's chick side, he cast another glance around the garage.

The building was hot, and no doubt the heat came from the oven she was currently pulling some metal pipe from. On the end of the pipe a ball of orange glowed molten.

"Holy shit. What is all this?" His gaze shifted to the shelves on the wall, and to the variety of blown glass.

"Glassblowing. It's a hobby of mine." Masterson nodded her head toward the fire. "That is a glory hole—and no jokes please."

His mouth curved in amusement, because she obviously knew a dirty reply had been on his tongue.

"And this—" she lifted the pipe slightly "—is a blowpipe."

She went silent as she dipped molten glass into what looked like crushed blue glass, rolling it around before walking back to the glory hole and placing the pipe and glass back inside.

Amazed and a little nervous she had such a dangerous-looking hobby, he shook his head. "How the hell did I not know this about you, Masterson?"

"I don't exactly put it on my resume. Now, quiet for a minute. I like to work in silence."

He kept his mouth shut, but with reluctance. From the way her small, defined muscles rippled in her arms, he knew the pipe was a hell of a lot heavier than it looked. It also just affirmed what a strong, hard woman she was, in and outside the agency.

Obviously deeply committed to what she was doing, she seemed almost unaware of him as she took a seat on a bench. Masterson braced the pipe on a ledge and grabbed some hollowed out wooden bowl type of thing.

Darrius was completely entranced as he watched her shape the ball of glass before she set it down and picked up something that looked like tweezers.

Deftly, and with the ease of a professional, she pinched and poked various parts of the glass, until it began to take on the unmistakable shape of a flower.

Then she grabbed another tool and began pulling and turning. The glass stretched, looking as pliant and sticky as taffy, becoming the stem of the flower.

It almost looked innocuous, but he wasn't stupid, that shit was hot.

Finally she moved across the room and gently removed the flower from the pipe. He followed her over to the table and stared down at the creation.

"That was pretty fucking amazing, Masterson."

"Thank you."

"What do you do with those anyway? Just blow them for fun?"

"Hardly. There's a small shop in Issaquah I'm contracted with who sells my flowers. I guess they're pretty popular."

He gave a slow nod. "I can see how they would be. They're nice. And if you enjoy doing it, why not? Nice little side biz."

"Glassblowing is therapeutic for me." She hesitated. "My dad was a glassblower by trade and had his work in several galleries in the Pacific Northwest. I used to sit in here and watch him create. It could be snowing outside, but he'd have the doors open and fire from the furnace kept the garage warm."

"Did he create flowers too?"

"No. He did bowls and vases. All kinds of utilitarian type of items that people get all excited over."

"So why flowers for you?"

Her delicate mouth curved into a slight frown. "I don't know, actually. It's just always been what I was driven to create."

But obviously the flower held some meaning to her, because she had a tattoo on the back of her neck that damn near matched it.

His gaze scanned the shelf, noting the similarities in her work. "And it's always the same type of flower? The same color?"

"Yeah. I guess that's weird."

"Nah, actually it's pretty cool. I'm glad I had the chance to see this side of you."

She made a barely audible *harrumph*, and the smile she flashed him was strained as she cleaned up her stuff and turned things off.

He had the feeling this wasn't something she shared with many people—or even wanted anyone to know about. But he'd blown that secret out of the water when he'd busted into her garage today.

He'd come here early this morning prepared for her to be a bit standoffish, but not prepared for an ambush of half-assed traps on her property. Or for her to fire a fucking bullet at his head through the door.

Mother fucker.

He reached behind him and plucked what felt like a thin needle from his shoulder area. And maybe not all her traps had been quite half-assed.

"So you wanted coffee?" She arched a brow and walked past him. "Come on, let's go."

He followed her outside the garage, his shoes crunching on the fallen, frost-covered leaves.

"So, what the hell is up with Fort Knox-style lockdown on your place?"

"Just being cautious." She shrugged and came up beside him as they crossed her lawn toward what looked to be the main house. "Sure didn't seem to slow you down any, though."

"I'm P.I.A. You should know better."

"So it would seem. I'll have to tweak a few things."

Hmm. Any more tweaking and he might lose an arm next time.

She opened the door to her house and strode inside. "I know I said coffee, but I don't drink the stuff. But I've got tea—hot or iced—and all kinds of fruit and yogurt for a smoothie."

"Really? I haven't had breakfast, and now that you mention it—"

"On second thought, don't say smoothie because that'll take far more energy than I'm willing to give you right now."

He laughed softly. This was the girl he was familiar with,

hard and sarcastic, not really that liberal with the warm and fuzzy.

"Tea is fine. Hot, please. It's cold as fuck outside."

"Well, that's kind of a backward analogy, because one would think fucking would be hot, but okay. Have a seat." She went to work filling up a kettle of water.

Darrius pulled out a chair at the round four-person table and sat down. He did a quick appraisal of the kitchen that was so tidy it almost seemed staged. Healthy food everywhere. Most of it fruit and veggies she could grab on the go.

And yet... He drew in a slow breath again and nodded. Maybe she had a small sweet tooth, because he'd bet his last paycheck she'd made oatmeal raisin cookies recently. Which was an image that didn't really come naturally.

Agent Masterson seemed the type to be far more comfortable with a Glock on a firing range than with a Kitchen Aid making cookies. Maybe they were store bought.

"So how are you?"

She turned from her spot at the stove at his question and watched him. "What do you mean?"

"Come on now, the question isn't exactly challenging."

She didn't even blink. "I'm doing just fine, thank you very much."

"You don't have to lie to me, Masterson. We're friends. I'm closer to you than any of the other guys on the team."

The kettle began to whistle and she turned away again, busying herself preparing their tea. He watched in fascination at the little metal ball she scooped loose tea leaves into. No pre-made tea bags for this one.

"Hilliard, I'm friends with everyone. I try not to play favorites," she murmured. "But really. I'm fine."

Like hell she was. Despite her positive words and casual demeanor, he could sense the turmoil inside her. Smell the fear just below the surface. She should have realized that too, should've known he'd never believe the lie. But then, she seemed to be throwing the lies in his face like verbal roadblocks.

Maybe he'd be more inclined to believe them, or believe there was a hint of truth to them, if he hadn't been there that night. Hadn't held her in his arms when she'd been at death's door.

The memory of it slipped into his thoughts, momentarily taking his breath away. She'd been so still. So pale. He'd heard her heart slowing. A few more days with that drug in her system and Grace Masterson would've had her name engraved in the memorial plaque at headquarters.

How the hell had she ended up involved in such a shady ordeal? It still blew his mind—the idea that shifters had willingly volunteered, accepted money, to be part of what could only be described as a horrific experiment to annihilate the species.

And Grace Masterson had been one of six to volunteer—though only five had come out alive, and it wasn't the drug that had killed him, but another P.I.A. operative on their team who'd been protecting the woman who was now his mate.

"Here you are. One mug of tea for my uninvited guest." She set a steaming mug in front of him. "Do you need cream? Sugar?"

When she moved to turn away, he caught her wrist, stopping her retreat. Her pale blue eyes widened and panic flickered in them.

"Thank you. The tea is fine as it is." He stroked his thumb over the pulse in her delicate wrist, felt it pounding faster than it should've been. "But you're not, Grace. You haven't spoken to anyone about what happened a couple months ago. Or how the hell you even got involved in such a mess. Why don't you try talking? Try talking to me."

Darrius watched the myriad of emotions flicker across her face.

Shock, pain, rage and fear again. He could pretty much pinpoint each one, and likely why she felt it, especially the rage. People didn't bring it up, didn't dare talk about it. *So how dare he?*

He could see the question in her gaze, the sudden rigidness in her shoulders, and yet she didn't pull away or try to remove his hand from her wrist. She seemed too stunned.

Everyone had been tiptoeing around the victims. Even though each one had been sent a request to be interviewed, none of them had agreed.

And what could they do? They couldn't force it. The line was a bit finer with Grace, because she was a federal agent. What she'd done could impact her job, and the consequences of her actions had still yet to be seen.

The most messed up thing about it was the whole experiment had been legal.

Though they'd wanted to prosecute the bitch behind it all, she'd covered her ass by having the shifters sign a contract indicating they knew exactly what they were doing and the risks involved.

Thankfully the drug hadn't worked, but instead whatever had been given to them caused them to shift almost continuously between wolf and human. It had nearly killed all the victims. Including Grace.

"I just don't understand why you did it. Why you would willingly sign up for such a messed up thing?" He shook his head. "You're a shifter, being part wolf is in your DNA. Why the hell would you sign up to be given a drug that tried to subdue that side of you?"

Grace flinched and he saw the flicker of agony in her gaze before it was gone.

"I'm not going to discuss this. Not now, not ever." She glanced pointedly down at his fingers that restrained her, and then back at him. "Do you mind?"

He found himself reluctant to release her, which startled him into obeying her request. He liked the delicateness of her wrist. How soft her skin was. The smell of her lotion—

What the fucking hell was wrong with him? She was an agent on his team, and he'd damn well better remember that.

Darrius pursed his lips and curled his hands around the

mug in front of him instead.

"I apologize."

"Thank you. I don't like being touched." She hesitated. "More so lately."

And yet in the garage, right after she'd been ready to blow his head off, she'd seemed to melt into his arms, cling to him almost desperately. Unless he'd imagined that.

"I'm trying to be real with you," he said with quiet determination. "Maybe the other guys will dance around with what happened. Maybe they're fine ignoring you and just letting you bounce back when you're ready, but I'm not willing to go that route."

Her mouth tightened. "Well, doesn't that make you an insensitive asshole."

"So what if it does. I want you to talk about it. Otherwise I don't think it's going to happen."

"You don't think *what's* going to happen?" Exasperation radiated through her words.

"Unless you start facing what happened, I don't think you're *going* to bounce back."

Chapter Three

I don't think you're going to bounce back.

Agent Hilliard had no idea how close he was. Grace swallowed with difficulty. He wasn't even trying for small talk now. Hilliard had sailed right over discretion and was plunging into the dirt she had no desire to dig up.

If he only knew. But of course he couldn't, and likely never would discover why she'd willingly signed up to be experimented on like some laboratory rat.

She was proud of her shifter blood and would never have tried to rid herself of the ability to shift. Until she'd had no choice…

Talk to him? He couldn't be serious. And yet one look at the resolve on his face and she knew he was. Jesus.

She hadn't even spoken to the P.I.A. therapist, despite heavy pressure from her superiors to do so. From the first day she'd regained consciousness, Agent Larson, their commander and alpha, had encouraged her to seek help. Pleaded even.

She shook her head in silent denial to Hilliard's request, but also to shake the hold he seemed to have over her with the intense plea in his dark gaze.

And when his strong, calloused fingers had held her wrist, she'd found her thoughts a bit foggy as well.

But it wasn't fear. She wasn't afraid of Agent Hilliard. Not today and never before on the job.

She'd lied to him a moment ago about not playing favorites. Darrius had always been her closest friend on the team. And though a tiny part of her desperately wanted to open up to him and have a meltdown worthy of a reality show, she knew it was far too dangerous.

And the danger extended beyond her well-being. She slid her gaze to the hall that led to the back of the house and where Aubree was likely watching television.

Grace moved back to the sink and gripped the counter, staring outside at the fog. Right now she needed to put physical distance between them. The idea of sitting down at the table, drinking tea and chatting about life as if it were all sunshine and roses just wasn't going to happen. Some things needed to stay buried. The last two months being the perfect example.

"Grace, tell me why you signed up to be a part of those experiments." His tone changed, became more urgent, as if he sensed she wanted to talk about it. "The guys think you must've had some kind of hunch about what was going on and you went in on your own undercover. Is that true?"

Undercover. If only it were something so heroic and brave. She swallowed the bitterness that formed a lump in her throat.

"It doesn't matter why I did it. The fact is, I *did* do it." She couldn't help but add on a whisper, "And you guys have every right to be pissed off."

"Grace, listen to me. No one is pissed off at you—what we are is damned concerned."

Concerned? She didn't deserve a shred of concern from them. Why were they so quick to give her the benefit of the doubt?

"Look, Hilliard, as much as I appreciate what you're trying to do here, I'm just not ready to talk about it." And she somehow doubted she'd ever be. "So I'd appreciate it if you'd just drop it."

He sighed, not seeming to be taken aback by the sharpness of her words. "All right."

"Thank you."

"You don't need to talk to me. Yet. But you do need to give me one of your cookies."

What the hell? "Say that again?"

"Oatmeal raisin, right?"

"How did you—"

"You bake them yourself?"

Her mouth worked, but no words came out. She could feel her cheeks warming. Talk about a change of attack.

"I don't bake."

"Maybe that's what you want everyone to believe, but I smell cookies. Fresh. Not the packaged crap."

Damn hypersensitive shifter senses. He was right. About her baking them, and about her not wanting anyone to know. Especially her fellow agents, who probably equated baking with dithering females who'd be better off tending the household.

The last thing she needed was any damn domestic, Betty Crocker-style jokes at the office.

"I ate the last one this morning, and for your information someone made the cookies for me."

"Did they now?"

She didn't answer because it was obvious he knew she was lying. He seemed really good at that. Knowing when she stretched the truth.

He gave a slow smile. "You didn't eat them all."

"Oh for God's sake. Are you for real?" She let out a huff of air and moved to grab the plastic container on top of the fridge. She pried off the lid and then set the bin in front of them. "Take them all if you'd like."

"Thanks. One'll do." He grabbed one of the palm-sized cookies and took a bite.

It distracted her for a moment, the way he closed his eyes and made a groan of approval. For a moment she saw Hilliard through the eyes of a P.I.A. groupie. Out of all the agents who could've had a fan club, Hilliard was the leading candidate.

Darrius Hilliard had that potent combination of looks and charm. His personality and humor was almost boyish, but his body was all man. He made her solid oak table and matching chairs seem frail with the way his tall, dark, muscled body was stationed around it.

"These are good." He nodded and took another bite. "How come you never bring us some of these? The guys would love you."

"Oh let's see... Pretty much so I don't have to deal with reactions like this. I'd rather be known for my ability to save your ass than bake cookies for it."

"Damn good point." He grinned and polished off the cookie. "I'll keep your baking life a secret, but in exchange I'll need you to keep one as well."

"Sorry, I don't do blackmail." But the minute her glib words were out, she realized what complete bullshit they were and swallowed a bitter laugh. Clearly she wasn't immune to blackmail, not if the stakes were high enough.

Hilliard leaned back in his chair and his expression became uncharacteristically somber. "Look, I didn't show up here today just to get you to talk."

A shiver of premonition raced through her. It wasn't going to be good. Whatever it was. Still standing, her grip on the chair in front of her tightened.

"I never thought you did. So just tell me."

His gaze didn't waver from hers. "Thom Wilson is dead."

She needed to sit down. Now. Desperately. Before she ended up in a heap on the floor. Or threw up on it.

Almost blindly, Grace sank down onto the wooden frame of the chair she gripped.

Thom was dead? No. Oh dear God. No.

She closed her eyes as images from not long ago flashed in her mind.

"We'll get through this," Thom vowed as he gripped her hand.

The cement walls seemed to be closing in on them. The floor beneath her was icy cold against her nearly naked skin. The smell of urine and feces coated her nostrils. Some of the shifters couldn't even control their bowel movements anymore, let alone their ability to shift.

Pretty soon she'd be just like them. They were about three injections ahead of her. It wouldn't be long now.

She shook her head, fighting the desolation. The terror.

What the hell had she gotten herself into?

"They're coming back for us. There will be another round of injections. Don't you see it's getting worse with every one?"

Thom cast a nervous glance at the other shifters. "Not necessarily. Everyone reacts differently."

"Jesus, Thom. You know just as much as I do that it's bullshit. We need to try and get out of here." She glanced around, trying to figure out if there might be a way out of this holding cell. "They're not going to let us go if we ask nicely. Not at this point."

They'd been told it was for their own protection.

"We only have to finish out the week, Grace. Just a few more days! We committed to it. We're getting paid a heck of a lot of money."

She watched as the man across from her began to shift again. Fourth time in the last minute. She saw the anguish in his eyes as his mouth opened on a silent scream.

And then his body morphed. Skin retracted, claws came out, and his growl of pain shook the walls of the building.

"This is too high of a price to pay," she said savagely. "I don't even need the money."

"But I do," Thom pleaded and grabbed for her hand. "I can't leave. I need money for college for my kids. Janie is heading off to UCLA in the fall. Shit, I have a mortgage I can't afford. Don't fuck this up. We'll be okay, the contract promised it."

Words on paper. That was all it came down to. Another shifter began vomiting against the wall.

Grace shook her head and whispered, "I don't think so. In fact if we don't get the hell out of here, some of us might not make it out at all."

A loud, metal door slammed somewhere down the hall and dread coiled her muscles into heavy ropes.

It was too late. They'd already come back.

She dragged herself out of the horrific memory and forced her gaze to meet Hilliard's.

"I don't believe it."

The middle-aged, pudgy, genuinely nice—and a little too naïve—father of two couldn't be dead. But of course he was, because Hilliard wouldn't lie about something like that.

Grace tried to drag in a slow breath, but her lungs felt crushed. "How did it happen? *When* did it happen?"

"Apparently his wife found him dead, sitting in his car in the garage two days ago."

"Carbon monoxide poisoning."

"Yes."

Hilliard's expression gave little indication of his thoughts, but the steadfast way he watched her made her think he was curious to read hers.

"Hilliard, they don't... They can't possibly think it's a suicide."

He didn't answer, but he didn't need to.

They thought Thom had killed himself. That he'd taken his own life after nearly losing it two months ago.

She blinked, stunned into absolute silence. Thom had survived fucking hell on earth, only to come back and kill himself? It didn't make any damn sense.

Or maybe in an awful, tragic way, it did.

A dark heaviness settled over her, familiar and unwanted. She struggled against it, just as vehemently as she always did.

Yes, there were some mornings she didn't want to get out of bed. Where the bleakness of her reality threatened to overwhelm her and it was easier just to go numb and not feel. But she fought it. Dammit, of course she fought it. She had to, for herself, and for the one person who still needed her.

But what if Thom wasn't as strong as her?

She heard a soft beeping and was vaguely aware of Hilliard digging for his cell phone.

"Shit. I want to stay and talk, because there are things that need to be said."

But apparently he had to go.

"So stay," she blurted, realizing how desperate she sounded now. A minute ago she'd been ready to kick his ass out the door, now she was begging him to stay.

But she needed to know more, needed details about Thom. And there *was* more Hilliard wasn't telling her. She could sense it.

He stood, almost reluctantly, before he shook his head. "I can't. Sorry, Masterson. I could have my ass chewed out for telling you what I did, but I wanted you to hear if from a friend first. Thom's death is still being kept under wraps while P.I.A. investigates. You're on leave right now, meaning it's not your problem."

But it was her problem. Thom was a survivor, just like her. They were connected by the same horrific situation.

"And if I came back?"

Hilliard froze on his way to the door, but didn't turn around. "To the agency? Will you?"

Her heart accelerated and her mouth went dry. Could she go back? How could anyone within the agency possibly want her to return?

Dammit, her job as a federal agent was to protect their species, not try to eliminate them. Tears burned at the back of her eyes and she bit back a helpless, frustrated growl.

It was so much easier to stay here. Bury her head in the sand, so to speak. To spend her days making glass creations and not give herself time to think about what had happened. To not put herself anywhere near the people who would be the constant reminder of what she'd endured.

And how she'd betrayed them...

When she didn't answer, he turned to glance over his shoulder. She saw it now, the brief flicker of sympathy in his gaze, before it was gone.

"Come back, Grace. Your team needs you." He opened the

door and took a step out. "And you need us, far more than you're willing to admit."

Then he left.

She wrapped her arms around her waist and drew in a ragged breath. Her body trembled now as she struggled to absorb the news of Thom's death.

Suicide.

There was so much wrong with that scenario.

A floorboard in the house creaked, and her gaze darted down the hall. She'd almost forgotten.

"Bree?" Grace strode briskly through the house and checked every room.

But they were empty. Her sister had fled when Hilliard had arrived.

Grace's chest swelled with the sharp breath of disappointment she drew in. She was close to her sister, even if six years separated them with Aubree only recently turned seventeen. She looked forward to their visits and the time they spent together. Sometimes Bree snuck out to visit when she wasn't supposed to, but Grace knew her sister usually escaped any repercussions because her brief disappearances had gone unnoticed.

But Bree had been skittish lately, and when she'd shown up this morning Grace had gotten the impression her sister had wanted to talk about something. And they likely *would've* talked after she'd finished with her glass, had Hilliard not arrived when he did. But he'd scared her off, though Grace wasn't quite sure why.

Frustration from multiple sources clawed at her, and the wolf within her skin begged to come out.

So why not let it?

She jerked off her clothes, stripping down to nothing, and then slipped out the back door. Her bare feet skimmed over the grass, and she barely noticed the chilliness of the autumn morning or the dew between her toes.

She picked up speed as she disappeared into the tree line

of her property. Grabbing the band that held her hair up, she pulled it free and let her hair fall heavy and wild down her back.

Her skin stretched and she unfisted her hands as her claws appeared. Her itchiness abated as her fur came out and the change took over.

She threw her head back, letting out a howl that was laced with frustration before she took off running in her animal form.

Exhilaration and relief spread through her as she moved off her property and explored the Cascade foothills. She merged with nature and breathed in the crisp scent of the mountains.

For a moment, she felt it. Someone out in the woods watching her, maybe following her as she ran. She hesitated, slowing her pace. But then, when nothing revealed itself, she brushed it off as being paranoid. As she'd just proven to herself with Hilliard's unexpected visit, she seemed to be prone to it lately.

She was safe now. She wasn't locked in a filthy lab. Naked. Being done God knew what to—maybe it was a blessing she couldn't remember much.

Hell, maybe she did need therapy. Someone to talk to...but for now, these were the moments that were therapeutic, the ones she loved the most. Being alone and in her wolf form. And besides the time she spent with her sister or at work, she was always alone.

The wolf was who she was and the side of herself that she embraced the most. And yet everyone who really knew her now assumed the worst. That she'd wanted to rid herself of this side.

Never.

She quickened her pace and leapt easily over the stump of a fallen tree.

Somehow, someway, she'd gain their respect once more. And hopefully their trust.

Chapter Four

Darrius pulled his Dodge Ram to a stop just behind Donovan's Range Rover at the edge of the forest.

He climbed out of the truck, already spotting the other agent doing stretches at the trailhead. He braced himself for the shit he was about to take for being twenty minutes late to their weekend morning run.

Donovan cast a glance his way. "About time, Hilliard. You lose track of time jerking off in the shower?"

Darrius grinned and grabbed his heel to pull his calf muscle into a stretch. "Came in five minutes, what with your pretty picture taped to the bathroom mirror."

Before he could blink, Donovan had grabbed a pinecone from the trail and chucked it as his head.

Darrius dodged it just as fast. "You throw like a girl."

"I'll take that as a compliment if we're talking about Masterson, otherwise, fuck you."

Grace. A sliver of tension raced through him, and Darrius wondered briefly if the other man suspected where he'd been this morning.

A couple of joggers appeared on the trail, making their way back to the parking lot. Darrius and Donovan gave small nods in greeting as the man and woman passed.

Unfortunately, due to the popularity and proximity of the trail to the city, they would be running in human form. At least at the beginning of the trail. It was too risky to try and shift without being spotted.

On occasion they diverted from the path and allowed themselves to transform, then run wild into the dense brush where most humans didn't stray.

But not today. There wasn't any rain, which meant there'd be more humans out than normal.

Once the couple had driven off in their cars, Donovan glanced his way again.

"Ready?"

"Let's do it."

They took off onto the trail, their pace was almost impossibly swift. Definitely faster than the average human.

As their running shoes ate up the dirt, the wolf inside Darrius itched to come out. He curled his fingers into fists and drew in slow steady breaths, more than accustomed with how to keep it restrained. It was always like this when he ran; his wolf side begged to take on its true form. There was far more freedom running in the shape of his animal side than being hampered by clothing and the human body.

But having the wolf just below the surface also had its benefits. It kept his instincts and senses honed razor sharp and gave him an advantage over the general human population.

Not even slightly out of breath, Donovan asked, "But seriously. You're never late. Where were you?"

Shit. Maybe Donovan didn't know exactly where he'd been, but he suspected something.

"Overslept."

Fortunately Warrick Donovan wasn't the alpha of their pack, or even the leader of their team. Which meant he didn't really owe the other man any kind of explanation—though the fact that he considered Donovan a close friend did leave a dent in his conscience.

But he couldn't fess up to visiting Grace this morning. He shouldn't have been there in the first place, and really shouldn't have given her the news he did.

Donovan grunted and swerved slightly to avoid a low-hanging branch. "Really. You gotta know I'm not going to cuss you out for going to see her."

Fuck.

Darrius didn't reply.

"You're carrying her scent like a red flag."

This time he glanced sharply at his friend, about to bite off another sharp lie, but then he remembered. Remembered the feel of Grace in his arms in her garage, just before she'd completely lost it. Her scent was literally plastered all over him. Of course Donovan knew where he'd been.

"Well, next time, bro, why don't you save us time and the masturbation jokes?" Darrius flashed him a lopsided smile. "You going to say anything?"

"It's not my place. What you do in your time is your own business." Donovan glanced his way, his brows drawn in concern. "Just tell me how's she doing?"

She was a mess. Jumping at shadows and ready to blow the head off of a squirrel if it came too close to her property. But he knew Grace wouldn't want him to say any of that.

Grace. Hell, when had he even begun to think of Agent Masterson as *Grace*. When he'd held her through the night, wondering if she was going to die on him and praying like hell she wouldn't.

She'd been so close to telling him something in the kitchen, he'd sensed it. And then she'd panicked and emotionally backpedaled, retreating back into her thoughts. He'd realized how thin her emotions were, the anxiety under the surface, and had quickly changed the conversation. Asking for a damn cookie instead of answers. Shit.

Though that cookie had been pretty amazing.

"You going to answer me, man?"

"She's about how you'd expect." It wasn't a lie. It was probably too close to the truth.

"Is she coming back?"

"Doubt it."

"Shit." Donovan shook his head. "She's a good agent. It'd probably be good for her to get back in the field."

"Yeah it would." And it frustrated the hell out of him that no matter what he said, she seemed to withdraw farther away. He'd hoped by showing up at her place today he'd be able to talk her into returning to the agency.

But she seemed pretty damn content spending her days blowing glass in her secluded rambler on the outskirts of North Bend—which was already a good half hour or so from Seattle.

"I guess time will tell." Damn if wasn't a clichéd phrase, but it was just the kind of non-committal bullshit he needed to put a close to this conversation. And just in case it hadn't, Darrius asked, "How's your wife doing? She adjusting all right?"

Donovan's expression relaxed and his mouth curved into a smile. "Sienna's doing pretty damn good. I'm actually a little surprised just how well she *has* adjusted."

"No kidding. That's one helluva curve ball to be thrown." Sienna, who had thought herself completely human, had not only stumbled upon the secret shifters species, but had discovered in a brutal way that she carried the wolf gene as well.

So much had changed in the last couple of months. For her, and for the entire shifter population.

Darrius drew in a deep breath, his lungs expanding with the crisp morning air as they increased their pace.

"She's lucky to have you, Donovan."

The other agent shook his head, his expression tightening. "I'm lucky to have her. She's my fucking world, and I'd destroy anyone who tried to change that."

Something close to envy pinched at Darrius's heart, but he turned his gaze back to the woods around them and thrust it aside.

What Donovan and Sienna had was amazing. Sure the shifter population mated, and they had strong feelings for their mates, but what those two had was like some fierce, indestructible, love-on-steroids type of thing. He didn't doubt for a minute that the newly married couple would each give up their lives to save the other one, if needed.

Maybe once, he'd had the possibility of having the same thing. But those dreams had faded over a decade ago.

"Hang on." Donovan slowed down and dug into his pocket,

pulling out his phone a minute later. "Just got a text from Larson."

Darrius came to a stop and rested his hands on his hips, his ever-alert gaze searching the forest around them for any threat as Donovan read the message from their alpha.

"So what the hell did you say to her, Hilliard?"

Darrius scowled. "Say to who?"

"To Masterson this morning." Donovan slipped his phone back into his pocket and arched a brow. "Apparently she's returning to work on Monday."

He was dead.

The discovery should've sent far more elation through her. There was a tiny prick of satisfaction, but it was quickly overshadowed as everything inside her turned hard and bitterness once again rose to create its acrid, unpleasant brew in the depth of her stomach.

Jocelyn set her cell phone down on the table and curled her feet beneath her on the supple, handcrafted leather sofa that had just arrived yesterday.

Dead. And by his own hand it appeared. Perfect…

Her gaze slid over the Seattle skyline and onto the dark waters of Puget Sound. The view was almost as priceless as the penthouse condo itself. The condo rarely went on the market, and the bidding war to purchase it several years ago had been ludicrous. But she'd won. She *always* won.

Though the past few months had been a setback. After investing a billion fucking dollars in that drug, one would assume it would've worked. That it would've cured those heinous shifters from their ability to shift.

But it had failed. The whole experiment and testing had been quite the clusterfuck. The drug had not only *not* worked, it had given shifters who were only half-blooded, who'd never before had the ability to shift, the ability to.

Just thinking about it sent ice through her veins and had

her breath catching. It was horrific. Absolutely, without a doubt horrific, and it went against everything she fought for.

She closed her eyes as the room almost started to spin. She grounded herself again and drew in slow breaths.

The drug hadn't worked, but there were other ways to deliver her vengeance. To make those creatures regret the day they were born. And she was well on her way to achieving it.

"Your martini."

Her quiet afternoon was interrupted by her assistant as he entered the sitting room. He carried his tall frame with self-assurance, but his gaze never met hers.

"Thank you, Andy." She reached to take the drink from him.

He had shifter blood in him, but not enough to make her disgusted by him. Initially he'd been hired to work with the shifters who'd undergone the experiments, but once that project had disintegrated she'd recruited him to be her personal assistant.

Andy was a recent college graduate who suited her needs perfectly. *All* her needs, as of recently. He'd been struggling to pay his student loans and she'd been on the prowl for some sensual entertainment. They had an unspoken agreement that worked well for them both.

Jocelyn allowed her gaze to trail over his body. A golden boy, literally. Blond with blue eyes. He was young—though not too young—with a hard, toned body. And he had the kind of stamina that would've won him a gold medal had it been an Olympic event.

She knew he waited to see if he'd be dismissed. Knew she really ought to send him off on some other chore. But she was in no hurry.

A celebration was in order after the phone call she'd just taken. Only she had no one to celebrate with. Not really. Her husband had died years ago, and the man who'd been her lover, who'd been at her side for the past three years, had been killed over the summer.

Her fingers tightened around the stem of the martini glass. Brutally murdered by those *fucking shifter savages* in an old warehouse.

Which had left her once again alone. Which was rather inconvenient. And, though she loathed to admit it, lonely. But loneliness could always be eased, at least temporarily.

Jocelyn plucked the skewer of olives free from her martini and captured one green morsel with her teeth, pulling it free before chewing slowly.

Vodka and salt burned on her tongue and she savored the taste. Savored the news of Thom's death again.

Yes. A celebration was most definitely in order.

She leaned back against the couch, shifting to force the silk of her robes to part and reveal a hint of cleavage.

"Why don't you sit, Andy?"

Though his cheeks hinted at color, he didn't hesitate, but moved immediately to the couch beside her.

"I know you're off in an hour, correct?"

"Technically, yes. But I have no plans."

"Hmm." She reached out to toy with a button on his black, pressed shirt. "Would you like to help me with my plans?"

"Anything you wish, ma'am." His gaze darkened, and she could practically hear his heart quicken with anticipation and lust.

Oh, there was no doubt that he could charm himself into any girl's panties. But there was the difference; she was not a giddy, impulsive college girl. She was a grown woman.

She wasn't foolish. She was quite aware of her aging looks. Her skin not as supple as it once was; her beauty had faded. But she *was* still beautiful—could still bring a man to his knees.

And she would enjoy bringing this one to his.

"I thought I told you to call me Jocelyn." She unfastened the silk belt at her waist and the robe slid from her shoulders, leaving her naked.

"Jocelyn." Hunger flashed in his eyes and she allowed a small smile. She caught his hand and dragged it to her breast, reveling in the strangled groan he made.

"By the way, I should mention my plans include coming at least five times before dinner."

Soon she wouldn't be thinking about those damn shifters—she wouldn't be thinking at all. She'd be deep in an oasis of passion where she could forget.

At least for the next two hours.

Grace cradled her tumbler of Earl Grey tea between her hands and glanced out the doorway to the agency, where the members of her team were gathering to head out on their assignment.

Her nerves were still riled after the debriefing yesterday down at the Seattle agency. But they'd given her the thumbs-up to come back and so here she was. And any minute she'd be going out with her team.

It felt weird to be back. Weird, but good. She breathed in the familiar smell of coffee and disinfectant that couldn't quite hide the mustiness of the old government building.

Her cubicle offered a bit of seclusion and comfort, but most important, a familiarity. It was where she did the paperwork, spent her downtime when she wasn't out in the field. Sitting behind her desk used to be the worst part of her job, but now she almost looked forward to it.

"You sure you're ready for this?"

She glanced up as Larson's head appeared over the edge of her cubicle wall. His question was light enough, but there was concern is his dark eyes.

"Yes, sir."

Larson stared at her, his gaze intense as he obviously tried to read her. She resisted the urge to squirm—to flinch—and met his gaze steadily.

Finally he nodded. "All right then. Good to have you back,

Masterson."

"Thank you. It's good to be back." Though that had yet to be decided. "So anything on the schedule for today?"

"I'm sending Hilliard and Yorioka, who you haven't met yet, out to interview Thom Wilson's family this morning. You, Donovan and I will be investigating a murder of a female human—it's looking as if the perp might be a shifter. So we're opening our own case quietly in addition to human law enforcement."

A murder case? Any other time she'd be all over this, but not today. She needed to get placed on that Wilson assignment.

"Could I..." Grace tightened her hands around her tea. "With all due respect, sir, I'd rather go with Hilliard."

"Is that so?"

His tone still held that soft drawl, but the thread of steel indicated he didn't quite approve of her request.

Crap, and she really needed to be careful being it was her first day back at work. But she needed to be involved with that case—needed to talk to Thom's family.

"I would prefer it, yes."

Larson eyes narrowed on her. "You're emotionally connected to that case, Masterson. Which is the reason I didn't put you on it. It would be a conflict of interest."

"I realize that." She bit her lip. There was no turning back now. "I won't let my emotions rule my judgment. You know I'm a better agent than that."

The silence that ensued screamed a thousand words. Oh yes, maybe once Larson had *thought* she was a better agent than that.

"Please, sir." Despite her intent, she heard the faint note of desperation in her voice.

He was going to say no. She could see the denial in his eyes, but then his jaw hardened and he gave a terse nod.

"I know the answer I should say." He paused. "But the truth is, Thom's family has been asking to speak to you."

Her heart leapt into her throat. "Seriously?"

“Fuck.” He shook his head and slapped her cubicle wall. “Don’t make me regret this, Masterson. Get your shit in order and be ready to leave with Hilliard and Yorioka in a few minutes.” He turned to walk back down the hallway, calling out, “And if I even suspect you’re out of line, I’ll pull your ass off this case before you can blink.”

“Understood.” Elation soared through her as she gathered her belongings.

Had Larson really just given her the go ahead to investigate Thom’s death? Her heart quickened and she stumbled in her brisk stride as she followed her team leader outside to the government vehicles.

She’d work well with Hilliard—they complemented each other like oil and vinegar. And whoever this new agent was, this Yorioka guy, well, she was sure they’d do fine together too.

Grace followed Larson out the glass double doors of the agency and pulled her black sunglasses from her bag. Her hands were so unsteady the glasses fell from her hand as if greased and hit the pavement with a clatter.

She’d just bent to pick them up when Donovan’s voice rang out across the parking lot.

“Well hell. I heard it was true, but I didn’t believe you were actually coming back.”

Grace straightened and slid her sunglasses on, grateful for the small barrier against them being able to read eyes for emotion.

Donovan closed the distance between them and pulled her into his arms for a quick, hard hug.

“Damn good to have you back, girl.”

Her heart swelled a bit and her throat tightened. These men were so much more to her than just coworkers.

She forced herself to keep her tone light as she murmured, “I’m not that easy to get rid of.”

She slid her gaze over to Hilliard, who leaned against one of the agency-issued vans. His arms were folded over his chest in a way that defined the muscles in his arms and shoulders. And for some stupid reason her pulse stuttered as his gaze slid over her.

Was it her imagination, or had his gaze lingered a bit longer on her breasts?

Grace resisted the urge to tug the edges of her suit jacket closer together. For some reason lately he made her ultra aware of femininity, and she felt all too soft, emotionally and physically. It was a sharp reminder that she was the only female on the team and how much she tried not to fall into the stereotypes trap.

"Good to have you back," Hilliard finally murmured, quirking an eyebrow.

Grace dipped her head in acknowledgement. "Thank you."

"I don't believe you've met the agent who replaced Rafferty," Donovan said.

"No, I haven't." Some of the blood left her head, and the world around her wavered.

Rafferty. She hadn't thought about him too much. Deliberately. He'd been the double agent who'd been up to his elbows in dirt with the Shifter Elimination Project. He'd been aware what was being done to her—the hell she'd been living through. His desire for money had outweighed his loyalty to his species, and in the end it had cost him his life.

"Masterson, let me introduce you to Agent Chris Yorioka."

The agent who stepped from the shadows was so slight she hadn't even seen him standing there.

"It's nice to meet you," Grace said quietly and accepted the hand the other agent held out to shake.

The daintiness of the hand that gripped hers had Grace's gaze darting back to the other agent's face for a closer look.

Framed in a round, flawless and obviously *female* face, dark eyes watched her with polite tolerance.

Larson gave Grace a light slap on the back, and grinned. "That's right. We've got another woman on the team."

Chapter Five

Another woman.

How rash of her to assume Chris had been a man's name. Chris was likely a nickname for Christine or Kristin. She'd missed the femininity of the agent with the way her sleek black hair was pulled back into a tight ponytail.

Grace struggled for words—tried to get out the appropriate greeting—but just gave small grunt as she shook the woman's hand.

Another female on the team. She'd spent so long earning her place, proving she could work as hard as a man that it had never occurred to her another female would take on those other struggles beside her.

"Well, it's about time to head out, right?" Agent Yorioka pulled her hand away and turned her back on Grace, but not before she'd seen the flicker of disgust in her eyes.

So even though they were only just acquainted, the other agent didn't care for her. Though it stung, Grace couldn't blame her. Surely Yorioka had been briefed on her background, the circumstances of why she was on leave.

Really, she was surprised the other men on her team weren't watching her with wariness or disgust too. She'd expected it and tried to prepare for it. But there wasn't even a hint of unease from them.

Her stomach clenched. They gave her more credit than she deserved.

"We're going to head out to the murder scene." Larson shot her another warning glance over the top of their tinted-window car. "Don't get into too much trouble."

She held on to that warning the entire drive to Thom's

house.

They pulled up in front of a split-level, dark brown house about fifteen minutes later. The curtains were drawn and there was a beige sedan in the driveway.

A chill raced down Grace's spine as she glanced at it. Was it the vehicle Thom had taken his life in? Most likely not. It would've been taken away as evidence yesterday.

Thom's family, being shapeshifter, would've called the emergency P.I.A. line to report his death. It was the number all shifters were given to call in case of an emergency, because calling 911 would invite too many questions and chaos. It upped the potential for a memory wipe of the human, should they learn too much.

Most humans weren't even aware of the existence of wolf shifters—the only exception being some members of the federal government and the occasional human recruited to work for the P.I.A.

"Are you sure you're up for this?"

Hilliard's soft question was meant for her ears only, but it was pointless being that the three of them had heightened senses anyway. Agent Yorioka would've easily heard the question from the backseat, even over the Beyoncé song playing.

The realization and question itself pricked irritation through her.

"Of course I'm up for this. If I wasn't I would never have come back to the agency. Let alone begged to come with you to see Thom's family."

Surprise, and something else—amusement?—flickered in Hilliard's eyes. "Begged to come with me, huh? So you're saying I'm the reason you came here today?"

She opened her mouth, but no words came out. She was momentarily distracted by the slight quirk of Hilliard's full mouth. Did he really think she'd come out here today for him? That would be ridiculous. Thom had been her motivation. One hundred percent, all the way.

And yet her breath caught, because she couldn't deny a tiny part of her relaxed at the comfort of being with Hilliard. There was an ease and familiarity that was unmatched with the other guys. He would make her first day back much easier.

Still, like his ego needed any further inflation.

"Charming guess, but no, Hilliard." She flashed a hard smile, one hand on the handle of the car as she readied herself to climb out. "This is another day at work for me, so don't for one moment think you had anything to do with my motivation."

"Oh for fuck's sake, really?" Yorioka gave an irritated sigh from the backseat. "As charming as this passive-aggressive flirting is, I've got a job to do. See you both inside."

The other agent slipped out of the car before her or Hilliard could reply. Grace could feel the color stealing into her face. Jesus, what was wrong with her? She'd just made herself look ridiculous, and once again, completely unprofessional. Why was she allowing Hilliard to get under her skin so easily today?

She tugged on the door handle. "I'm going in too."

"Hang on." Hilliard reached beyond her to tug it closed again. "I'm sorry."

"Don't worry about it."

"I mean for yesterday. For scaring the shit out of you and forcing you to face some things you may not have been ready to deal with yet." He hesitated and looked away. "I sure as hell didn't want to get you in over your head back here if you're not ready."

"It's okay. Seriously, I'm ready." She paused. "I've been ready. You just gave me the push I needed. I missed you guys—missed the team."

Her gaze slid to Yorioka who now knocked on the front door of Thom's house. Though part of the team, the new girl seemed to have already written her off.

"Don't worry about Agent Yorioka." Hilliard must've sensed her thoughts. "She'll warm up to you."

Not likely. The other female agent's mind seemed to have been made up. She didn't have the energy to point that out, and just murmured, "We should go inside too."

"Yeah we should."

Grace had reached to open the door again when Hilliard suddenly caught her other hand in his and squeezed lightly.

"You say the word if it gets too much, and I'll get you out of there, you hear?"

She cast him a quick look, trying to ignore the undercurrent of warmth that seemed to race between where his hand held hers.

Why did he care so much? Why was he trying to take responsibility for her?

"There's no shame in it, Masterson. So promise me you'll let me know."

He could read her so well. She knew there was the potential to fall apart inside that house—she'd be speaking with Thom's widow.

But she'd hold herself together in front of them, dammit, even if she had to have a silent meltdown in the bathroom for a few minutes.

"I promise."

"Good." Hilliard pushed open the door for her and winked. "But for the record, I think you'll do great. Now get your ass in there."

The heaviness on her heart lifted a bit knowing he had her back and that he'd given her an out—even if they both knew she'd never take it.

Together they walked up to the house and entered the open door, following the sound of voices and soft weeping.

The smell of flowers was overpowering, and the first thing she saw was endless arrangements along the banister and in the kitchen. This family, Thom, was well loved.

They entered the living room and Grace stumbled, almost physically forced backward by the wall of pain and grief radiating from the woman sitting on the couch.

Thom's widow. It had to be. The slender woman, probably in her early fifties, sat hunched over on a floral coach. She had her brown hair held in a sloppy bun on her head, her fists were pressed against her mouth, her face blotchy, and her eyes were swollen and red. She looked like a woman gripped by the hellish talons of grief.

Immediately aware of Hilliard and Grace's presence, the woman's gaze leapt from the shag carpet and up to them. She barely looked at Hilliard before her now rounded gaze locked on Grace.

"Mrs. Wilson, this is Agent Hilliard and Agent Masterson," Yorioka began in a gentle tone, shooting them a warning glance. "We hope our visit won't upset you, but it's imperative that we speak with you again and collect evidence."

"You're her." Mrs. Wilson didn't seem to acknowledge Yorioka's statement, but stared at Grace as she spoke.

Ice swept through Grace's blood, as well as a numbness that she was nearly used to by now. Did this woman blame her? Hate her on sight? She couldn't fault her for either and braced for it.

"You're the female agent who was held with my Thom." The widow rose unsteadily to her feet and moved toward Grace.

Grace braced herself, ready for anything. Biting words. A slap across the face that Grace wouldn't stop.

Mrs. Wilson's face distorted. From misery, to frustration, and then to pain. When she lifted her arms, it took everything within Grace not to flinch. Instead she waited, sensing the sudden tension in Hilliard and knowing he'd step in to protect her if needed.

Don't, she warned silently, knowing he couldn't hear her, but hoping he'd sense her wishes.

But when the older woman closed the distance between them, it wasn't to hit her, but to wrap her arms around Grace. To pull her into a comforting hug that stunned her to the core.

"I am so very sorry for what you have gone through, my dear."

This woman, who'd just lost her husband, was comforting Grace. Why? Hilliard's gaze collided with Grace's and she could see the gesture had surprised him too.

"Thom spoke of you often. You were such a rock to him during the ordeal. And you're so very young yourself..." Mrs. Wilson broke off and squeezed her harder. "I'm so sorry."

Tears burned behind Grace's eyes and a lump formed in her throat. Without realizing what she was doing, Grace closed her arms around the woman and returned her embrace.

"I am so sorry, Mrs. Wilson." Her words weren't quite steady, but it didn't seem to matter now. "I can't tell you how sad I was to hear of Thom's death."

"You may call me Elaine." Her arms tightened further around Grace. "And thank you."

Grace's gaze slid to a framed picture on the wall of Thom, Elaine and two girls in their teens. It must've been taken several years ago. The print was faded and Thom and Elaine looked younger, but they all appeared quite happy.

"I promise." Grace swallowed with difficulty. Her words were husky. "We will investigate all possible causes in Thom's death."

Elaine pulled away, her expression weary. "Thom took his own life, my dear. As much as I may wish otherwise."

Grace's heart leapt into her throat and she struggled not to shake her head. So even Thom's wife was convinced it was suicide? Didn't she even suspect it might've been foul play?

"Did he show signs of depression in the days leading up to his death?" she prodded. "Any indication he might do something like this?"

Elaine hesitated. "Thom struggled with depression some, yes, but quite honestly he did so before the experiments. Ever since he was laid off from *The Seattle Times*."

That made sense. Grace was aware money had been Thom's driving factor to do the experiments.

"Did Thom leave a note?"

"No." Elaine's eyes brimmed with tears as she shook her head.

No note? That was a little odd. Though it was entirely

possible Thom's death was exactly what it seemed. A tragic suicide spurned by one man's depression and conscience. But there was the niggling sense of unease, that something didn't quite add up. Because she just couldn't comprehend how he could walk away from those experiments, so grateful to be alive and be reunited with his family, only to take his life.

"So you were the one who found Thom?" Grace asked carefully.

"Yes, and I'm thankful for the fact. If it had been one of my daughters who'd found their father..." Elaine swallowed visibly, appearing shaken. "I'm so glad that's not the last memory they have of him."

"Mrs. Wilson, I just had a couple more things to go over with you if you don't mind?"

Hilliard, keeping his voice quiet and gentle, took over the questioning, and Grace couldn't have been more grateful. She pulled away from Elaine and moved down the hall, giving herself the moment she had hoped she wouldn't need. She wound up in the garage after following Yorioka's voice.

Crime tape still cordoned off the chilled garage, but Grace slipped under it to join Yorioka, who was in discussion with a guy from the forensic unit.

"The car was taken into evidence then?" Grace asked when their conversation died.

"Yeah, the day the body was discovered. We're just back today tying up a few loose ends and lifting some prints." The forensic guy cleared his throat, picked up a small laptop and began typing.

He looked familiar, but she struggled with his name. Pete? Rick? Their paths had crossed on more than one crime scene.

"Did the call history on the cell phone get checked?"

"Call history was empty," he answered without looking up.

Or deleted. That was a definite red flag in her eyes. "Someone should've submitted a subpoena to the cell provider."

"Probably."

Grace waited for them to pick up their discussion, but from

the growing silence, she realized that wasn't going to happen.

He knew who she was, she realized. He was aware of her connection with Thom and the experiments, and this guy wasn't any more thrilled by her than Yorioka.

"What's your name again?" Grace finally asked, determined to stay professional at all cost. "I know we've worked together in the past."

"Rick." His gaze still wouldn't meet hers.

"Right, I remember now. Rick, have you guys found any indication this could be more than a suicide?"

"Okay, this is bullshit," Yorioka interrupted harshly. "Look, Masterson, I'm sorry if a murder would lessen the guilt load on your conscience, but the evidence is pretty damn clear Thom Wilson took his own life."

Grace's jaw clenched as she turned to face the other woman. If Agent Yorioka wanted to have this out now, than why the hell not?

"Did I do something to offend you, Agent Yorioka?"

Genuine amusement and disbelief flickered across Yorioka's face before she scowled again. "What, are you effing kidding me? Your entire presence within the P.I.A. is offensive after what you did."

"You sure are good at playing judge and jury without having the facts—"

"I know enough. I know that you betrayed your team and volunteered for something equivalent to an extermination project." Yorioka strode across the empty garage until they were almost toe-to-toe. "What kind of agent does that? You should've resigned."

"The P.I.A. means everything to me and I work damn hard at what I do."

Rick cleared his throat and muttered something about using the bathroom before disappearing out of the garage.

"Sure you do," Yorioka scoffed. "You should've been fired."

Anger rose in Grace's blood, bringing her wolf close to the surface. Her voice thickened as she ground out, "I'm a damn good agent, which is why they didn't fire me."

"Whether you're a good agent or not is, I'm sure, subjective." Yorioka flashed a hard smile. "You have a lot to prove before I'm convinced of your worth."

"I don't have to prove shit to you, and the sooner you realize that, the better."

"Everything all right in here?"

Grace stepped back from Agent Yorioka as Hilliard entered the garage, his wary gaze sweeping between the two women.

"We're fine," Yorioka murmured succinctly. "Just getting to know each other a little better. Isn't that right, Masterson?"

"Exactly." Bitch. Grace arched a brow and forced a slight smile. "In fact, we should do lunch sometime soon when we can have more time to chat."

Yorioka didn't bother to hide her bark of a laugh, but instead stepped out of the garage and back into the house.

"Looks like I missed out on all the fun." Hilliard switched the notebook he held to his other hand.

"Yeah, had you been here a few minutes earlier, you would've had the joy of watching me become a human piñata. Always a blast." Grace glanced at the ground, trying to calm her temper a bit, before meeting Hilliard's gaze again. "Did you question Mrs. Wilson further?"

"I did. But this is already the second round of questioning for her. She's a little emotionally drained and pleaded a headache. She's lying down in her room now."

Grace could relate to the emotionally drained part. She'd thought she was ready to come back, to deal with everything. But, hell, maybe it was just another bad decision.

"If we haven't already, I think we should subpoena Thom's cell phone records. The call history was deleted."

"Not a bad idea. I'll check into that." Hilliard nodded. "Let me grab Yorioka and we can head back to the office early for some paperwork."

Needing to get outside, away from the reminder of Thom's

death, Grace bit her lip and pushed past him. "I'll meet you at the car."

Darrius watched her go and swallowed a sigh. The truth was, they could've stayed a bit longer. Perhaps asked to speak with the daughters again, but chances were they wouldn't get any more out of the girls now than they had last time. And beyond that, Masterson was struggling. He could see it in the tension in her shoulders and the haunted expression in her eyes.

Maybe she regretted coming back to work. *And you basically pushed her into it.* Guilt stabbed at him as he went to find Yorioka to let her know they were leaving.

"We're going to head out," he said after locating her.

She glanced up from her notes she was currently scrawling on, and nodded.

"If you don't mind, I'm going to stick around with Rick, the guy from forensics. I want to be here when he checks the victim's computer." Yorioka's expression was laced with excitement. "He already said I could catch a ride back from him."

Yorioka knew what she was doing. She might look young, but she'd been with the P.I.A. for twelve years, and had only recently transferred from the Dallas office. He knew she was trained in forensics and as a field agent, but it was clear which she enjoyed more.

"You get the okay from the office?"

"Of course."

"All right, we'll catch you later then." Hilliard turned to leave, and then hesitated, before turning to face her again. "Masterson is a good agent. I'd appreciate it if you'd give her the benefit of the doubt."

Yorioka's expression closed off. "I was probably a little hard on her, but I don't understand how you—how any of you—can justify what she did."

"We don't justify it. The truth is, we don't know why she did it." Some of the agents had their theories—that Agent Masterson had been trying to go undercover without permission, but Darrius didn't buy it. "What we do know is she's young and has an incredible amount of potential to be a stellar agent—she was already on her way to being one. And the agency must agree, because they allowed her to come back."

"They interview her?"

"Of course. Right after the rescue. She was debriefed and interviewed extensively by someone from the agency."

Yorioka's lips curled into a sneer. "And they invited her to return to work."

"Yes. Whatever her motivation for doing it was, it must've been good."

"But you don't know why she did it. No one does."

"She's not obligated to share why with us. Nor is the agency."

Rick, the forensic guy, walked past them back toward the garage, and gave a slight chin jerk in acknowledgment. The guy was a bit of an arrogant prick, if Darrius remembered correctly. Still he nodded back.

"I don't know. I trust the agency, but I've got to say that you all treat her like a delicate porcelain doll."

Hilliard laughed and relaxed a little. "She'd likely throw you down if she heard you call her delicate."

"Charming, but Masterson isn't my type."

Yorioka made it no secret she was gay. Hilliard and the rest of the team had met her partner within the first couple of weeks that she'd started. Her partner, sweet and a bit shy, was the main reason Yorioka had transferred out from Dallas.

"Just, ease up on her. Okay? She's been through a lot."

Yorioka stared at him for a moment, and then gave a terse nod. "I'll try, but I can't make any promises. I call out bullshit when I see it."

"Deal, but you won't find much of it with her."

Yorioka grunted and turned away. "I'm going to have a cigarette. Catch you back at the office, Hilliard."

Darrius made his way out of the house, anxious to climb into the car with Grace and reassure her that she'd done well today.

Which was weird. He had to wonder if he'd be having the same reaction with any of the other members of his team. What was it about Grace that had him so damn protective lately?

Once outside the house, he spotted her across the street, leaning against the car, apparently waiting for him and the keys. She didn't see him right away as she stared off down the road, and he took a moment to check her out.

Her dark hair was in a loose ponytail that hung over her shoulder. She wore minimal makeup, but didn't need it. He wanted to be closer, to see if her lips were full and glossy from a tube, or if it was natural.

Her arms were folded across her chest, making the blazer and blouse beneath it gape a bit. The blood in his veins pulsed a bit harder with lust and his wolf rose closer to the surface.

Darrius blinked in shock, feeling like he'd been sucker punched. Son of a bitch, there was no doubt about it. He was definitely having some kind of physical reaction to Grace. That moment in her garage the other night hadn't been some weird fluke.

This was going to be a problem. A big fucking problem.

Unsettled, he jerked his gaze back to her face and felt like he'd just gotten decked again. She'd seen him, and Lord almighty did she look ticked off.

She straightened from the car and started toward him. "You know next time you feel the need to come to my rescue, don't."

Wary now, he tilted his head. "You gonna elaborate on that?"

"I don't need you defending me to Yorioka." She shook her head and gave him a tight smile. "Or, hey, maybe next time you decide to do it, at least try and make sure I'm far enough away not to hear."

So she'd heard that little discussion between him and the

other agent a few minutes ago.

"She was out of line."

"Doesn't matter. I can take care of myself." Grace spun on her heel and started back toward the car.

Danger. He sensed it before he saw or heard anything.

Darrius was already moving before the squealing tires sounded. His feet flew across the pavement and he had both arms around Grace, jerking her across the road just before a black minivan went barreling past them.

Chapter Six

They smacked into the agency vehicle, Grace first and Darrius against her. Adrenaline ravaged his blood, making him on the brink of shifting. His claws came out, piercing through the material of Grace's jacket as he gripped her.

Her pupils were dilated with shock and her body trembled.

"Where did that come from? How did I… I didn't even see it."

He could hear the frantic pounding of her heart and knew it nearly matched his.

"Are you okay?" he rasped and forced his claws to retract, thrusting his wolf back into the depths inside him.

She nodded, almost bobble-head like. "Yes. I think so. A little bruised, but fine."

But she was as shook up as him. His gut was twisted up like a pretzel and a sheen of sweat gathered on the back of his neck.

Fuck. *Fuck.* Someone had nearly hit her. Had nearly run her down. Had they both just been so caught up in arguing that they'd been completely oblivious to the approaching minivan? Was it even possible?

But it hadn't even slowed—never braked as it raced past them.

This wasn't an accident. He knew it deep to his core. He glanced down at Grace again, who was still in his arms and seemed in no hurry to pull away, and found her eyes shining with fear and wariness.

"Bet you don't mind that kind of rescuing," he somehow managed in a light tone, reminding her of the angry words she'd hurled at him just before the van had nearly run her down.

Her gaze, a bit unfocused, darted back to his.

"I guess there can be exceptions every now and then." Her attempt at humor was obviously forced. "I don't suppose you caught the plates on that guy?"

"Fuck, I wish."

"What the hell happened?" Yorioka rushed out from the shadows of the house, dropping her cigarette on the ground and crushing it with her shoe. "Jesus, did I see that right? You nearly got taken out by some soccer mom."

Darrius's jaw clenched, and he jerked his gaze back to Grace. She gave a subtle shake of her head.

"I was distracted," she called out flatly. "I didn't see it coming."

Which was bullshit, because neither of them had. That minivan had barreled around a corner determined to hit whoever had been in its path. And that person was Grace. Still, it was clear she wasn't ready to admit that to Agent Yorioka.

"You're sure?"

Grace finally looked over at the other agent. "I'm sure. I'll be fine. Obviously, they missed me."

This time.

"All right. Whatever you say," Yorioka grumbled, obviously unconvinced, before she jogged back into the house.

Darrius didn't move, and Grace still made no attempt to free herself from his arms. Which made him think she was still frazzled.

And yet...her heart had slowed, but then sped up again. He'd heard it. Could hear the unsteadiness in her breathing as her fingers gripped the material of his button-up shirt. He could sense the fear leaving her, replaced instead by something else. Something hot and potent.

His blood mimicked hers, rushing and pulsing in response to the slender, feminine curves pressed entirely too close against him. The wolf inside him rose to the surface, but this time it had nothing to do with danger.

Her gaze darted to his, and he saw the shock and

awareness in her eyes. She felt it too—was aware of the sexual electric current between them.

"Hilliard." His name was husky on her lips, and it seemed to shock her back into their surroundings. She blinked once, hard, and then shoved away from him. "We need to get back to the office."

The pounding of his blood slowed and his wolf withdrew. Darrius let out a breath between his teeth and swore silently. What the hell?

Good thing she'd shoved him away, or who knew what might've happened.

"Yeah, we do. Climb in. I'm driving." He knew she was shaken up still from nearly being run down, whether she'd admit it or not.

Thankfully, Grace simply nodded, before climbing into the car.

Grace steered her sports car into a tight spot on the steep downtown Seattle hill, ignoring the sign warning that there was no parking until after six. It was five thirty. She'd take her damn chances at being towed or ticketed.

Slamming the door to her car, she jogged toward the entryway of the posh, shiny black building. She ignored the main elevator options and walked past the concierge to the elevator tucked away in a corner of the floor.

The doors opened after she pressed the button, but that would be as far as she went without the appropriate key.

Grace pressed the speaker button inside the lift and waited for someone to answer.

"How may I help you?" The voice came through the speaker, crisp and a bit bored.

"I'm here to see Ms. Feloray."

"Is she expecting you?"

"Yes." Not officially, but Jocelyn Feloray wouldn't be surprised by her sudden presence.

"And your name?"

"Grace."

"Grace? Uh, one moment." There was silence for nearly a minute, and then, "All right, stay where you are and you'll be brought up."

Grace didn't bother to stop a derisive laugh, even though she knew he'd disconnected.

The elevator doors whisked closed and the shaft eased upward in a slow, steady pace. It climbed the innards of the building until reaching the top floor.

When the door slid open, Grace stepped outside into the hallway of the penthouse condo.

"Grace?"

She hadn't seen the man practically hiding to the left of the elevator, and irritation pricked as she swung to address him.

"Yes?"

Jeez, he was young. Beautiful Abercrombie face and a chest to match. Had Jocelyn been trolling the community college for a new assistant?

"I'm Ms. Feloray's assistant." His gaze slid over her. Quick. Appraising. A move he'd probably mastered at the local nightclubs and bars. "Come in, she's expecting you."

"Thank you."

"You look familiar. Have we met?" he asked lightly, his gaze intense as it searched hers.

Really? Not so original with the pickup lines, if that's what this was. Though she doubted she was anywhere near his type.

"Trinity nightclub. Bathroom stall for, oh about, five minutes. Wow, I'm flattered you'd remember me."

He swung back around, disbelief and embarrassment reddening his face. "Labor Day Weekend? Wait, that was you?"

Damn. She'd been spot-on about his type.

"No." She flashed him a hard smile. "Thanks for the escort in, but I can take it from here."

She moved past him, repulsed by his sleaze. Not to mention

there was something else that was just off about him. She stepped out of the hallway and through the front door of the condo. Floor-to-ceiling glass windows revealed a view that must've cost millions. Beyond the handful of smaller buildings in front of them, white ferries glided across the choppy waves of Puget Sound.

She wasn't interested in the view from the penthouse, but more the owner of the condo.

She crossed the opulent living room and followed the scent of some kind of tomato sauce simmering in the kitchen.

The woman who stood next to the extravagant stove hardly looked a day over thirty, though she had to be pushing fifty now. Her slender body was attired in what looked like a designer dress—probably costing more than Grace's monthly salary.

"Well now, how domestic is this? Jocelyn Feloray doing her own cooking." Grace's voice dripped disdain as she moved into the other woman's line of vision.

"I enjoy cooking every now and then." Jocelyn looked up and offered a slow, predatory smile. "It's Grace, right?"

If Jocelyn's intent had been to goad her into anger, she'd be disappointed.

Grace leaned back and braced her elbows on the marble countertops. "I'm sure it would be all too convenient for you to forget my existence, but I'm not that obliging to disappear so nicely."

"A bit of humor, darling. Forgive me. It's just been so long since I've seen you."

"Yes. What, probably about fourteen weeks now?" Grace's jaw flexed, and she wasn't quite able to hide the bitterness buried within her. "If I remember correctly, the last time I saw you, you were looking on as some disgusting pig shoved a needle in my thigh."

"Mmm. True. Except he wasn't a pig, he was a wolf." Jocelyn shrugged. "Or half, if we're being technical. Not that there's much of a difference between full-blooded and half any longer."

Jocelyn's pleasant veneer cracked a bit as Grace spotted the flash of fury in her eyes. But then it was gone, and she was once again stirring her sauce and back into faux domestic goddess mode.

"Yes, I really should thank you for that. It's one thing you did right—creating a drug that gives all my half-shifter brother and sisters the ability to change into the wolf they were destined to be."

Jocelyn shuddered, obviously trying to suppress her anger now. "That is disgusting and was never my intention."

"I don't know. I thought it was karma at its absolute finest."

Setting the spoon on a holder, Jocelyn turned to face her. "Is there a reason you've come here today?"

"Oh, I think you know why I'm here. Did you have something to do with Thom Wilson's death?"

She arched a brow. "Who?"

"Don't screw with me. You know *exactly* who I'm talking about. He was one of the victims of your horrific experiments."

"Victims? Oh, please. You all signed up willingly to be a part of the test phase of the drug, darling."

Grace let that little remark fly. For now. Willingly was stretching it. "He was found dead over the weekend. A suicide."

Though Jocelyn's brows rose appropriately, Grace didn't miss the flash of satisfaction in her eyes.

"Well now, that really is tragic."

"Fuck you."

"Such language," Jocelyn mocked. "Your mother should've taught you some manners."

White-hot fury exploded inside Grace, and her fingers curled into fists as she felt the wolf demand to come out and draw blood. Her nails pricked the palm of her hand and she had to slow her breathing to restrain herself.

"Had she lived long enough, I'm sure she would've. Not that I'd waste manners on a lowlife like yourself," she ground out and pulled away from the counter, advancing on the older woman. "Did you send someone to try and kill me today?"

Genuine shock flickered in Jocelyn's eyes now. "Kill you? No. What happened?"

Grace stared her down for a moment, and then turned away. So it was possible Jocelyn wasn't behind the death-by-minivan attack this afternoon.

"Don't worry about it."

"But, Grace—"

"We're done here." She shook her head and headed out of the kitchen. In the doorway she paused and glanced back at the woman who'd made her life hell. "I'd better not hear about anymore *suicides*. Do we have an understanding?"

Jocelyn just lifted a shoulder and gave another brief smile. "Ultimately, the choice was his? Was it not?"

Grace turned and walked away. "I'm still waiting on the autopsy."

"Beer? Whiskey?"

Darrius studied the two options on the table in front of him, then glanced back up at Larson.

"You look like you could use one or the other," Larson added.

Reaching for the beer, Darrius gave a jerk of his head to mark his appreciation. "Thanks. I think I do, actually."

The bar they were in was dark, near empty, and filled with the tormented voice of Kurt Cobain from an old Nirvana album.

The Doornail was an unspoken shifter hangout located in a hole in the wall in Pioneer Square. The building had to be over a century old, and the pub itself had resided on the first floor for nearly as long. It had been owned and operated for three generations by the Neilson shapeshifter family.

"Good choice." Larson tossed back the shot and wiped the back of his hand over his mouth. "It's fucking weird not having

Donovan here as much."

"The guy's married now, has a wife to take care of, and all that jazz."

Larson's mouth twitched. "Sienna can take care of herself pretty damn well, from what I understand."

"Yes. But there's the love factor and being mated bit. Makes you all crazy and not want to be away from your significant other for any longer than necessary."

"Sienna works for the P.I.A. now. She's right down the hall from him when he's in the office."

"Yeah, but he's not in the office all that much," Darrius pointed out. "We've been in the field more often."

"Yeah. Speaking of. What happened today? The truth, not just what you wrote on the report."

Shit. Larson wasn't just their team leader, but the alpha of their pack. Lying wasn't anywhere near an option.

"Interviewed Thom's widow. Spoke with the forensic guy for a bit. Then left." Darrius paused to take a swig of cold beer. "And that's when Gra— Masterson was nearly run down by some jackass in a minivan."

Larson cursed. "Did you catch the plates?"

"I don't think I'd be here right now if I had." No. He'd be out pounding some guy's face into the pavement.

Darrius's fingers tightened around the beer bottle until he felt the slight cracking of glass. He eased up, forgetting his strength.

"You don't think it was an accident."

"No. I don't." There was no point in lying to his alpha. "But Masterson would have my balls if she knew I was telling you this."

"Tough shit. It's your goddamn duty to tell me these things, and I sure as fuck don't want any of my agents getting hurt."

Colin, the pub's owner, came over at that moment to say hi and grab their food order. Darrius asked for ribs, but wasn't really hungry. He didn't even want to be here right now. Everything inside him was coiled tight with the need to check on Grace. To see her again and make sure she was all right.

"Now tell me. Who would want to hurt Agent Masterson?" Larson asked once Colin had left to deliver their orders to the cook.

"I don't know. Feloray Industries? Maybe they want to off all the survivors of the experiments."

"That'd make them pretty fucking stupid. And obvious."

Which was around the same lines of what he'd been thinking. "I don't know who else it could be. Who else out there wants her dead?"

"Maybe not dead. Maybe just messed up a little. Hell, who knows? But I think we'd better keep a closer eye on her."

"Already am," he admitted, before thinking whether it was wise or not.

"Is that so?" Larson paused as their food was delivered. "Are you going to tell me what's up with you lately?"

"What do you mean?"

"You seem a little...protective of Masterson." He cut into his steak, then lifted his hard gaze again. "A little concerned—more than normal, really—with what's going on with her."

He was, and there was no way he could deny it. He couldn't explain it either. Not to himself, and sure as hell not to Larson.

"She's a fellow agent. Of course I'm concerned about her."

Not replying, Larson just crooked an eyebrow as he chewed his steak.

"Look, if you're thinking we're sexually involved, you're wrong. I've never crossed that line with Masterson."

Larson pointed the blade of his steak knife at him. "Maybe not yet, but you'd like to."

Hell yeah, he'd like to. Which was becoming an intensifying problem.

"It's probably not a good idea, you know." Larson's warning was a little too casual as he continued to eat.

"Well, sleeping with a coworker is never a good idea." Darrius forced his usual shit-eating grin and picked up his ribs.

"Makes things messy as hell at the office if things go sour."

"To say the least. And Masterson is probably a bit vulnerable right now."

"I'm not sure that's the word I'd pick for her."

"You know what I mean. After the shit she went through, she doesn't need you seducing her for a quick fling. If anything, she needs to find her mate. Someone who will be there for her for the long term."

Ouch. But his alpha was right. And Darrius didn't do long term. Why bother when he knew that none of the women would ever be his mate?

Larson's words were a sharp reminder that he wasn't the only one feeling protective of Grace. The whole team had always kept a close watch on her. And Larson probably felt extra responsibility as her alpha.

Mouth twisting into a hard smile, Darrius shook his head. "Look, the last thing I want to do is get into Masterson's pants." He couldn't keep the terseness from his voice this time, maybe that came from the bitter taste of lying. "You seem awfully concerned with everyone's love life, Larson."

"Are you questioning my right to be?" Larson gave a soft laugh, but there was a steel edge in it that reminded Darrius of his place.

They might be friends and shoot the shit out at a bar, but at the end of the day, everyone on their team and pack answered to Nathan Larson.

"No, I'm not that fucking stupid," Darrius muttered and finished off his beer. "But since we're on the subject, how's all that romantic shit going in your life right now?"

He watched the flicker of irritation and wariness in his alpha's eyes. It was almost as if Darrius had asked about a bad case of hemorrhoids instead of his love life.

"It's fine."

It was common knowledge that Larson was recently engaged to the daughter of an alpha from another pack. A gorgeous, spoiled redhead who screamed high maintenance.

The mating had been predicted for years, and would be good politics between the two packs when it ultimately happened.

"When's the wedding and mating? You're the head honcho, Larson." Darrius couldn't resist fucking with him a little. "Your pack is getting eager for you to settle down and start producing the next generation."

"Fuck you, Hilliard." Now Larson's expression went completely sour. "I hear it enough from the elders, I don't need it from you too. There's plenty of time for that business."

"There is, and I was just giving you shit. Take your time and make sure she's the right one."

"Right one? Sure. As if I have that luxury." Larson gave a hard laugh and took a swig of beer. "Anyway, what about you? There are plenty of girls you could have fun with for a nice little distraction." Larson glanced around the bar to where a group of women sat in the corner, watching them and giggling quietly. "See that? The girls love you. Bet you could take any one of them home tonight."

Oh, he didn't doubt it. And some nights he'd done just that. But tonight the idea left him a little cold.

"I could."

"You should. Usually you do. But now that I think of it, I can't remember the last time you left this bar with a chick. Certainly had to be before that whole rescue op on the feral shifters." Larson paused, his eyes narrowed. "When we freed Grace."

Shit, it hadn't been that long. Had it? Dismay and unease had Darrius shifting in his seat.

"I think whatever you're feeling toward Masterson is probably just you needing to take the edge off." Larson jerked his head to the right. "Look there. The pretty blonde seems like she'd be willing to help."

Darrius didn't miss the way his alpha's voice had lost its lightness, but now took on an edge. A warning that reiterated it would be a bad idea to get involved with Grace.

Maybe Larson was right. Maybe if he spent the night with

another woman, it'd ease up on this sudden need for Grace. Right now he felt like a shaken bottle of soda with the cap still on.

Darrius glanced back at the table of girls, and sure enough the blonde was watching him with extra interest. She was his usual type. Why was he even hesitating? Any other time he would've been brushing up on his seduction skills in a heartbeat.

You've got this. He forced himself to give her a slow smile and waited.

She giggled, whispered something to her friends, and then stood up to make her way over to him.

"You know, Larson," Darrius muttered, feeling more confident by the moment, "I think you might just be on to something."

Chapter Seven

Grace stared out the kitchen window into the evening darkness, replaying all aspects of her day. It took the whistling of the kettle to jerk her back to the present.

She moved away from the counter she had been leaning against and plucked the kettle from the hot stove.

Her first day back had been both cathartic and a complete nightmare.

It had felt so good to be back into her normal routine. To be with her team and feel their love and support—whether she deserved it or not. They'd invited her for drinks after work, something pretty common in the past. But she'd turned them down.

She'd already planned to go see Jocelyn, but if she let herself admit it, she also wasn't quite ready to face sitting across from any of the guys in a social setting. She wasn't ready to shoot the shit or get back to normal. Did she even know what the hell normal was anymore?

Stifling a yawn, she already envisioned the evening ahead of her. A book, a blanket and the couch. Perfect.

She loaded her tea ball with leaves and set it steeping in a mug of hot water before making her way to the bathroom.

Grace angled her body so she could lift her T-shirt and see her back in the mirror. The pale skin was unmarred. After Hilliard had tackled her out of the way of harm, pushing her against the car, she'd had a dark bruise running up her spine.

Nodding, she allowed her shirt to fall back into place. That was another perk of being a shifter. Her body healed fast. So fast that scars were a rarity. Though some injuries took longer than others to heal.

She flinched as she almost felt the sting of a whip against her back. Some images from her captivity during the experiments were easily remembered, some not quite as much. Which she realized she should probably be thankful for.

As she left the bathroom, she froze, hearing the sound of the front door handle turning.

Even knowing the only person who could easily get on her property and into her house, she still braced to fight. The tension didn't ease until her sister stepped inside a moment later.

"Oh, so you *are* here." Aubree smiled tentatively and closed the door behind her. "I called several times, but there was no answer."

No, there wouldn't have been, because she'd been avoiding all phone calls since this afternoon. Guilt pricked lightly, because she knew better than to cut her sister off that way—unintentional though it may have been.

"I'm sorry, I put my phone on vibrate and it's been in the bottom of my purse."

Aubree crossed the room to hang up her coat. Her slight limp was as much a part of who she was as the blue eyes they'd both inherited from their mother and the chestnut brown hair they attributed to their dad.

The limp had never slowed Bree down in life, though. Really, how could it when it was nearly all she'd ever known?

The same tragic accident that had killed their parents had left Aubree with a horrifically broken leg that even with shifter genes had never healed right.

Since toddlerhood, Aubree had always walked with the limp, and she'd never been able to shift without substantial, debilitating pain.

Grace's heart broke a little every time she thought of her sister trying to shift as a child. How her body would begin to morph, but because her bones had healed abnormally, her body was never quite able to make the transition to her wolf side without a trip to the shifter hospital afterward.

Over the years Aubree had become better at restraining the shapeshifter side of her, so she rarely went into the shifting process. She had never known the freedom of being in wolf form, or probably couldn't remember the few times she had during toddlerhood.

Aubree would never know the earth intimately, or become one with it in the way a shapeshifter did. Often Grace wondered if her sister felt trapped, depressed by being held prisoner by her body. Only Aubree never seemed to be burdened by her disability, instead seemed to be eternally optimistic about life, though maybe a bit shy and withdrawn.

Just as she was right now. After hanging her coat, she tucked a strand of hair behind her ear and moved to embrace Grace.

"I've missed you. How was your first day back at work?"

"It went all right." Grace ignored the second flare of guilt.

Aubree didn't know why Grace had taken so much time off. In fact, as far as she was aware, her sister didn't even know anything about the experiments or Grace having been a subject for them. If Grace had it her way, she'd never know.

"And I've missed you too." Grace pulled back to look her sister over. "I swear you're getting skinnier, Bree. You're a teenager, aren't you supposed to be eating anything that's not nailed down?"

Her sister's smile faltered and her gaze slipped away. "I'm not very hungry lately. And, besides, I'm pretty sure I've stopped growing and am about as tall as I'm going to get. Five four. That's not bad, right? And in like five months I'll legally be an adult."

Grace winced. "That soon, huh? Time is flying."

"Not fast enough." Bree stepped away and moved to the kitchen. "I look forward to being independent and not having to answer to anyone."

Grace, who'd begun to follow her, nodded. Valid point. Actually, pretty damn valid.

"Well, you know my offer stands. The minute you hit

eighteen you're welcome to move in here. It'd mean switching schools—"

"I'd do it in a heartbeat." Bree grabbed an orange off the counter and stabbed a fingernail into the thick rind to peel the fruit.

Grace pulled out a chair and sat down. It would be so much easier with Aubree under *her* roof and not stuck in some private shifter boarding school their aunt had enrolled her in.

There was no love lost between Grace and her aunt. They'd always had a toxic relationship, and Grace had left the moment she'd turned eighteen. And she'd felt the guilt of leaving Aubree behind every day since.

"I wish I could move in now."

Grace's heart ached at the way her sister's voice cracked, but she forced a gentle smile. Was this what her sister had wanted to talk about when she'd come over Saturday morning?

"We've tried that. Unfortunately, the courts won't allow it, remember?"

"Don't remind me. They think *she's* more suitable and prepared to take care of my disability." Aubree popped a piece of orange into her mouth and chewed slowly. She swallowed a moment later. "*Disability*. I'm not an invalid—I can take care of myself just fine. Maybe one leg is a bit of a mess, but the other is great."

She hated defending their aunt, but she tried to do so for her sister's behalf. "Still, there's always the possibility of help from a specialist, and you're under her insurance."

"Of course she's taken me to specialists, but none of them can quote unquote *fix me*." Aubree gave a soft sigh and finished the rest of her orange.

"Oh, Bree, you're perfect. Don't worry about it." Damn, this conversation was just bringing them down. Maybe it was time to change the subject. "So, hey, I wish you would've stuck around Saturday morning. You left in such a rush, and I thought you were going to help me blow some glass."

"Oh, I really wanted to. I love making those pretty flowers."

Aubree leaned back in her chair and gave Grace an apologetic smile. "I'm sorry I left without saying anything. I figured you might have wanted a bit of time alone with your friend."

Hilliard. Just the mention of him took her off guard. Grace thought about this afternoon and that heated moment when he'd pinned her to the car.

What had happened there? Some kind of adrenaline rush from nearly getting killed? Wanting to jump the first person of the opposite sex you saw? She was usually a pretty logical person, but she was hesitant to admit she might be attracted to Agent Hilliard.

"You work with him, right?" Aubree quirked a brow. "He's one of your super badass agent friends?"

Grace laughed softly. "Super badass? Nice. Don't let him hear you call him that or it'll inflate his ego even further."

"One of those guys, huh?"

"Yeah. Popular with the ladies." A little too popular. Which was another reason it would be a bad idea to get involved with him. "What about you, Bree? Any boys out there catch your attention lately?"

Aubree's smile faded and for a moment she looked almost sick. "No. Not at all. Guys pretty much suck, and I really don't have time to date anyway."

Whoa. Something had happened there. Usually her sister was all too eager to talk about her life. Social, love, all aspects really.

"All right, you can't drop the 'guys suck' bomb without elaborating. What's going on, Bree?"

Aubree bit her lip and kept her gaze on the tabletop. For a moment she looked as if she might respond. A solid knock on the door stopped her, and she shook her head.

"It's nothing. You should probably get that."

Wanting to probe further, but equally concerned by who could possibly be at her door, Grace finally relented and went to check who was outside.

Speak of the devil earlier and he appears... Hilliard stood outside, hands thrust into his pockets as he scanned the property behind him.

Again? He'd shown up at her house *again*? Really?

She opened the door and shook her head. "Showing up unexpectedly at my house has become a habit of yours, Hilliard."

He turned to face her again and gave a diluted version of his usual charming grin. "Probably, but hey, I knocked this time."

"Mmm. I suppose I can give you brownie points for that." She stepped back and gestured for him to come inside.

"Those little alarms and traps you've got set up must've taken you forever. Is there a code to deactivate that stuff or something?"

"Yes. I have it." Aubree stood up, her gaze bright as she looked him over. "But then I'm family. Hi there, I'm Aubree. I've heard a lot about you since Grace became an agent. It's so weird you'd show up now. Were your ears burning?"

"My ears?" Hilliard's pensive gaze slid between Grace and her sister.

Oh this was just too damn awkward. Grace let out a slow breath and gave a *who knows* shrug, hoping Aubree would drop it.

"We were talking about you," Aubree continued cheerfully.

And so much for dropping it.

"Were you now?" Hilliard slid his attention back to Grace. His gaze was entirely too knowing and thorough. She curled her fingers into fists and willed herself not to squirm. Heat had begun curling through her and her cheeks felt suddenly warm.

What the hell was this? Hot flashes? She was way too young for this crap.

Finally, as if Hilliard could sense the sensory turbulence inside her, he seemed to take pity and looked back at her sister.

"It's nice to meet you, Aubree." He reached out and caught her hand, kissing her knuckles. "You are just as pretty as your sister."

There he went, turning on the charm for another female. She knew his flirting was harmless. Still, when her sister let out what sounded like a giggle, Grace resisted the urge to roll her eyes.

"Well, aren't you too sweet?" Aubree pulled her hand away and grabbed her backpack from the floor. "I'm going to leave you guys alone and get some studying done. Grace, do you mind if I take over the back room for a while?"

"Not at all." Grace waved her away and watched her sister leave the room. A moment later she heard the door to the back room close. It wasn't loud, but the sound was an ominous reminder that she was left alone with Hilliard.

Even without looking at him, she was aware of him next to her, leaning against the counter, arms folded across his chest. She could feel his gaze on her as her nostrils flared to take in the faint scent of cologne or aftershave—something. Whatever it was, he smelled good. And it irked her to realize she'd noticed.

The silence swelled, and she knew she'd have to break it before she went a little nutty. Would have to ask why he'd come here in the first—

"So you have a little sister." He spoke before she did.

She cracked a small smile. "Happens sometimes. You know, parents really get into that family bit and keep popping them out."

"Any other siblings?"

"No. It's just Aubree and me."

The familiar twinge of sadness hit to think of how brief her time with her parents had been. Even less for Aubree. Her little sister had no memories, and just a handful of pictures to remember them by.

She finally glanced at Hilliard. "How about you?"

"A younger brother, and two older sisters."

"Big family."

His shoulder lifted in a slight shrug. "It sure made the fight for a morning shower fun."

She liked this, Grace realized. The small talk. The comfort

of having Hilliard hanging out with her after hours. Which was weird, because maintaining a friendship after work hours always made things a little tricky.

And dammit, after today she was starting to wonder if she wanted more than friendship. Which was really, really bad.

She finally dragged her gaze away from his charming smile that had her heart tripping all over the place. It was imperative that she get him to leave, and fast.

"Why are you here again?"

Chapter Eight

Darrius hesitated, not even sure how the hell to answer that. Maybe he didn't have an answer.

It was a little hard to focus with Grace wearing her pajamas—pink plaid boxer shorts and a skintight tank top. She'd obviously showered. Her hair, still damp, hung in loose, dark waves down her back. And she smelled sweet. Whatever soap or lotion she wore had to have some kind of cinnamon scent to it.

Every breath he took in just upped his awareness of her—made him want to gather her into his arms and press his lips to the curve of her neck. He needed to find out if she tasted as sweet as he knew she would.

Knowing she waited for his reply, he finally settled for saying the only thing that he could think of. The only thing neutral. "I figured you might want to talk about what happened today?"

He watched the tension invade her body, the wariness flicker in her eyes.

"Which part?" She pulled away from the counter and held up her hand. "Actually, don't answer that. You figured wrong. No, I don't want to talk about any of it."

She walked past him, away from the bedrooms and toward what seemed to be the living room.

His gaze unwillingly slipped to the curve of her ass, and his blood rushed south. His jaw flexed as he took in the long, pale legs that ended in bare feet. Feet that were nearly running through the plush carpet to move away from him.

"It's late. You shouldn't be here anyway."

He caught up with her and grabbed her arm, swinging her

around. “You think I don’t know that?”

“So why are you here?” There was desperation in her voice now, as if she dreaded the confrontation that had been building.

“I don’t know. I don’t fucking know. I just found myself driving here instead of home tonight.”

“Okay, you know what? Not an acceptable answer.”

“Maybe not. But here’s what I *can* tell you.” His fingers slid over the soft skin of her upper arm, holding her still as she tried to pull away. “There was this cute blonde at the bar tonight and we were in her car. She was all set to let me fuck her.”

Shock flared in her eyes, and then disappointment, before her gaze turned hard and cold. “What, is crude the new charming with you, Hilliard? Look, I don’t doubt you can get laid. No one is going to dispute that,” she ground out, “but I don’t need you to show up at my house to give me a blow by blow, okay?”

“I think you do need to hear this, because you’re part of the damn problem.”

She stopped trying to pull away and let out a growl of fury, going toe to toe with him now. She was several inches shorter than him, but she could intimidate the hell out of most people.

But instead of intimidating him, the anger and passion in her gaze lit a spark to the embers inside him. Made what little control he’d had when he arrived, snap.

“I am *not* part of your problem. If for some reason Little Hilliard didn’t want to get up and play, they have convenient blue pills for that. So why don’t you go bum one off your dad and hightail it back to the bar and finish where you left off with your blonde friend?”

Hilliard stared at her for a moment, letting the words sink in with disbelief. And then he laughed.

“You think I…” He shook his head and laughed harder, but it wasn’t really driven by amusement. More so frustration. “I didn’t sleep with the woman, because I couldn’t even kiss her without thinking about you.”

That shut her up. Grace sucked in a breath and she seemed at a loss for what to say.

"But I tried." His jaw flexed. "Because wanting you is a damn inconvenience, Masterson."

Again she didn't say anything, but he didn't miss the dilation of her pupils or the way her breath quickened.

He released her arm and used both hands to push back her hair over her shoulders before cupping her face. "I'm tired of running from this. So why bother trying anymore?"

Realization flickered in her eyes. "Hilliard, don't you dare."

Too fucking late. The wolf inside him had taken over the reins and was playing the game his way now.

He pulled her hard against him and covered her mouth with his. Expecting her knee in his crotch, he was shocked when instead her fingers curled into his shirt and she tugged him closer. She wasn't fighting him, but matching him with everything she had.

Her mouth parted beneath his, her tongue already meeting him halfway to tangle and tease. Sweet. Dammit all to hell, but she tasted like the inside of a candy store. So amazingly good, but so bad for you.

He pushed aside the human voice inside him—the one that told him to come to his senses before this was too late—and gathered her tighter in his arms. Her soft breasts flattened against his chest and his cock pressed through his jeans to her belly.

Deepening the kiss, he commandeered her mouth. Tasting and exploring every tempting inch.

More. He needed more.

Darrius slid his mouth from hers, giving in to the urge to explore. He traced kisses over the curve of her jawline, before moving to the tantalizing hollows her neck offered. The pulse in her neck a silent call for attention his tongue was all too eager to answer.

"Damn, you smell so good," he muttered when lifting his lips for just a moment. "I want to taste you. Everywhere."

Her body shuddered at his words and she let out a breathy whimper. "It's the Cinnamon Roll body wash. My sister gave it to me for my last birthday. Oh God, my sister who is just down the hall."

He laughed huskily and buried his lips against her neck. "It's not the body wash that's doing this to me. And your sister is studying in a room at the other end of the house. We're fine." Darrius sucked the curve of her neck and closed his eyes, intoxicated by the scent of her. The softness of her skin beneath his lips.

She melted into him again, surrendered to whatever crazed passion had them in their grip. He caught her mouth once more in another searing kiss, while easing a hand between them to tease his fingers up her toned stomach and onto the soft roundness of one breast. Her nipple poked into the curve of his palm, and he was hit by the fierce need to know what it would taste like in his mouth. To suck it until it was teased and distended and Grace was begging him for more.

"*Yes*." She stilled and then pulled away slightly. "And either you brought your Glock home in your pocket, or...wow."

He flicked his thumb over her nipple and was rewarded by her gasp.

"Wow, is the answer you're looking for." He couldn't stop a smug smile. "Little blue pill, my ass."

She laughed, a solid, throaty sound that was all confidence and pleasure.

"What's wrong with us? Why am I feeling like this with you? Like I could throw you down on the floor right now and ride you until I can't see straight?"

He groaned, his cock lurching into further hardness. "Shit, sugar, are you trying to make me lose it?"

"Mmm, I'm undecided..."

"I don't know what's going on with us. Hell, I've been trying to figure it out myself." His lips brushed the pulse in her neck again. "However, I do have what is probably a completely asinine theory."

She sighed, teasing her fingers up the back of his neck. "I'm torn between wanting to hear it, and wanting you to take off my shirt."

Oh shit. Had she just given him the green light to remove her clothes?

She nibbled on his bottom lip. "But you'd better tell me your theory."

Damn. And there came the yellow light. "I stayed with you when you were feral, and held you that one night. You were so close to dying, and I'm wondering if we somehow bonded in a way."

She froze in his arms and lifted her head, horror flashed across her face. "Crap, you didn't do anything to me, did you? I just... I have so few memories of that time. I mean, we're not mated or anything?"

"No, of course not. I've never bitten you." His fog of desire for her lifted a bit as the familiar sting of pain pinched his heart. The reminder that he wouldn't be biting her, or anyone else. "I never claimed you. You probably would've known."

Her cheeks reddened before she blinked and glanced away. The relief on her face was evident. "Right, of course. And I mean, why would you have? You're right, we would've known. So you think there's some kind of subconscious bond then?"

"Hell, I wish I knew. I have no idea what happened, but ever since that night... I feel responsible for you. Protective."

She gave a broken, distressed laugh. "You sound like you're offering to be my nanny."

"Grace, what I want to do to you is not suitable for kids."

A tremble ran through her and she laid her forehead against his chin. "You need to stop, because dammit, this is *so* inconvenient."

"You think I don't know that? Hell, Larson already warned me to stay away from you."

"What?" Her head lifted again and she finally did step back. "Larson knows about this? How? I mean, dammit, Darrius, *I* didn't even know about this."

"He sensed my growing attachment to you."

"Attachment?" Her laugh rose to a higher pitch as she began to pace the room. "That's such a strong word, how about we *not* use it. What happened tonight was lust. And we made the mistake of acting on it. Which I'm thinking won't be happening again."

The fact that she'd called him by his first name didn't slip his attention, but he didn't call her out on it. He actually liked the intimacy of it—he'd begun calling her Grace when they weren't at work. Masterson was too damn formal for the things he wanted to do to her.

"Maybe it is lust," he agreed mildly and crossed the room and caught her hand, lacing his fingers through hers. "But I can't ignore what happened between us tonight. I want you, Grace."

For a moment it almost seemed like her eyes got misty, and then her mouth thinned and she gave a terse shake of her head.

"Well, news flash, this isn't just about you, Hilliard. So forget tonight happened, because it was a one-time deal."

"Why? We're both consenting adults. Why would acting on it be a mistake?"

"One, Larson already told you to back off—"

"He's worried that I'll hurt you."

That threw her for a moment, and finally she laughed. "Well, out of all my concerns, that's not one of them."

"Okay, then what's the other reason you're against us exploring this?"

"Jesus, you're dissecting this situation like a frog in high school biology." She cast him a look of disbelief. "We work together, becoming fuck buddies is not a good idea."

He barked out a laugh. "You think we'd be the first coworkers in history to get it on? Come on."

"It's different with us. I work in a male-dominated field. You don't understand what that's like."

With suddenly clarity, Darrius did understand. He

understood exactly what this was about, and where she was coming from.

"I get it. Before Yorioka you were the new agent and the only girl. Did you feel like you had to prove yourself to us?"

She blanched, and judging by the wariness in her gaze, he'd nailed it.

"It doesn't matter."

"I can promise you the guys have never disrespected you in any way, Grace. You've always been one of us—we don't see gender."

That last bit was a lie. The team had always been a little more protective of Grace because she was a woman. The wolf sides of the men were genetically programmed to protect the females in the pack—it was as much a part of them as breathing.

Still, he had no doubts Grace was as good of an agent—if not better—than any of the men.

"And if anything did happen between us, that's where it would stay. Between us. I'm not the type for locker room conversations." He brought her hand up to his lips and flipped it to kiss the inside of her wrist. "We'd be good together, you know it as much as I do."

She closed her eyes and he felt her pulse quicken beneath his thumb.

"I understand rejection may be something of a novelty to you, but I promise the slight sting to your ego will fade."

When she opened her eyes again, her gaze was a vacant, hard stare that indicated she'd withdrawn emotionally. And as much as he wished it might be, it wasn't his ego that stung. It was on a much deeper level.

What the hell was wrong with him? Of course he'd been rejected before, and he never had a problem bouncing back. And yet here he was nearly begging Grace to go to bed with him? For real? Shit, he needed to get the hell out of here and come back to his senses. Big-time.

Darrius released her hand and stepped away, finally

remembering another reason that he'd shown up tonight. Concern. "I'll leave. But do me a favor."

With her arms folded across her chest, she gave him a wary glance.

"Be careful. I'm not convinced that near hit by the minivan today was an accident and I don't think you are either."

She hesitated just long enough to validate he was right on his hunch.

"I just wasn't paying attention to my surroundings."

And yet still she lied. Irritation gripped him as he turned and made his way back toward the door.

"You're a damn shifter. You're always paying attention," he called out as he left. "Just take my advice and keep alert."

Grace waited until the door shut and then ran unsteady hands through her hair.

Shit. Make that shit times a billion.

She'd just had the hottest make-out session of her life, and it was with Darrius Hilliard.

This was so wrong in so many ways. She'd chalked it up to lust. Okay, maybe. But, she'd had lust before. Lust pretty much ruled you between the legs and had little to do with the heart and mind.

Whatever had happened between Darrius and herself had been like lust on crack. The intensity of it had dug into the marrow of her bones and held on. She'd basically kicked him out, but in no way did it diminish the need and heat still burning in her body.

Damned inconvenient was an understatement. She didn't want to get involved with any man right now, but if it had to be someone, why couldn't it have been with some random guy she met at the dry cleaners or something?

But a fellow agent and friend?

Darrius hadn't taken long to figure out why she was freaking out. He'd pinpointed it right away. But she had set rules for herself when she joined the P.I.A.—it was strictly business with the guys, not a damn nightclub to get her flirting on.

Not that she flirted. Ever, really. She wasn't *good* at it. As a teen she'd been the girl who liked to spar with the boys in martial arts, not for the chance to flirt and feel feminine, but to prove she could fight just as well as any boy.

In college it hadn't been much different. Instead of the dance clubs, she'd frequented the shooting range.

And it wasn't like she didn't like men. Every now and then she had the urge to sleep with one, though nothing like the urge that had hit tonight with Darrius. She wasn't a virgin—she'd had sex before. It, like flirting, was something she didn't consider herself good at. Which she would never admit aloud, because who the hell failed at sex?

If she rated her sex life to this point, it'd be meh to decent. But she knew, without a doubt knew, by what had happened earlier that if she slept with Darrius the rating would be off the chart.

"Bad idea, Grace. Really bad idea," she muttered to herself.

The sound of a toilet flushing had her attention snapping back to the fact that her sister was still in the house. Aubree came out of the bathroom a moment later and then just stood in the hallway, not moving.

"Bree? You okay?"

Her sister jolted, her glance sliding toward Grace. Obviously she hadn't seen her at the end of the hall.

"Grace...yeah, I'm fine." Aubree looked away. "I just think that something I ate isn't agreeing with my stomach."

Pushing Darrius to the back of her mind, Grace strode forward, brows knitted with concern. Her sister did look awfully pale.

"Can I get you something? Antacid? Some milk?"

"No, I'm fine. I think... I'm just going to go home. Did your friend leave?"

"Yeah, a few minutes ago. Can I give you a ride? Or did you drive the Jeep out here?"

"I drove. I'm fine, really." Aubree gave her a quick hug, avoiding her gaze, and then scooped her backpack off the floor. "I'll talk to you later."

As the door slammed shut, Grace flinched. Was it possible her sister had heard, or even seen what had happened between Darrius and her? If so, no wonder she'd left.

Sex had never been a topic that frequented their conversations. Maybe because Grace rarely had it, and Aubree was so much younger than her and likely still a virgin. Walking in on her big sister in a hot and heavy make-out session would probably have sent her running.

With a sigh, Grace locked and bolted the door again before heading back to the kitchen to clean up her dishes. She glanced up at the clock and frowned. Almost eight? Yikes, the night had gotten away from her.

She was only on her second dish when someone pounded on the front door. "Grace!"

Her sister's frantic voice drifted through the thick wood and Grace rushed back to unlock it, concern sweeping through her.

"What's going on, Bree?"

Pale and trembling, Aubree stepped into her house, folding her arms across her chest. "My tires are flat."

"You have a flat tire?"

"*Tires.* All of them." Looking dangerously close to tears, she bit her lip. "Grace, I think... I think someone might've slashed them."

Grace barely let her finish before she'd pushed past her and out the door to investigate for herself.

The long gravel drive was shrouded in darkness; just the small motion light on the side of the house illuminated the black Jeep.

Crouching down, she ran her fingers over the tire and felt the definite split in the rubber where someone had indeed slashed them.

Son of a bitch. Her pulse quickened and her jaw clenched with unrestrained fury. Was it possible that whoever had come after her today was back?

She stilled at the sound of branches snapping deep into the woods off her property. So faint, a human wouldn't have heard it.

"Grace?" Gravel crunched as Aubree made her way back outside.

"Go in the house," Grace ordered, her voice soft and offering no opportunity for argument. "Lock the door and don't open it until I return and tell you it's safe."

"But what are you going to do?"

Ignoring the fear in her sister's voice, Grace stripped herself of the clothing that would hinder her shift.

"If someone tries to come inside there's a gun on the top shelf in my bedroom closet," Grace said firmly. "You understand? You don't ask questions, you just shoot."

"You want me to shoot someone? Grace, I've never even used a squirt gun."

"I don't think you'll need it, but if you do, you'll have to be a fast learner."

Naked now, she glanced behind her to see her sister still hesitating by the Jeep. "Dammit, *go*, Bree."

Her sister gave a cry of distress, but spun on her heel and moved as quickly as her limp leg allowed.

Hearing the door slam shut, Grace turned and sprinted across her yard. Her body shifted as she leapt over the wooden fence and when she hit the edge of the forest she was all wolf.

She followed the sound of branches cracking as someone ahead of her moved quickly through the trees.

A growl of fury erupted past her muzzle as she tried to gain on whoever the hell it was. One thing was for sure, the fact that he'd dragged her sister into this was a big mistake. *Big.*

The flash of movement ahead meant she was getting closer. Grace quickened her pace, weaving between trees and leaping over large branches that blocked her path.

She spotted him up ahead. Another wolf. Driven by rage, she leapt at him, catching him on the back just as he turned to face her.

Snarling, his canines flashed white in the darkness as he slid away from her.

Driven by rage and fear, she couldn't process the realization that his scent was familiar to her. But it made her pause long enough for him to get the upper hand and knock her to the ground.

She struggled beneath him, attempting to roll him off her as her teeth snapped at his neck and her claws dug into his sides.

But he was too quick, and much stronger than her. And only when his jaws closed around her neck—not enough to puncture, but enough to take control of her—did his scent fully sink in.

Her gaze snapped to his, and the fury there had her flinching in her wolf's skin.

Seeing the silent command in his eyes, she allowed herself to shift back to human as he did the same. Her awareness returned with the occasional sounds in the forest and the smell of the evergreen trees.

"What the fuck do you think you're doing out here?" Darrius ground out.

Chapter Nine

It was almost hard to breathe, let alone talk, with the weight of his body pinning her to the damp dirt of the forest floor.

She tried not to look at the bulging biceps that bracketed her head. But the hips that pinned hers down, and the thickness of his cock that pressed against her stomach were a bit harder to dismiss.

"Jesus, Grace, I almost killed you."

Still in the grips of shock, partly from their position, she couldn't stop the derisive laugh. "Sorry, buddy, but I think you have that backward. I believe I'm the one who nearly ripped your throat out."

"Bullshit." His glower indicated he didn't share her amusement. "Now answer my question. Why the hell did you follow me?"

"Because I didn't realize it was you."

Darrius cursed softly and then pulled himself up and off her. Thankfully he was too close still and the darkness of nightfall kept her from seeing more than his naked chest. And lowering her gaze would just be stupid. Tempting, but stupid.

For a moment there was almost a sting of disappointment, and there was no way she was going to analyze it.

"That wasn't too smart coming out here like that. You need to be more careful."

"I can take care of myself." She brushed some small twigs off the backs of her legs.

When she glanced back up to give him a hard look, she caught his gaze sliding over her. The flare of his nostrils and sudden hardness in his jaw meant he struggled to control his reaction to her nakedness.

Though he shouldn't have, because nudity was part of the shifter lifestyle. Clothes were shucked before shifting, or everyone's clothing budget would be through the roof.

Still, she couldn't quite desensitize herself completely with Darrius as she did with other shifters. And it was clear he struggled with the same thing.

His dark body was toned and tight in all the right places. The slash of a six-pack cut over his belly, and for just the briefest moment she imagined what it would be like to trace each square with her tongue.

Shaking that sensual thought free, she brought her mind back to the situation at hand—which was not Darrius's abs.

"I came out here because I was chasing someone who slashed the tires on my sister's Jeep." A possibility snaked around in her mind and she took a step back from him, suddenly wary. "You wouldn't know anything about that, would you?"

"What the hell are you talking about?" His mouth flattened into a tight line. "Someone sabotaged your sister's car?"

"You tell me."

"Wait, you think I did it?" He barked out a harsh laugh. "Don't be stupid."

"Well, you were still on my property, the only other person around that I've noticed."

"I'm not the only one around." He turned and strode around their immediate area.

Oh my God, his ass is like marbled perfection. The thought flew through her head before she could stop it. Thankfully his back was to her, so he couldn't see the way her face flamed red.

"When I left, I heard someone on your property and went after him."

That got her attention. Her gaze shifted from his perfect-ten behind and upward again. Dammit, he'd turned around just in time to catch her staring at parts of him she really ought not be staring at.

"You heard someone? Did you see anyone?" she asked.

He gave a brisk shake of his head. "No. I think I scared him off when I left. He must've struck while I was inside."

And while I was distracted by your tongue in my mouth. Shit. She needed to be so much more careful.

So Darrius had heard someone too. She hadn't really suspected him capable of slashing Aubree's tires, but the question had needed to be asked. Besides, what would his motive have been? Darrius charmed women, he didn't terrorize them.

"Well, thanks," she murmured grudgingly. "For chasing away whoever the bastard was. Probably some teenage prank."

She turned to walk away, but his words stopped her.

"You don't believe that any more than I do. Why are you making excuses when so many messed up things are happening?"

She paused and turned back to face him. "Because until I decide whether they're messed up or not, I'm not hitting the panic button."

"Let me stay with you tonight."

Her sharp laugh was swallowed up by the trees around them. "Didn't you just try that line back at the house?"

He moved toward her. "I'll sleep on the couch. You can trust me. My request this time isn't motivated by me wanting to have you flat on your back."

The air in her lungs suspended at that last line, and she tried to exhale, tried to say something, but all she could focus on was the image his words evoked.

"You don't play fair," she finally managed to choke out.

"What do you mean?"

"Stop talking about sex."

"I just said this wasn't about sex—"

"Oh, I heard what you said, but you had to tag on that last line that completely screwed up my ability to think."

His gaze smoldered as he took another step toward her.

"Really now? I have that much of an effect on you? Agent Masterson—always so damn cool and calm."

Oh like there was any denying it now? "You know you do. You proved that back inside my house. Which is why you're nuts to try and ask to come back."

He was so close now, his breath feathered across her face. "I'll take the couch. I promise to behave myself. I just want you protected tonight."

Why wasn't she offended by his admission? Normally she would've bristled and snapped out some harsh response at the idea that she needed protecting.

But something inside her softened a little. Clung to the idea that someone wanted to protect her. The concept was almost a novelty. Since she'd lost her parents, she and Aubree had been on their own. Guardians or not. Grace had been the protector.

And now here was Darrius, forcing his way into her life. Forcing her to face fears and memories she didn't want to revive.

How easy and wonderful would it be to crack a little and accept his help?

She struggled between the yes that hovered on her tongue and the no that was nearly an automatic reply.

Curling her hands into her fists, she finally shook her head.

"I'll be fine. You know I will. Thanks for checking on me tonight." She turned to walk back to her house.

Strong fingers curled around her elbow, halting her retreat and spinning her back around into his arms.

"I'll respect your decision. But before you go..." He caught her jaw with one hand and before she realized what he was doing, he'd covered her mouth with his own.

As his tongue slid past her lips to claim hers, the ground beneath her seemed to lift and fall. Or maybe that was just her legs giving out.

If the first kiss tonight had been her sexual resurrection, this one was its rapture.

The nocturnal noises of the forest slipped into the background and all she became aware of was the taste of him. The increasingly familiar scent of Darrius.

It raced through her blood like wine, making her heady and impulsive. Where she'd agree to almost anything. And maybe he knew it, because he released her mouth just as abruptly as he'd captured it.

"Go." The one word was ragged from his lips, even as the thumb that swept across her swollen mouth encouraged her to stay. "Get your ass back home and fast, Grace."

She nodded, still not completely back in reality.

"But know this," he warned, "even if you're outright refusing my help tonight, you *will* be safe."

Still she didn't move. Her body hummed and ached, and she could barely remember why she'd come out into the forest in the first place.

Tires. Slashed. Bad guys... *Right.*

Darrius set her aside and closed his eyes. "Dammit, *go.* Now. Before I do something I know you'll regret in the morning.

With clarity returned, Grace let out a strangled moan and then spun on her heels, shifting back to wolf a moment later. Before he could make good on his words, or she begged him to, she rushed back home.

"I need you and Masterson to do surveillance on a POI in Thom Wilson's death."

Darrius snapped his attention from the email he was typing, and reached up to catch the piece of paper Larson dropped before it could hit his desk.

Hell, the morning was already off to a busy start.

"Person of interest? Are you saying that the agency believes this may be more than a suicide?"

The alpha's expression remained unreadable. "At this point we're still leaning toward a suicide. All the other survivors have remained unharmed. But some prints showed up in the garage that weren't easily explained. Not family, doesn't seem to be anyone they knew."

"Definitely sounds like it's worth checking into." And Grace would sure as hell be excited to hear about the POI.

Grace. That's all it took. That one brief thought of her and he was hurtled back to the night before and that moment on the path. When he'd been flush on top of her, both of them naked.

Jesus. That situation could've ended so differently. Like him buried balls deep in her, instead of sending her scurrying off like a damned frightened rabbit.

It had been damn hard not to nudge her thighs apart and slide into her welcome heat. And she would've taken him. When he ultimately sent her away he could smell her arousal, could almost feel the slickness of her body wrapped around his dick.

Instead he'd told her to run. Damn smart in retrospect, but at the time it had nearly killed him.

But the danger last night had far outweighed his need for Grace—even if just barely. When he'd been leaving her house, Darrius had sensed someone on her property. He hadn't seen the slashed tires on Aubree's car or heard anything more than a rustling in the trees along her property, but that and gut instinct was enough to make him give chase.

"So this guy." Larson leaned back against the wall to the cubicle. "Wesley Parker, he lives out in Tukwila. Has a record of domestic violence."

So their person of interest was also a piece of shit. Nice.

Darrius scanned the paper. No jail time or conviction—his wife had dropped charges, but at least had had the sense to divorce him.

"You hand this off to Masterson yet?"

"She knows, and is wrapping up a morning session with Wedgewood. They know to meet out front at the top of the hour."

Wedgewood, the therapist. Larson didn't say it, but it was clear what Grace's session was about—the dark days during the drug trial.

Good. Relief eased through him and he nodded. Actually it was *damn* good that Grace was finally opening up about it. Maybe it wasn't to him, but it was to someone.

When Grace joined him in the agency car, the lines around her mouth were tight and her gaze was haunted. Talking to the therapist had obviously dug up some wounds she might not be ready to deal with.

He clenched his fingers around the steering wheel and tried to stop his body's automatic response to the scent of her. To the primal wolf side of him that immediately rose to the surface.

Forcing aside the lust clouding his mind, he started the car and focused on a safer subject.

"How did your session with Wedgewood go?"

The tension in her body snapped back like a tautly released rubber band.

"You know that's confidential."

Maybe not the safer subject, he realized, pulling out into traffic. "Yeah, I realize that. And feel free to tell me to fuck off, but just know I'm asking as someone who cares about you, not as your fellow agent."

Silence ate up the space between them, before she finally gave a small sigh. "I don't know, I guess the session was fine. I'd rather not do them at all."

"Then why do you?"

"Because it was one of the conditions of my returning to work."

And clearly she resented it. "You can't blame them. It's only natural they'd want you to seek help."

"Oh hell, of course I don't blame them. Not at all. My God, it's amazing they even took me back."

"They'd be crazy not to. You graduated from Charter Academy top of your class," he said, referencing the training academy all agents had to complete.

But she didn't respond. If anything, she seemed to draw deeper into herself as she struggled with the demons that obviously tormented her since the experiments.

"Talking to Wedgewood will help. You *will* heal from this."

She muttered something under her breath. He wasn't quite sure what, but it sounded along the lines of not deserving to heal. His chest tightened as frustration consumed him. He wanted to heal her—wished there was some way to help. Because the guilt she held on to was thick enough to dam a river.

"Anyway, it looks like you may have been on to something, Grace." Since they were alone, he made no attempt to call her by her last name.

And from the way her expression remained impassive, it didn't seem to bother her too much.

"How do you mean?"

"Did you see who we're watching? POI on the Wilson case."

"Oh right. That." She smiled slightly, but her attention slid, almost distracted, out the passenger window. "You don't need to hear me utter 'I told you so'."

No, and she wouldn't anyway. Grace wasn't the type.

"It's not a smoking gun. The POI could've been any guy who'd come over once or twice." He threw it out there casually, knowing she'd argue it.

"Or he could've killed Thom and was a stupid enough son of a bitch to leave his prints."

He laughed softly, genuine amusement at the sarcastic drawl in her voice. "I'm glad we got assigned to do this together."

"Why? Yorioka not giving you the warm and fuzzies?"

"Yorioka's fine. She does her job well enough." He pulled the vehicle onto the highway. "But you and I, Grace, we have a chemistry."

He sensed the tension running through her body without glancing her way.

"I hope you mean in a compatible coworker way."

"I mean in an every way, sugar." Now he did look at her, just in time to see her scowl deepen.

"Save your pet names for your girl of the week, Darrius. I thought we covered this last night. I'm not interested in you."

He made no attempt to hide the knowing smile. "Really? *Really?* Last night on the trail, I could've had you on your back—"

"Oh Christ, will you shut it? We're at work. I don't want to discuss this."

Another quick glance her way showed his comments had gotten beneath her skin. Her cheeks were flushed, he could hear the racing of her heart, and her hands were knotted in her lap.

Deciding to take pity on her, he changed the subject. "How's your sister?"

Some of the tension left her shoulders and she shook her head. "She's all right. I drove her home and then called in a favor from a friend who owns a garage. He's hooking her up with some new tires today."

"Any idea who'd do this? She have any enemies?" *Or is it one of yours, sugar.*

"I really couldn't say. She may not be prom queen, but I don't think she has anyone with any kind of grudge against her. I mean, Bree's a good kid. Crap, and almost not a kid anymore," she muttered almost under her breath.

"How old is she? She looks young."

"She's seventeen."

Still in high school. He couldn't resist teasing, "So you're, what, two years older?"

"Five. Which, I'm sure you've read my file and already know."

Christ, she was young. He had almost a decade on her. He could often forgot how young—how much of a rookie—Grace really was. She seemed older than her years and fit in with their team like a seasoned veteran.

Again he had to wonder how the hell she got involved with

the experiments.

"There's the house on the right." Darrius nodded his head to the gray house, but kept driving. Only at the end of the street did he swing the car around and slide parallel into a spot along the curb.

They were far enough away to avoid being spotted, but with a pair of binoculars trained on the house. Though they barely used the tool—which seemed almost primitive nowadays. With their ability to see longer distances with incredible clarity, they relied more on their animal senses that always gave them the advantage.

Darrius made quick observances, noting the lawn that was probably a foot high with uncut grass and weeds. The gray paint on the house appeared weathered and dated, chipping in places and peeled completely off in others. A couple of rusty bicycles littered the front yard, and what looked like a basketball.

The house stuck out in a neighborhood that was probably middle class. The icing on the cake of their POI's meth-lab-looking home was the peeling beige station wagon in the driveway that had to be from the seventies.

"This feels a little like profiling," Grace murmured, her voice laced with amusement. "Shitty house where the POI lives? I mean, I was kind of hoping for a nice condo on Lake Washington or something."

"If our POI had that kind of money, I doubt he'd have fallen to the level of involvement this case has."

"Hmm. You'd be surprised. Sometimes money has nothing to do with it."

Something in her voice—the slight harshness in the word nothing—made him suspect Grace wasn't talking about their POI anymore. This was personal and likely went back to the experiments. If money hadn't been her motivator, then what had? Not that he'd ever suspected she'd gone in for the money.

Grace seemed financially stable, and from what he understood and had learned recently, she brought in a nice sum for those glass flowers she blew.

"Do we know if this guy is a shifter?" she asked.

"According to the notes Larson gave me, it looks like it. Wesley Parker. Twenty-nine, not married but has weekend custody of two children."

"Hmm. Hope his kids have tetanus shots if they're riding those bikes."

Darrius laughed, falling into the usual ease they had together. When Grace decided to use it, she had a wicked sense of humor.

"I'm trying to figure out whether the guy is home—" he jerked his chin toward the house, "—because really, does that car even look drivable?"

"Maybe…with some jumper cables and duct tape."

"Yup. Definitely spotting some silver tape on the front fender."

"Oh jeez." She laughed softly and then glanced his way. "Did you eat breakfast?"

His smile grew, knowing where this was going, and he met her gaze. She'd relaxed a bit, seemed more in her element and was back to the usual Grace he knew on assignment.

Often one of the agents would bring breakfast or snacks along when they knew they'd have an early morning or stakeout. He hadn't known they'd get assigned to do surveillance, but he'd brought in breakfast anyway this morning.

"I had a protein shake before I left his morning." He reached behind him and snagged a brown paper bag. "But I picked up some maple bars from Top Pot on the way in."

Her eyes lit up even as her mouth compressed. "I thought I smelled something pretty awesome. But, donuts? Really? Isn't that a little clichéd for what we do? Not to mention a total sugar rush."

"Says the woman who denies making oatmeal raisin cookies." He grabbed one of the bars and cocked an eyebrow. "And are you complaining? 'Cause don't think I won't eat the whole damn bag of these and not share." To make his point, he licked the glaze off that had spilled down the side of one bar.

He hadn't meant the move to be sexual, but the small hitch in her breathing didn't go unnoticed. Nor the dilation of her eyes—which he suspected had nothing to do with donuts.

"Yes. I don't doubt it." Her words sounded choked as she snagged the bag from him. She lowered her gaze from his mouth and pulled out a donut.

Satisfaction slid through his blood and he made no attempt to hide the arrogant smile that curved his lips. She could deny it all she wanted, but she wasn't immune to him by any means. Grace apparently hadn't been able to erase last night from her mind any more than he had. Though if she had any idea of his smug thoughts right now, she'd likely slap the smile right off his face.

Darrius turned his attention back to the house, but there hadn't been any movement since they'd arrived. Maybe the POI wasn't home. Which seemed more like a possibility if he had a nine-to-five job. Though looking at the house, the POI didn't exactly scream suburban dad who worked five days a week at a local bank.

Grace made a noise of satisfaction, then murmured, "This maple bar is good, no matter how damn bad it is for me. Thanks."

"Anytime, sugar." He finished off his donut and glanced her way. "Hey, how well did you get to know Thom Wilson?"

Darrius hadn't realized he was going to even ask the question, but it had been rolling around in his head for days now. Maybe he'd finally asked because they were so at ease now, so relaxed and back to the norm.

But clearly Grace didn't like going there mentally, because the tension was visible as her shoulders stiffened and her brows drew together.

"I knew him from the experiments. That was it."

"Did you ever talk after? When you were both freed?"

She hesitated, and he could sense she was debating answering honestly. "Once."

He didn't doubt she was telling the truth. Why lie about that. But would she elaborate? "Did he contact you?"

She gave a slight nod—seemed to be focusing extra hard on their POI's house as she ate her donut.

"He was depressed. Needed someone to talk to who understood what he was going through."

Crap. The donut he'd just eaten revolted in his stomach. Her words didn't bode well for ruling out suicide, and if Larson were to figure out she'd met with Thom...

"And I know what you're thinking, but you're wrong. I'll never believe it was a suicide. Thom Wilson would never kill himself." She paused and seemed to be struggling with her own demons. "You don't know what we went through—how every day was just a struggle to *not* die. We were survivors."

The last statement was almost inaudible, but he'd heard it and she was absolutely right. It was pretty much a damn miracle any of the volunteers had survived the experiments.

Seeming to lose her appetite, Grace chucked her half-eaten donut back into the bag.

Seeing her now, here, so alive and determined, was such a potent reminder at how close they'd been to losing her. His heart stuttered a bit just thinking about it, imaging the seat next to him empty, or permanently filled with another agent. It disturbed him on the deepest level to think about *what if* she hadn't been rescued in time.

Even now he could almost feel the dead weight of her body as he'd cradled her in his arms. Begged her to hold on just a while longer while the P.I.A. created an antidote to the drugs she and the others had been given.

"You're supposed to be watching the house, not me."

Her wary gaze met his, briefly, before she glanced back at their assignment.

Not even realizing he'd been staring so hard, Darrius shifted his attention back to the house. But he couldn't stop the quiet words. "I thought we were going to lose you. You were sicker than any of the other ferals. You had one foot in death's door."

"Well, clearly I stepped back out." It was obvious that she tried to sound detached, but there was a hint of pain behind the two words.

Maybe it was a shitty idea, but he wanted answers. He wanted her to trust him enough to confide in him.

"Do you remember anything from that week, Grace? I know the contract was iron tight, but maybe something happened that is grounds for prosecution. Maybe you remember something we could convict them on..."

Chapter Ten

Did she remember anything? Grace kept her gaze on the house but didn't really see it. Instead her mind flashed through a half dozen memories, at least she assumed they were memories. They were detached and moved through her head kind of like those floaters you get in your eyes. And every now and then her mind locked on one, but it slipped away just as quickly.

"I wasn't raped, if that's what you're asking. I was told an agency nurse did a full examination on me after the rescue—but even that's hazy."

Another memory flashed through her mind now. Briefly. Darrius holding her, his face above her and his dark gaze intense and full of worry. There were emotions tied to the image as well—desolation, and yet peace. A peace that came from knowing she'd die in the arms of a man she trusted?

Grace clenched her teeth and forced back the sting of tears that burned her eyes and made her throat tight.

She hated going back to that time in her head, hated that she was being forced to do so in therapy. And yet, somehow she didn't resent talking to Darrius as much as she did the therapist at the P.I.A. There was some relief in opening up to him.

"I remember you," she admitted grudgingly. "You seem to be the strongest memory that I apparently don't mind keeping."

She couldn't resist casting him a quick glance from beneath her lashes. His emotions were mixed, and blatant in his eyes. Frustration, and yet pure masculine pleasure that had her stomach flipping. He'd been right, they did have a connection; it was like an invisible electric wire between them that sizzled and snapped. It had fed her energy then, and did so now. It kept her alive, kept her going.

His gaze slid back to the house, and she didn't realize he'd reached for her hand until his strong fingers threaded with hers.

She didn't draw away, literally couldn't have if she wanted to. Her hand felt almost fragile in his large one, and she squeezed his fingers, accepting the energy he gave.

"I couldn't let you die."

His words weren't quite steady, and it shocked her a bit to realize how much those dark days had affected him as well.

"How did you hear about the experiments?"

He changed the subject, and she wasn't really surprised. Darrius didn't seem like the type of guy who liked to stay deep emotionally. He was the joker. The sensitive, funny guy who liked to keep things light.

And though it was easier now to open up to him, his current question was tricky. She didn't want to lie to him, but oh, God, she didn't want to tell him the truth. Didn't want to tell *anyone* the truth.

"Well, the experiments were very quiet. I mean, they had to be. Feloray Laboratories couldn't just throw out an ad for shifters to come in and sign up for a study." That much was the truth. Humans weren't aware of shifters, which meant everything was kind of done on the sly. "It was mostly word of mouth, and it eventually got back to me." That much was...a partial truth.

"And so you volunteered to be a participant?"

"The whole thing sent alarm bells off in my head." She drew in a slow breath, and plunged on. "So, yeah, I signed up and went in undercover, figuring I could bring back some information for the P.I.A."

Lie. The biggest, filthiest, most blatant lie and she hated that it was now between them. She should've been used to it by now, because it was the same one she'd told the P.I.A.

There was no response, except for the subtle tightening of Darrius's fingers around hers.

As the moments passed and he didn't say anything, her pulse quickened and her throat went dry. He didn't believe her. The realization sank in with the gentleness of a brick.

He didn't need to argue, question her further, or even give any indication he'd heard her. She absolutely had no doubt he was screaming "bullshit" in his head.

But why? She was sure the therapist had bought the same story—and was pretty sure the agents on her team would too if she fed it to them. Hell, Darrius had at one point told her they already suspected that was her reasoning.

"That's both stupid, and admirable." Darrius stroked his jaw line with his free hand. "Though I'm leaning toward stupid."

His words gave every illusion that he believed her, but she wasn't a fool. Which mean she had to try harder.

Her pulse quickened. "Look, I know it was absolutely stupid. I should've come to the P.I.A. with my concerns instead of taking it on myself."

Had her words sounded as desperate to him as they did in her head? She waited for him to reply, but he remained silent for too long.

Finally, "What was it like at the beginning of the experiments? Do you remember that much?"

Not exactly a response to her words, more a diversion from them. Which was okay, because she could answer this part honestly. She blinked and slid back to that day in her mind.

"Lots of paperwork, and everyone was really friendly. It all seemed so innocent." She smiled faintly. "The volunteers who signed up to be a part of the tests were excited—I mean, it was a lot of money."

"Yeah, well I doubt it was worth the cost you all paid. Feloray Laboratories basically got away with attempted murder."

He was absolutely right. "And I want them to be held accountable more than anybody, but those contracts were too thorough." Her voice thickened with every word. "I would be perfectly content to see Jocelyn Feloray burning over a spit in hell. She'll be there. Someday."

Darrius's gaze narrowed on her, as if her vehemence had surprised him. But murmured, "That bitch has gotta be Satan's go-to woman."

"She's on his speed dial."

Darrius's laugh was low and sexy. It died too quickly, a soft sigh replacing it. "It just doesn't make any sense to me. Why would anyone want an anti-shifting drug? Why would someone want to deny their wolf side?"

"It wasn't so much about denying that side of them." She had to help Darrius understand. "Someone like my sister, for instance. She had a horrific break in her leg as a child and it never healed properly."

Darrius grunted. "I noticed she had a limp."

"She's had it for nearly her whole life. For her to try and shift is excruciating, but you know how it is. It's instinctive. It's not an easy thing to control, especially when we're children."

Shapeshifter children were watched carefully. The community couldn't afford to have a child shift in front of the human population. Until shifter children learned to fully control their instincts, they were kept close to home. Home schooled and only allowed to run free in areas where no humans would spot them.

In the rare instances a human did spot them, the human was given a memory wipe. A quick, painless procedure that could wipe the memory of the human, or shifter, for as far back as needed.

"I suppose I can understand someone with those circumstances." Darrius traced a finger lightly over the palm of her hand, and the seemingly innocuous gesture sent tingles through her body, momentarily distracting her. Until he added, "So why not sign up your sister to be tested?"

Cold washed through her, draining the blood from her head and leaving her a bit dizzy. He was so close to the truth, pretty much running parallel to it now. And she'd led him right to it.

"Because it was the experimental stage. The drug was new

and untried." She tried to keep her voice casual. "No one knew the side effects."

"Ah, right. Of course."

Except Jocelyn Feloray. Helping the shifters had never been the woman's intention—she'd wanted them dead. She hated the species with a passion that was unbelievable. And Grace hated her with an equaled passion. Because she'd walked in the doors of that run-down lab fully aware that she might never walk out again.

"Well, it's a good thing Aubree didn't find out about the experiments then. Sounds like something she might've been foolish to try and sign up for—kind of like her big sister. Then we would've had to worry about rescuing two Masterson girls."

A good thing was an understatement. A bit emotionally drained now, she couldn't do much more than nod.

Darrius dropped her hand and sat up straight. "We've got movement."

What? Shit, she'd completely lost focus on what was going on. Her gaze steadied on the house just in time to see a man exit the front door and make his way to the rusty station wagon.

Tall and skinny, the man definitely looked like he spent his days smoking meth out of a pipe.

"I say we tail this guy," Darrius murmured. "See where he takes us?"

"I'm in." Because she was betting her money there was a good chance he would take them to Feloray Laboratories.

The Doornail was packed for a weeknight, and many of the patrons were agents with the P.I.A.

Darrius slid his attention across the table to where Grace had recently sat down in one of the wooden chairs. Her arms were folded across her chest and discomfort flickered every now and then across her face.

This wasn't her scene at all, and yet he and Donovan had

convinced her to come tonight. They were celebrating, because apparently Grace's instincts were pretty damn kick-ass.

She'd been the only one to say Thom Wilson's suicide might not be a suicide. He'd been skeptical—hell, all of them had. She'd stuck to her guns, and tonight they were given the shred of evidence that she might've been on to something.

After tailing their POI, it was clear the meth-head definitely had some kind of ties to Feloray Industries, because he'd been parked outside their lab for over an hour and a half.

It was by no means a smoking gun, but it was definitely a connection they were going to further investigate.

Her gaze finally skimmed to his, and a slight smiled curved her lips. Amusement flickered in her eyes. She gave a slight shake of her head, as if to say *I can't believe you got me to come here.*

He winked. "I'm buying you a beer, Masterson."

"You're not buying me a beer, we've got work in the morning."

"If he doesn't, I will." Donovan gave her a light slap on the shoulders as he stood up. "We've all got to work in the morning. Besides, what do you think we come here for? The food?"

As he walked off to the bar, Yorioka shrugged and said, "I don't know. The fish and chips are pretty killer."

They'd all come out tonight, the entire team, which was rare, but nice. Larson had even brought Alicia—the uptight socialite fiancée who looked as if she'd rather be anywhere but in a dark, loud pub. Her hands were folded in her lap, her mouth compressed, and her gaze narrowed with repulsion.

Darrius shook his head and wondered if the two would really end up mated, and if playing politics in the shifter community would really be worth putting up with someone like Alicia.

Agent Yorioka had also brought her partner, Denise, a quiet, soft-spoken Asian woman, who was currently in a quiet discussion with Larson.

But Yorioka seemed more focused on Grace, watching her

over her beer with an expression of derision and irritation. Obviously, Grace still had a long ways to go before she earned the other agent's respect.

Well, fuck it, she didn't have to go out of her way to prove she was a good agent to the new girl. Grace had *been* the new girl, had already spent months working her ass off. Obviously he and the rest of the guys trusted her, so Yorioka was just being an idiot if she let her own judgment cloud her view.

"We're celebrating your instincts tonight, Masterson." Larson gave her a steady glance and took a swig of beer. "They're not bad. Not bad at all."

A flush filled her cheeks and pleasure flickered in her eyes. "Thanks."

"I'll bet you the agency will have a search warrant on that guy by morning," Donovan added as he returned to the table from the counter. "And I've got your beer."

Darrius watched her accept the beer with a laugh. She looked good. Happy, and yet maybe a bit uncertain of the attention she was getting.

His smile faded a bit and he looked away. He couldn't quite ignore the instinct that told him she'd lied in the car this afternoon. Everyone was so eager to believe—maybe they just wanted to—that Grace had sent herself into the experiments undercover.

But he knew she wouldn't have made such a stupid move, no matter how new she was. Grace was damn smart and cared about her career. She'd never have risked it by pulling a stunt like that.

So why was she lying? What irked him more was that she not only lied to everyone, but kept lying to *him*. Didn't she trust him? Whatever she was hiding, she didn't want it revealed. Which just made him all the more determined to figure out what the hell it was.

"You guys give me way too much credit." Grace sipped her beer and shrugged. "You all would've done the same."

Her gaze lifted and collided with his. He saw the pleasure

leak out a bit, and the guilt that slipped in. But then, when he didn't look away and their eyes stayed locked, her expression shifted. Heat flickered in her eyes, and an awareness appeared that he knew she wouldn't want him to see.

She lowered her beer and her tongue flicked out to catch a drop on her lip. Hunger lashed through him, instantaneous and potent. His blood heated and his body stirred.

Shit. Why was his reaction to her so immediate lately? It was almost violent in its intensity, and equally confusing to him.

He jerked his gaze away, urging the dominant wolf inside him to back the fuck off.

"I thought my wife said she was coming tonight," Donovan muttered, glancing around. "Do I need to kick someone's ass at the agency for working her too hard?"

"I work hard by choice, so stop your nagging, honey."

Donovan, whose back had been to the door, stood and turned around, then swept his wife up into a huge hug, before planting a kiss on her lips.

"Easy with the PD-fucking-As," Darrius called out, but again felt that stab of jealousy at the bond they shared.

From what Darrius had heard they'd always known each other, but had drifted apart. They'd only reconnected during the experiments when Donovan caught Sienna trying to free the feral shifters, while the agency team was inside the lab trying to do the same. Though strange as it was, it was pretty cool that something so positive could come from such a horrific event.

Sienna pulled away from her husband, and her gaze slid over the table before landing on Grace. The petite blonde let out a noise of excitement, before making her way around the table.

"I heard you were here, but refused to believe it until I saw you." Sienna gave her a hug. "I'm so glad to see you out with everyone tonight."

"Thanks. It's really good to see you too." Emotion thickened Grace's voice and she blinked hard. "I'm sorry, I just haven't been very sociable lately."

"I absolutely understand, and promise I'm not criticizing." She glanced back at her husband. "Warrick, will you please get me a glass of red wine? I'm going to catch up with Grace."

Darrius didn't bother to hide his rumbling laugh as Donovan immediately got to his feet to go to the counter.

Whipped. A hundred percent. But Sienna was beautiful, smart as hell and pretty damn amazing so he couldn't fault him. She was the perfect match for Donovan.

Sienna took up his abandoned chair next to Grace and drank a sip of his beer. "Now tell me, how have you been?"

Darrius didn't mean to intentionally eavesdrop, kept his gaze scanning the bar, but it was hard not to listen to the women's conversation.

"I've been better. I've been worse," Grace said softly.

"Yeah, I can believe it. If there's ever anything I can help with, please let me know."

"I will. Thanks, Sienna. It means a lot."

He hadn't realized the two knew each other so well, or had gotten close. Though it made sense, now that he thought about it. He'd been aware that Sienna had checked up on Grace several times after the recovery—often bringing food and flowers. It was a natural progression to friendship.

"So, I think we should do a girls night out," Sienna suggested brightly.

"A girls night, hmm?"

"Count me in," Alicia called out from across the table, seeming to finally perk up. "I'm always in for some wine and a spa day."

"Oh, yes, wine!" Sienna agreed. "Everything's better with wine."

Now that just sounded like trouble. Darrius flicked a casual glance back at Grace and found her watching him. Instead of blushing or looking away though, she kept her eyes locked on his.

Everyone around them seemed to fade away, and her gaze slid to his mouth. Still watching her eyes, he saw the hunger there, and the vacillation.

"Wouldn't it be fun? Some sushi and definitely some wine. Good call, Alicia. And maybe we can catch a movie, or do the pedicures thing…" Sienna trailed off.

Darrius broke his attention from Grace and glanced at Sienna—found her watching the both of them with open curiosity. Great. The last thing they needed was Sienna getting the wrong idea. Or maybe it was the right idea, and there lied the problem.

Grace cleared her throat. "Right. Pedicures," she said quickly, her voice a bit strained. "That could be fun."

"Good." Sienna nodded slowly and accepted the wine from Donovan as he returned. Fortunately her attention seemed to shift back to her husband. "You don't mind if I just keep your seat, do you, honey?"

"What's mine is yours." Donovan grimaced, but moved to sit in an empty seat by Darrius.

Whipped, he thought again, but maybe that wasn't such a bad thing.

Grace nodded at what Sienna was saying now—something about the new drug they were creating for shifter infants—but she couldn't slow her heart or her thoughts of Darrius.

All too often tonight her gaze would slip to him, and most of the time she found him watching her. It didn't matter whether he was talking to Donovan or shooting the shit with Larson and Yorioka, his gaze always seemed to stray back to her.

It was a bit unsettling. And thrilling.

How long had it been since a man had pursued her? Been interested in her? She didn't make it easy for them to do so, and had always been more closed off from developing relationships—romantic or otherwise.

She'd learned early on that when she did open herself up, she inevitably got hurt. Maybe the ones you loved left you alone in this world by dying, or maybe they betrayed you. Either way it resulted in the same pain.

But the moment she'd joined the P.I.A. and been assigned to her team, everything had changed. Her heart had cracked a bit and she'd allowed the guys in. It'd been like gaining a bunch of protective older brothers. She'd become just as determined to protect them as she knew they would her.

Her gaze lifted and moved across the table to Darrius. He was talking to Larson, but he'd been watching her out of the corner of his eye. She could sense it.

A tingle of awareness started at the back of her neck and raced through her body.

Somewhere along the way, Darrius had lost that brother vibe. It still freaked her out a bit, this whole thing between them, whatever it was. But it was becoming harder to deny it. Despite the walls and roadblocks she put up, he seemed entirely too apt at knocking them down.

"So when should we do the girls night?" Sienna asked, dragging Grace's mind away from Darrius again.

She put up another wall, vowing to give the other woman her full attention. At least for the rest of the evening.

The time passed by too quickly, filled with drinks, laughter and wonderfully distracting discussions.

Flushed from the two beers she'd drunk, Grace excused herself to use the bathroom.

The restroom was in the hallway of the building and was shared by several businesses. The hallway itself was cold with a faint musty smell. One of the overhanging lights was nearly out, wheezing its final breaths as it flickered on and off.

Familiarity raced through her, but not because she'd been here before. It reminded her too much of the lab they'd been kept in during the experiments. Her slight buzz from the beers vanished as darkness and fear swept through her blood.

Irritated with herself, that this is what she'd been reduced to, Grace forced herself to keep walking and eventually made her way into the bathroom.

She'd just picked a stall and locked the door when the bathroom door squeaked open again. The hairs on the back of her neck rose and she went still, her hand on the lock. She listened to the muted footsteps that came inside, heavy and measured.

You're being paranoid. It's just some other chick coming to use the bathroom.

Even still, she slid her hands silently into her oversized leather purse, closing her fingers around the thick handle of her Glock. Only with the cold metal in her grip did her pulse start to slow, and did she feel the familiarity of self-control return.

Whoever had entered the bathroom had moved into the stall next to her. She slid her gaze to the floor, then to the left.

Maybe they weren't sexy heels, but the shoes next to her were definitely a woman's. Still, she couldn't shake the sense of unease, and she'd never been one to ignore her instincts.

Abandoning any pretense of using the bathroom, Grace knew she needed to cut and run. She had the gun, but the last thing she wanted to do was use it. Shifters didn't draw unnecessary attention, but if it came down to that, someone would get a hole in their chest.

She pushed back the bolt of her lock and opened the door, exiting with calm caution. Walking backward toward the exit, she kept her gaze—and her gun—trained on the stall next to her.

Her heart thudded in her chest. Just a few feet and then she'd be out of the bathroom.

But the door to the stall remained closed, and her brows drew together with uncertainty. The woman still hadn't made any indication she was leaving the stall.

Oh, Grace, you've flat-out lost it. She had to be bordering on unhealthy paranoia. Had she just completely freaked out for nothing?

Some of the tension eased from her shoulders. Still, she didn't lower the gun even as she reached for the door handle.

Her free hand closed around the brass knob and she twisted it, the safety of the hall, as ridiculous as it seemed, just inches away.

Pulling open the door, her chest expanded with a breath of relief. But the air ripped from her chest again as the door slammed into her. The force of the impact sent her sprawling back into the bathroom where she smashed into the floor, her head greeting the tile with an unhealthy crack.

She saw stars. Or wait, maybe she thought she did in the darkness that suddenly enveloped her. Whoever had smashed in the door had turned off the lights.

Grace tried to scramble up, raising her gun and forcing her gaze to adjust to the darkness and find the threat.

The arm that wrapped around her neck coincided with the cold barrel of the gun that pressed against her temple.

"Drop your weapon, Agent Masterson."

Chapter Eleven

Son of a bitch.

"Drop your fucking gun. I don't like having to ask twice." She dug the barrel deeper into her forehead.

That voice. She knew that voice. It was a woman's, and obviously disguised into a low rasp, but still something jarred in her memory. She couldn't pin it down, though, not while her brain whirled for a way to escape. A way to not give the attacker the advantage by putting her own gun on the floor.

The woman grabbed her ponytail, jerking her head back so her throat was exposed. In the darkness she could almost make out her shape, the whites of her eyes, but no features.

That's when she felt the sharp prick of a knife at her throat and the weight of another person's body straddling her waist.

Male this time. Large. Heavy. Not defeated, but also not dumb, she didn't resist as the man pried her gun from her fingers.

There were two attackers, but of course that made sense. One had been in the stall next to her—she should've just shot the son of a bitch—the other had been the bastard to nearly knock her out with the door.

"You never were very good at taking orders, Grace," the man rasped.

He knew her? Unlike the woman, she didn't recognize knife guy's voice. Or did she?

She drew in a slow breath and tried to place their scent, to figure out if they were familiar. But they'd come prepared, probably doing a thorough body wash with heavily diluted bleach to mask their scents.

"What do you want?" She moved only her lips to ask the

question, not messing with the tip of the knife that hovered above her carotid artery.

The woman seemed to relax a bit, as if she were relieved the man had control now. Hope flared inside Grace, even as the woman didn't move away completely, but eased the pressure of the gun against her temple.

"Aren't you afraid?" The man with the knife lowered his head, his voice still raspy and almost a whisper.

Raw panic gathered in her throat, forming a scream that she knew they would silence harshly. But the position—being held down and threatened—was so like her time in the lab that she felt the fingers of hysteria tracing over her.

Stay angry. Focus on the rage. How have these bastards gotten control of you?

"If you were going to kill me, you would've done it by now." It was amazing how calm her words were when she was anything but.

"Maybe I like to hear my victims beg."

A memory slashed through her mind. A new one she'd never remembered until now.

She'd been curled up in the cell at the lab, naked and bruised from the continuous injections and restraints. And a man had stood above her, circling with a digital camera in his hands as he snapped pictures.

She'd begged him to stop—to seek help for the shifters. The memory fizzled a bit. Had she vowed retribution? Or was that a thought she'd added now in her current fury?

He'd been there with her during the experiments. She was certain of it.

"We've been in here too long." The woman was obviously getting nervous—not a good sign when she had a gun at Grace's head.

Yes, they had, and Grace was hoping like hell someone would walk in any minute now. Though, dammit, that might just put more people at risk.

"You're right, though, Agent Masterson. We're not here to

kill you." The man used his free hand to touch her cheek and she was unable to stop the shudder of repulsion, even as she formed a plan.

You just let down your guard, asshole. Big mistake.

"We're here to warn you," he continued, his breath so close to her face now she could smell the hint of ginger on it. "Let Thom Wilson rest in peace, or this might get ugly."

Thom Wilson... They were here about Thom? Her mind stored that bit of information and then moved on to what she had to do next.

"It's already ugly." Before he could blink, she'd grabbed his now lax wrist and forced it above her head.

The shocked cry of pain from the woman was the only confirmation she needed to know that the knife had connected with her face.

Grace rolled free from them in the chaos. She barely took a second to get orientated, before knife guy was lunging at her again.

"That was pretty stupid, you bitch."

Before he reached her she had a second to slam her foot into his belly with a strong sidekick, and he stumbled back into the wall with a muffled *oomph*.

Triumph surged through her, but it was short lived as she realized too late she'd lost track of the woman. She made her presence known—and her anger at being cut—by slamming her gun into the back of Grace's head.

And then it was too late to fight, because unconsciousness was already taking over.

"So...you hoping for twins, Sienna?" Darrius couldn't resist jumping into an animated ribbing over when and how many kids Sienna and Donovan were going to have.

"No, absolutely not." Sienna glared across the table. "No twins. No triplets. No anything. My eggs are staying unfertilized for at least a few more years." Her gaze shifted to her husband.

"Got that, Warrick?"

"Gross." Darrius groaned, but his grin slipped as his gaze jerked suddenly toward the hallway that led to the bathrooms.

Unease had hit quickly and intensely. How long ago had Grace left to use the bathroom? Two minutes? Three? Something was off. He knew it with a certainty that he didn't want to question.

His pulse quickened and he pushed back his chair. "I'll be back in a second."

"Hilliard."

Darrius ignored the sharp warning from his alpha. Larson knew he was going after Grace and was making his disapproval known, but fuck it. Darrius wasn't going after her to shove his tongue down her throat in the hallway, he was making sure she was okay.

He slipped out the pub door and into the hallway. The sight of two people in black wearing masks, hightailing it out a back entrance was enough to make his blood go cold.

A growl erupted from his throat, his canines slid down and his nails slid free as the wolf inside him readied to shift and give chase. Barely, just barely, did he have enough sense to cast a quick glance at the closed bathroom door. Seeing it was dark inside, he knew his first priority was Grace.

Darrius sprinted back to the door to the bar and took in the handful of people still at their table. "I need help!"

Seeing the alpha quickly rise, along with others at the table, Darrius rushed back to locate Grace. He ran back to push open the bathroom door, but it resisted, moving slowly inward, as if something on the other side blocked it.

"What's going on?" Larson snarled from beside him, brows drawn with determination.

Darrius jerked his head toward the exit. "Pretty sure Grace got attacked. Two perps, all in black ran out the back door."

"We'll find them." Larson let out a growl of fury, and then he sprinted out the back door.

Darrius had already turned away and was easing open the

bathroom door, using his weight against the resistance.

"Grace, you need to answer me, sugar."

The door swung open, all resistance gone now. Darrius stepped inside and found Grace facing the mirror as she splashed some water on her face.

"Grace?"

It took a moment, but finally she lifted her head and met his gaze in the mirror.

Son of a bitch. The bruise on her forehead and trickle of blood running down her neck made something savage rise inside him. His claws slid forth, piercing into his palms as he stepped inside.

The urge to kill rode him hard, and now he regretted not giving chase with Larson.

Knowing it wouldn't be smart to show every emotion running through him on his face, Darrius filtered all out but concern.

"Are you okay?" He forced his voice to remain calm as he closed the distance between them. Unable to help himself, he reached out to use the pad of his thumb to catch the small droplet of blood.

"I'll be fine." She gave him a hard smile. "We heal fast, remember?"

Physically. *Fuck.* "What happened, Grace?"

"I guess I let my guard down."

Her words were flat and simple, as if that explained everything.

"Bullshit. We've talked about this. You don't get taken off guard. There were two of them," he said, not really asking it as a question.

"Yes. One I was aware of, she came in and tried to hide in the stall next to me."

"She? One of the attackers was a woman?"

"Oh yeah. Definitely." She grimaced as she wet down a paper towel and blotted her neck. "I tried to get out of the bathroom, where I'd stupidly cornered myself, and then the guy tried to smash my face in with the door."

"They both attacked you?"

"Yeah. The man had a knife to my neck, the woman had a gun to my head. They had turned off the lights, so I was pretty much fighting blind."

"Kind of hard to fight at all with the barrel of a gun at your head." No longer able to hold in his fury, Darrius let out a string of curses and slammed his fist into the wall.

Surprise registered on her face. "Hey, easy there. It could have been worse."

"You mean if they'd killed you?" he couldn't resist snarling.

"Obviously they didn't want me dead or we wouldn't be talking right now. You'd be pretty proud of me. I did this one counterattack that gave me the advantage." Her smirk faded. "Well, for a few seconds anyway."

"I'm always proud of you. You're a damn good fighter." But taking on an armed woman and man wasn't exactly a fair match. "We should get you looked at."

"I'm fine. Just a bit of a headache and suitably bruised, as they intended me to be. Besides, by the time you found someone to look at me I'd be healed," she pointed out.

Turning back to the mirror, Grace touched the bruise along her forehead and he couldn't argue that it was already fading due to her shifter blood.

She was right, but it didn't ease his concern or fury.

The encounter had shaken her up. He knew it, even if she hid it well under the bravado, it was in the slight tremble of her hand and the way her gaze wouldn't quite meet his.

"It's okay to be afraid, Grace. You don't need to be so strong all the time."

He watched her in the mirror, saw her bite her lip as the shimmer of tears in her eyes caught the light. Shock raced through him as he realized she was trying not to cry, he could sense it.

With a muffled curse, he strode forward and turned her to

face him, before pulling her into his arms.

"It's okay, you're safe now."

He expected her to jerk away and/or plant her fist into his belly, but instead her arms slipped around his waist and she pressed her head against his shoulder.

"You don't need to be strong *all* the fucking time."

"I'm not strong, I've just gotten really good at faking it," she whispered raggedly. "And if you tell anyone about this—"

"This is between you and I, sugar." He pulled her tighter against him, and smoothed a hand gently down her back. "But you gotta stop worrying about what others will think, they know you're a good agent."

Her body trembled in his arms and she sighed. "I don't know about that."

Irritation eased through him. Darrius pulled away just enough to catch her chin between his fingers and tilt it up so she had to look at him.

"I do." His gaze locked with hers, and he could see the frustration there that likely had little to do with what had just happened.

Then the emotion shifted, her gaze darkened and her breathing grew heavier.

"You need to trust me."

"I do," she whispered. "Sometimes a little too much, and that scares me."

Her words wrapped around his heart, raising the protective and possessive side of him. They also sparked the need to touch her—to taste her again.

Unable to stop himself, he lowered his head to brush a kiss across her mouth. It was supposed to be quick and comforting, but he should've known better. The moment his lips touched hers, the spark of need lit inside him and threatened to become a full-on bonfire.

Grace made a murmur of surprise that morphed into a sigh of pleasure. Her fingers slid up his chest and her mouth parted beneath his.

She was beginning to trust him, had just admitted it, and she no longer fought the attraction that was between them. The realization sent a rush of cold through Darrius.

When he'd first realized the chemistry between them, he'd written it off as a fluke that would maybe end up with them in bed together. But the sex hadn't happened yet, and a foundation much stronger than friendship was building. Only he knew the foundation was an illusion that could quickly crumble. It could never support a relationship if she was looking for one.

Dammit, what the hell was wrong with him? Why was he even kissing her in the first place after she'd just been assaulted?

Garnering what little self-control he had left, Darrius lifted his head.

Get your mind back in the game, asshole.

"Sorry, I didn't mean for that to happen."

She gave a husky laugh and pressed her forehead against his. "Don't be. It was probably the exact distraction I needed, and if we weren't in a public bathroom, I'd probably be asking for a hell of a lot more."

Her casual words had an immediate impact on his body. His cock tightened beneath his jeans and the air hissed out from between his teeth.

"Damn, sugar, you need to bite your tongue."

"Or what? You'll do it for me?"

Now he did laugh, and she joined him. But the break in tension was well needed.

"Not to bring the conversation back to the bad stuff, but what did they say to you? If they didn't want you dead, they must've had a message."

She stepped out of his arms and sighed. The wistfulness faded from her expression as she leaned against the wall, folding her arms across her chest.

"They told me to back off the Wilson case."

He barked out a laugh of disbelief. "You've got to be shittin' me. That's pretty damn brazen."

"Yeah that's what I was thinking. And I'm willing to bet they work for Feloray."

"But that would be so stupid. They've got to know we'll suspect them first thing."

"Oh, I'm sure they do. They sure weren't trying to hide who sent them." She hesitated. "And I think I know them. Or at least one."

"Really? I think when Larson gets back we'll file a report with the police—"

"No cops." She gave a fierce shake of her head. "You know how risky it is involving humans with shifter business. Besides, we'd have to explain my lack of injuries."

There was a sharp knock on the door before Sienna popped her head inside the bathroom.

"Grace? Oh my word, what on earth happened?" She strode in, eyes crinkled with distress. "Are you okay? I heard you were attacked."

"I'll be fine."

"You don't look fine. If you look this good now, I would've hated to see you five minutes ago." Sienna looked around. "Is my husband hunting down the jerk who did this to you?"

"Jerks," Darrius added. "I would've been out there with him, but—"

"Your first concern was Grace. Of course I understand." Sienna's gaze softened, became almost pensive as she looked between him and Grace. "It's only natural."

Only natural? Shit. Sienna was romanticizing this as if they were future mates. There was nothing between him and Grace besides a strong friendship and healthy dose of lust.

But even as he told himself that, the unease rode in on a cloud of doubt. What the hell? Grace couldn't be his mate—he knew that, so what the hell was going on?

The sound of footsteps in the hall had them all turning to see the others return.

"They're gone," Larson said quietly as he strode into the

bathroom. “Looks like they had a van running in the alley out back. We tried to follow it, but once they hit the main road it was over.”

Darrius gave a sharp nod. “You get a license?”

“No, it was deliberately covered, probably mud or some shit.”

“Wow, this place is becoming quite the little hangout.” Yorioka smirked, stepping inside. “Maybe we should take this outside the bathroom before it gets invaded by the gaggle of sorority girls that just showed up at the pub?”

Larson nodded. “Everyone back in the pub, we need to talk.”

Chapter Twelve

"Who's after you, Masterson?"

Grace clenched her hands around her half-drunk beer, but knew she wouldn't be taking another sip.

She couldn't ignore Larson's question, even if she wasn't quite sure of the answer.

"I don't really know, sir."

"We're outside of work, you can drop the formalities." Larson flashed her a hard smile, but there was little warmth. "I should be hauling your ass over to the police station to file a report."

"I think we all know that's a bad idea," she said mildly, basically repeating what she'd said to Darrius earlier. "We don't want to involve human law enforcement in a shifter problem."

"You think these two were shifter?"

"I'm certain of it. They know I am, and seemed to make an effort to cover their scent."

"And yet you have an idea who they are."

"Maybe, maybe not. There was something familiar, but I couldn't pin it down for certain."

Beneath the scrutiny of the alpha's stare, she struggled not to squirm. Something about the guy made you feel like you were a kid getting chastised. He was fair, both as their alpha and their team leader, but he was intimidating. No one would deny that.

His fiancée sat next to him, watching her with sympathy in her eyes.

"You're bleeding, sweetie. Do you want a bandage?" Alicia offered. "I have a first-aid kit in my purse."

No she didn't want a freaking bandage—though a shot of

tequila was sounding pretty damn good right about now.

"I'll be fine, thanks."

Larson grunted. "I understand there was some kind of accident the other day as well."

Her gaze snapped briefly to Darrius. Had he told the alpha about the near minivan hit? Or the tires being slashed? Either one she'd rather her alpha *not* have known about.

"I've had some bad luck lately, yes. It doesn't mean I'm ready to chalk it up to someone trying to intimidate me."

Donovan grunted from the end of the table where he sat quietly with Sienna. And when Grace glanced around, she noticed all the team members looked a bit skeptical. Yorioka included.

"You're not stupid, Masterson," Larson murmured. "You just had two people blatantly attack you in a public bathroom. How the hell does that leave any doubt in your mind?"

"Even if I accepted it, why me? Why not warn Darrius or Yorioka to back off the Wilson case? I'm not the only one investigating it."

"But you were the only one who was convinced it wasn't a suicide."

True. Though now that they knew their POI's prints were found in Wilson's car, and he was connected to Jocelyn Feloray, people were starting to get on board with her theory. It was one of the reasons they were celebrating tonight, wasn't it?

"And you are also one of the survivors from the experiments," Donovan pointed out. "And if they really are targeting them, you're going to be on their list."

She shook her head. It just didn't make any sense. "But they didn't kill me."

"I think you should come stay in the city. You're too damn isolated outside of North Bend." Larson scowled. "Hell, there's not even a Starbucks in sight."

Grace laughed. "Oh come on, there's a Starbucks ten minutes from my house."

"You can stay with Sienna and I," Donovan offered.

Sienna nodded, her eyes lighting up. "Absolutely, in fact I was just about to say the same thing."

"Look, you guys, I appreciate the offer, but there's not a chance I'm leaving my home because a couple of dipshits have decided to threaten me."

"Then I'll stay with you."

Darrius's quiet statement had all heads turning in his direction. Grace could feel her face warming, but she didn't reply, instead just waited for Larson to shoot down the idea. She knew he didn't approve of the possibility of her and Darrius getting involved.

"I think that's probably smart."

Stunned, she glanced at their alpha. Had she heard that right? He wasn't looking at her, though, but instead at Darrius.

"You guys can't just decide my future for me. This is my life—"

"Yes, and it's under attack. You've got choices, Masterson. Either stay with the Donovans, take the protection that Hilliard is offering, or I'll bring you into the agency and have you sequestered for your own protection."

Her heart thudded and her mouth went dry. Sequestered. Jesus, he thought it was that serious? Of course he did, or he wouldn't be threatening her with it.

She didn't want to leave her home, especially to be babysat by Warrick or Sienna. She needed to be there for Aubree anyway, so like hell would she agree to being *sequestered*.

Which left...

"Hilliard. He can stay with me." Resigned to the idea, she didn't hear anything else anyone said. She could only see her life spiraling out of her control.

"You tired?"

Grace jerked upright, not even realizing she'd nearly fallen asleep in the truck. She cast a glance over at Darrius, who was driving.

"Yeah. I'm a little tired," she muttered, not bothering to hide the grumpiness from her tone.

It was almost ten at night and she'd been up since five thirty. After the bar, he'd followed her back to her house so she could drop off her car, but then insisted she hop in his truck so he could drive to his place and pick up some things so he'd be prepared to stay a while.

They were on their way back to her house again, but overall it had made for an unpleasantly long night.

"You're a good sport, Grace."

She just barely stopped the derisive snort. "I don't have a choice. My alpha spoke and I had to listen."

Darrius shrugged. "You could've been sequestered. Or stayed with the Donovans."

"You know those aren't really options." She sighed. "I can't give up my life, and besides, Aubree needs me. If I'm in hiding I'm pretty much leaving her without protection."

"And does she need it? Protection, I mean."

More than he knew. "She's young and a little vulnerable. I'm really all she has."

"She's got your parents, right?"

Oh how she wished. "No. They've been dead for years now."

He cast her a sharp look. "I didn't know that. How did it happen, if you don't mind me asking?"

"There was an accident when we were on a family camping trip. I was eight." She glanced out the window into the darkness, trying as she had so many times before to remember that day. "We were up at Hurricane Ridge in the Olympic National Forest, hiking on one of the trails. And then..."

She shrugged. So much of that day was just gone, no doubt blocked for self-preservation. "I don't really remember. From what I hear the ground was saturated from heavy rain, the cliff already crumbling and we got too close to the edge."

"We?"

"My parents, my sister and I. We all went over the ledge. My parents were killed instantly from broken necks." Oh God, it never really got easier to say. “My sister’s leg got mangled, and I…was somehow absolutely fine.” The guilt that had always been a part of her surfaced again, gathering in her throat so she had difficulty swallowing.

“Jesus, I’m so sorry. I had no idea. That’s just horrific.”

“Yes.” It was the only response she could muster.

“So who raised you and Aubree?”

“Our uncle and aunt,” she replied in a flat tone that garnered her another sharp look.

“You don’t sound too happy about that. Were they not very nice? Did you have an awful childhood?”

“It wasn’t all sunshine and roses,” she replied honestly and sighed. “But they never intended to be parents and had two kids sprung on them. Aubree and I were happy, and have always been incredibly close. Aubree doesn’t remember our parents—our aunt and uncle were all she ever knew, and even then our uncle passed away five years ago.”

“I’m sorry. You guys sound like you had it pretty rough.” Darrius pulled his truck onto the dirt road that led to her house.

“Thank you,” she said softly.

“For?”

“For volunteering to stay with me.”

“Yeah, well I’d like to say my motives were completely altruistic, but I’d be lying.” He parked his truck next to her Eclipse and turned off the engine. The laugh he gave was husky and pure sensuality. “I want you. And the more opportunities I have to seduce you, the better.”

Her mouth dried out at his blatant statement. With just the darkness between them, her heart quickened and heat sizzled through her body.

“Darrius, has anyone ever told you you’re overly aggressive?” She attempted lightness, but his words had brought her body to life.

Just imagining the context of what he’d said had her nipples tightening and an ache blooming between her legs.

She wanted him. As much as she wanted to keep denying it to herself and to him, she knew it was pointless because he sure wasn't buying it.

"Well, that's just it. I think you like my aggressiveness, sugar."

Actually, she did. Which was odd, because with any other guy she would've told him to shove his hyped-up swagger where the sun didn't shine.

Turning in her seat, she stared at his dark profile. What would it feel like to finally give in? To have those full lips moving over her breasts and lie beneath the weight of his muscled body as he moved inside of her?

The ache between her legs became a full-out throb, and with sudden clarity she realized she didn't want to say no anymore. She wanted to think about something besides the awful attack tonight, and sex with Darrius might just be a damn good distraction.

"I do like your aggressiveness," she admitted softly. She inched her hand over the space between them and caught his hand, lacing her fingers through his. "But will you like mine?"

Taking over the role as aggressor, Grace tugged his hand over to her and placed it on her breast.

"Oh, damn," he rasped, shock and pleasure in his tone. Yet he still curled his hand to mold her flesh against his palm. "I was not expecting that."

"I like keeping you on your toes," she confessed with a breathy laugh.

He flicked his thumb over her nipple and she couldn't stop the small gasp that escaped.

"Grace, are you sure about this?"

She leaned over her seat toward him, her body ablaze as his fingers pinched the sensitive peak of her breast.

Positioning her mouth just above his, she murmured, "Put it this way. When we get inside the house you don't need to take the spare room. I want you in my bed."

Darrius groaned before his mouth crushed down on hers.

He plunged his tongue deep, while his skilled fingers teased her nipple into full alertness.

Head spinning and her body on fire, Grace slid fully into his lap. She answered his demanding kiss by rasping her tongue against his, tasting him and exploring the hidden contours of his mouth.

She lifted her head and dragged in a ragged breath. "If we don't get inside, you may end up taking me here in your truck."

"I'm trying to think of an argument on why that would be bad." He unbuttoned the top three buttons of her shirt.

"Me too." Oh he couldn't stop now.

She cried out when he slipped a hand inside her shirt and beneath her bra to discover bare flesh.

So good. It felt so good to finally have him touching her like this.

"I mean, there's a bed with a mattress inside," he pointed out, before lowering his head to brush his lips over the swell of her breast.

"Oh wow... Mattresses are good, but a little overrated." She helped unbutton the rest of her shirt and quickly removed her bra. "I could also just as easily ride you in the front seat of your truck."

Darrius groaned and she felt the immediate rise of his cock against her thigh. He cupped her breast again, stroking his thumb over her taut nipple.

"Damn, you are going to make me lose control and fast."

"That's kind of my goal. I'm tired of waiting and even two hundred feet to my bedroom seems too far right now."

"In that case..." He lifted her easily, so high that her knees fell open over his hips and her breasts were level with his mouth.

When his lips closed around her nipple she moaned her pleasure and slid her hands over his shaved head.

"Darrius," she whispered. "Oh, please don't stop."

"Not a chance. Not now that I've tasted you." He caught her nipple between his teeth, tugging lightly until she whimpered with need.

She was barely aware of anything but his mouth, until the brush of his fingers between her legs rocketed her into orbit. When had he unzipped her pants? Moved his hand inside and beneath her panties?

"You're so wet." He slid a finger into her.

Grace jerked against him, her nails digging into his shoulders now.

"So tight." He added a second finger and groaned. "If we were inside, I'd have my tongue inside you by now. I want to taste this sweetness so bad it hurts."

The imagery had her whimpering and clenching her muscles around his fingers.

"Later," she whispered. "You can make good on that promise later."

With the need inside her flaring to incinerating levels, she reached beneath her to free him from his jeans and underwear.

He was thick, hot and hard in her hands, and the drop of moisture against her thumb made her want to catch it on her tongue. But just as she'd promised him, that could wait until later.

"There's still too many clothes in the way." She moved off of him to slide out of her pants and underwear.

Darrius watched her through hooded eyes as he stroked himself.

Wow, he was big, almost in an intimidating way. But where there was the small shiver of nervousness, there was also the thrill of anticipation.

Even though she was completely naked, he was nearly fully dressed, with just his erection free from his jeans. Free and standing at attention.

"I can't do this."

Disappointment ripped through her, and her gaze jerked back to his. "But I thought—"

"You look so damn beautiful. Like candy laid out just for me. And I'm not taking you without tasting that sweetness first.

I want to make you come with my mouth." He reached beneath the seat and pulled the lever that had his seat pushing back.

How in the hell was he going to accomplish that? Not that she was complaining, because the idea of him going down on her had her body weeping with excitement.

Darrius caught her around the waist and maneuvered her so her legs fell over his shoulders and her upper back and head fell against the steering wheel.

Comfort was the last thing on her mind as his hot breath feathered across her sex.

"Love that you shave smooth, sugar. You're my own damn candy shop. Right here."

She was so open, so exposed, and her body trembled with anticipation. He made a small grunt of pleasure before burying his mouth between her legs.

Grace gave a sharp cry, her eyes nearly crossing with ecstasy as his tongue delved deep into her. His words had been the kindling to her fire, but his mouth was the accelerant that set her ablaze.

She traced trembling fingers over his shoulders, entranced by the sight of his dark head against her pale thighs. He took his time, almost seeming to taste and savor her like the candy he'd compared her to. His tongue slid in and out of her channel and then homed in to tease her clit. Paying special attention to the tiny bud in a way that guaranteed he was going to make her come fast.

"Oh my God, Darrius." Her thighs clenched around his head. "You're way too good at this."

He gave a husky laugh and his mouth slid over to her inner thigh to bite lightly. Not hard, but just enough that she knew it would be pink if she could see it.

"Trust me, you're not the only one getting pleasure. I want you to come."

He didn't seem to expect a reply, because he went back to tasting her and driving her wonderfully close to that edge of pleasure.

Cupping her ass in his large hands, he dragged her closer, sealing his mouth tighter to her sex. And when his tongue took the path back to her clit, she was a goner.

Grace gripped anything she could find to hold on to. The gearshift, the door handle, his thighs, it was all a blur as pleasure slammed into her body again and again.

There was a woman screaming. It had to be her, right? But the shudders of ecstasy that continued to rack her body made it hard to think straight.

Finally she became aware that he'd lowered her back onto his lap. Grace dragged in much-needed oxygen, burying her face against his shoulder as she gripped his shirt.

He moved slightly and she realized he was reaching past her to pop open the glove compartment.

A condom, she realized, he was putting one on. At least someone had the sense to remember protection.

"Amazing," he muttered and slid his hands into her hair, dragging her head down to his so he could kiss her.

His tongue plunged deep, making her taste herself, and the realization shot her arousal level right back up to scalding level.

The nudge of his cock at her entrance brought her back to reality a bit, a shiver of anticipation rushed through her.

"You're so beautiful."

"Thank you." Her cheeks flushed with pleasure, and more than anything she wanted him to just push up and into her.

"I can't wait to be inside you." He kissed her again, lifting his hips to enter her just a tiny bit.

"Yes. Please." She tried to ease down onto him, confused at why he was even hesitating.

"I want you so damn much. But before we go any further I need you to understand that this can never be more than sex."

It was almost like he'd injected ice into her heated blood. Her mind struggled to comprehend what he was saying, or more so why he'd be saying it.

"I—wait, what?"

He kissed her again, as if trying to keep her distracted. It almost worked, until he lifted his head again.

"If you're looking for a mate, then I'm sorry but I can't offer that."

Was she looking for a mate? Had she given off the impression she was looking for something serious? Where was this coming from?

The fog in her mind lifted enough to think clearly. He'd rattled off those words almost in monotone, like he'd gone into autopilot. They'd barely registered in her fevered brain, like a disclaimer at the end of some prescription drug commercial.

Which is probably just what he'd intended.

Her blood began to heat, but for a different reason now.

"Son of a bitch. You're *reciting* this, Darrius," she growled. "It's a line you use on every girl you go to bed with, isn't it?"

Shock swept across his face, and then the tiniest flicker of guilt that meant she'd nailed it.

"I'm *not* one of your usual shifter groupies. You can't just flash me that charming smile of yours and expect me to fall into bed with you."

Wariness flickered across his face now. "Grace, it's not like that..."

"Oh really? So how does it work, *Hilliard*? Do you get a girl so hot and bothered that you know they'll agree to anything when you spring this on them?"

When he didn't immediately answer she climbed off him, knowing his silence was the confirmation she didn't want to hear. "You know what? Fuck you. Or wait, let me take that back, maybe five minutes ago I would've. But now, you can just go to hell."

She pulled on her clothes, wishing her hands weren't trembling so hard from fury. "And I take back my offer to share my bed tonight. You can have the spare room."

Chapter Thirteen

Shit. Shit he'd messed up and royally.

Darrius struggled for the words that would stop her from getting out of the truck. That would convince her he wasn't a complete bastard.

But he lacked any because he was one, and he'd just shown his cards to the one girl he really did care about.

The realization jarred him a bit, until he clarified the thought in his mind. Of course he cared about her, they were friends—he'd held her when she was on the verge of death—only someone without a heart wouldn't get attached a bit.

Wincing, he tucked his erection back into his jeans. With a sigh, he tried again. "Grace, we need to talk. I just want you to understand—"

"Actually, I think *you* need to understand." She paused, her hand on the door handle. "All I wanted was an uncomplicated little quickie to distract me from a pretty shitastic day. I wanted it from a guy I trusted and whom I was attracted to."

And there she went laying it all out on the table. She trusted him and was attracted to him—that much sent a sizzle of triumph through him.

But she wasn't after permanent. It should've been a relief, but disappointment stung slightly. Which made absolutely no sense. Confused, he tried mentally to shrug it off. He couldn't claim her as his mate—he couldn't claim anyone. So why should he be disappointed that she only wanted sex?

"You were looking like you might be that guy," she continued and shook her head. "Well, right up until you started treating me like your flavor of the week."

He gave a small laugh, but wasn't the least bit amused.

"Are you trying to inflate my ego, or kill it?"

"I don't think it can get any bigger." She scowled and opened the door. "But, don't worry, I'll figure out another way to burn off this frustration."

The jealousy that rose inside him was instantaneous and violent. The wolf inside him went primal, possessive, and acted on instinct alone.

Before Grace had even slid one leg out the door of his truck, he'd moved across the seat to stop her.

With an arm wrapped around her waist to restrain her, he lowered his head to nuzzle the back of her neck.

"No need to rush off."

"Oh, there's every need." Her voice, husky with anger and desire, washed over him and upped his need for her.

"You can't honestly think I'll let you go out to find another man tonight, sugar?" Wanting to prove just how easily he could have her, he slid his hand upward and into the blouse she hadn't buttoned. "If you need help burning off energy, then I'll be the one to do it."

"The hell you will." She tried to tug away, but he tightened the arm around her waist. "*Darrius.*"

His intention had been to force her to stay and listen. But now, with his hand in her shirt and the soft warmth of her breast against his knuckles, he couldn't resist. He cupped her breast again, testing the weight and fullness of it in his palm, before capturing the nipple that rose to greet his fingers.

She let out a ragged breath. "You don't play fair. At all."

"And I'll never claim to." His lips brushed the back of her neck. Someday, some man would bite that sexy neck, and claim her as a mate. It wouldn't be him though.

The realization made his heart pinch and he drew in a ragged breath.

"I need you to listen to me."

"Fine. I'm listening, but do you have to touch me at the same time?"

"I wish I could stop." He moved his hand to tease the other

breast.

Unwanted triumph swept through him as a shiver ran through her body and she couldn't seem to stifle her moan.

He wanted this woman, probably more than he could remember wanting a woman, which shouldn't have been possible. And the idea of hurting her made everything inside of him cringe. Larson was right. Grace was still vulnerable at the moment, even if she denied it.

So why don't you let her go inside? Leave her alone? His conscience barraged him, but letting her go would be like denying himself oxygen right now.

He settled for honesty, she deserved that much. As much as he was loath to stop touching her, he released the sweet little breast cradled in his hand and turned her on his lap so he could look in her eyes.

"I shouldn't have pulled that shit with you, Grace. Shouldn't have used that *line*—because you're right, it was one."

She tensed and he sensed the immediate change in her, the animosity radiating in waves now—the unhappiness in her eyes.

"You should've known me better."

"I did. I do. Shit." He released her enough to rub the back of his neck. "Maybe it is a line, but it's also the truth. I would hate myself if I hurt you. And I know by us getting involved that's always a risk."

She paused, seemed to reflect on his words. "What you did hurt me more than any risk of us getting involved."

"I realize that now, and I'm sorry." He pushed back a strand of hair that had fallen across her cheek. "I completely own up to being an asshole. Give me another chance."

Her gaze slid to his mouth and she swallowed visibly. "I have a feeling you wouldn't let me walk away, even if I wanted to."

Impossible. He couldn't let her walk away from whatever they had right now. "I'd do everything in my power to stop you."

"I understand why you need to clear the air with women. Why you're up front that it's a no-strings-attached thing."

Her words, maybe unintended, came at him like unpulled punches. Hitting hard and deep, and leaving him strangely hollow and weary. Darrius Hilliard, the constant flirt. The player who all the girls wanted. It was the reputation he'd earned himself. It was half truth, half illusion.

"And no strings is exactly what I'm looking for right now." She seemed to falter, search for words. "My job, my sister, those are the priorities in my life right now. I'm too young, too busy, for serious right now."

The fact that she was so young was another reason he'd been hesitant to get involved with her. What if she got emotionally attached? What if she wanted more?

"When things started heating up between us, I knew exactly what that meant. It'd be casual. You're Darrius Hilliard—you don't *do* serious."

More punches that were well earned. Usually he just rolled with them and claimed the philanderer status that had been cast on him so long ago. It almost was his identity now, when initially he'd embraced it to deal with the pain.

If she only knew...

"But one day, it's *going* to happen." Her smile wavered slightly as she lifted her gaze to look at him again. In her eyes now, a glimmer of sadness. "You'll think she's just another lover, but you'll realize she's your mate. And you'll be completely blindsided, because all these years you've been emotionally pushing women away."

"Grace." The truth was coming now, there was no stopping it. It rode in on a tidal wave of emotion, driven by her gently chastising words.

"Look, maybe you don't want to hear it, but it's true. You're not exempt from falling in love, Darrius."

"Grace, listen to me. I can't have you as my mate—or any other woman for that matter." So few people knew the truth, and many had forgotten.

Irritation flashed in her eyes and she shook her head. “Seriously? It means that much to you? To maintain this playboy lifestyle and—”

“Grace, I'm already mated.”

It was almost like having her head slammed into the ground all over again, only without the crushing pain. At least to her skull.

Grace blinked, stunned and disorientated. She tried to latch on to his words—make sense of what he'd said. But they swirled around in her mind like a verbal tornado, too fast to grasp or comprehend.

Her gaze was frozen on the curve of his lips, which were now compressed into a tight line. But she kept hearing that phrase over and over again.

I'm already mated.

It couldn't be possible. She would've known, wouldn't she have? People would have told her.

“But just a few minutes ago we almost... You made me...” She trailed off numbly, unable to even speak the words.

Darrius was mated. She'd almost made love to a mated man? Had let him bring her to orgasm, when he already had a mate?

“I'm going to be sick.” She fumbled for the door handle, desperate to get away from him. To breathe in the cool air that would contrast against her flushed skin.

The iron-like arm around her waist halted her, dragging her back against her will.

“Grace, wait.”

“Let me go.” She slapped at his arm. Tried to pry his fingers off her one by one.

But when it was clear he wouldn't release her, she went limp against him, unable to stop the small furious sob.

Though his body front was pressed flush against her back, and the arm around her waist was dangerously close to her breasts, he made no move to touch her further.

His words were a soft tickle on her ear as he murmured, “Calm down a second, and I’ll explain.”

“Explain? I hate you so much right now,” she seethed. “You’ve never been monogamous in the time I’ve known you. I almost let you *fuck me* in the front seat of your truck. You’re staying with me. Protecting me. So unless your mate is dead, there’s not a hell of a lot you can say to explain.”

He stilled, seemed to hesitate. “Well, you got it. She’s dead.”

The fight left her with the swiftness of a water balloon hitting pavement. She let the heaviness of his words sink in.

How had she not known about this? Did anyone at the agency know?

Grace wiggled in his grasp, needing to see him to have the rest of this conversation. He eased his grip on her and didn’t protest as she turned to face him.

Even in the darkness of the truck, her gaze sought his. She looked for anguish there, or at least a hint of pain. There was a tinge of sadness, but the emotion that shone the most was weariness.

“How come you’ve never said anything? I had no idea.”

“Most people don’t. It was a long time ago.” He sighed. “We were teenagers when we mated, both just eighteen.”

Layers. There were so many layers to this man, and she was only now realizing it. The world saw Darrius Hilliard as a charming, funny playboy who only went skin deep. And apparently he’d been happy to let people make their assumptions, her being one of them. But now the truth was coming out as each layer was pulled back.

“How long were you mated?”

“Only a few months. ”

Her heart pinched as she imagined how strong his grief must’ve been—how much it likely still affected him, even if he hid it now.

His mate had died young. For humans, it would’ve meant Darrius getting on with his life and maybe finding another person to love. But he wasn’t human, and claiming a mate went so much deeper than love.

Shifters, when they mated, mated for life. You were connected to that person on a soul-deep level until you met again in the afterlife.

And they'd only had a few months together…

She caught his hand and gave it a gentle squeeze. "I'm so sorry."

His lips twisted, almost bitterly and he shook his head. "It was years ago—water under the bridge now. I've accepted that my future isn't like everyone else's. That's why when I get involved with a woman, I give them the same warning."

"Understandable." And it was. Explaining a dead mate every time he met another woman was probably far too painful. Was he trying to exorcise the pain—forget the gaping emptiness of a mateless future?

His choices and the women he'd bedded weren't for her to judge, but she almost understood them better now.

"You're not the only shifter to have lost a mate," she said hesitantly, tracing her finger over the palm of his hand. "Has there ever been a case of a shifter re-mating with someone new?"

Darrius gave a slight nod. "A handful, but it's almost an anomaly, really, and usually there ends up being some reason why the first mating never took. But it gave me hope. For fifteen years, I've dated, I've been with women, but it's never happened."

"What's never happened?" She hesitated. "How does it work?"

His gaze fell to hers. Disbelief in his gaze. "You don't know?"

"I mean I have an idea, I know the crux of it. Male bites female on the neck and they are mated, but I don't really understand what drives them to do it." She chewed on her bottom lip, hoping she didn't sound like a complete idiot.

Again there was disbelief in his gaze, as if he couldn't quite believe how naïve she was. And dammit, some things she was naïve about. But she'd never had many friends, and her aunt and uncle hadn't discussed the details of mating—really ever. She'd had to figure it out from locker room gossip during high school. Put the pieces together.

"When a male chooses his mate, he's driven by a need that is instinctive. Consuming. Most of the time, but not always, it happens during sex."

"See that's what I don't understand. Wouldn't the male get all worked up and bite any chick he's screwing?"

His laugh was soft and low, the sexy sound that sent shivers through her.

"You're a razor-sharp agent, but adorably inexperienced with mating."

"Oh will you just shut up." Her cheeks flushed, and she punched him lightly in the stomach. He caught her fist and lifted it to his mouth, brushing her knuckles with his lips.

Her stomach fluttered and she bit back a sigh. "You realize I'm not a virgin."

"No, I didn't think you were." His smile died and something blazed fiercely in his eyes. Something dark, angry, before it was extinguished as he drew in a slow breath. "I'm obviously not either. And every time I slept with a woman who wasn't my mate, I'd hope that maybe this time would be different. That maybe my canines would drop and I'd be compelled to mate again."

"But it doesn't happen."

"Never even came close." He kept up the featherlight caress of her knuckles. "And as much as I want to promise you roses and forever after, it won't happen with me."

There was another sharp sting to her heart and a lump in her throat, but she struggled not to show it. Why it bothered her, she couldn't say. She wasn't looking for forever after. Not yet, but hearing the finality in his words that it could never happen between them hurt with an intensity she couldn't analyze.

Knowing he was waiting for her response—probably

expecting her rejection—she forced a slight smile and nipped at his thumb.

"Well, fortunately it's like I told you. I'm too young for serious anyway." She lifted her gaze to his again. "But I'm going to need some time to take all this in and figure out what I want. Maybe we can just take it slow...see what happens?"

He gave a slow, skeptical nod. "I still want you, Grace. Pretty damn bad, but I'll understand if you want to run like hell now."

And she wanted him—that much hadn't changed. Even though she'd just come a short while ago, her body had begun to hum with need again.

"I'm not running," she said softly. "Though maybe tonight I might. It's a lot to take in, and I'm a bit tired now. Plus we still have to work in the morning."

"Absolutely. We should go inside. Get some sleep, sugar."

She wasn't sure what to think of the thrill that raced through her at the endearment. But every time he uttered it, she always felt a little happier. Sexier. Maybe that was just the Darrius effect. He charmed girls, and he was awfully good at it.

She reached for her door handle again, and then paused, another thought striking her.

"Just to clarify. You got pretty riled up earlier when I said I'd find another way to burn off energy. In case you thought I meant another man, you were wrong. I was going to head over to the garage to work on my glass."

He grunted and she thought she spotted relief in his eyes. But his smile was pure seduction. "I like my plan for sex better."

She laughed softly and climbed out of the truck. "I'll bet you do. But if you don't mind... I still think you should take the other room. At least for tonight."

Darrius climbed out as well and walked around to her. "Agreed. I don't want to rush you. I want you to really think about this."

She turned and stepped into his arms. Cupping his face,

she brushed a light kiss across his lips.

"I will. I promise."

Though she knew her heart had already made its choice, she wanted Darrius. Even if it was only for the short term. She just hoped it wouldn't hurt too much in the end.

Grace stirred in her bed. Sleep still curled around her body and mind, but she blinked past it to glance at her clock. Ten minutes before her alarm was set to go off.

The house was silent, and as she stared at the ceiling she remembered everything from last night. Remembered that Darrius, all six-foot-two hard male of him, was asleep in a bedroom not too far from hers.

And he'd been mated. The reminder hit her almost as quickly.

Her stomach clenched and her heart twisted before she drew in a slow breath and her body relaxed again.

Sighing, she rolled over onto her side and stared at the wall.

Just the idea of Darrius mated sent toxic emotions through her head. Jealousy. Sadness. And something dangerously close to heartbreak. But why? She'd told him up front she wasn't looking for serious—hadn't even considered the possibility of him being her mate. It was what she'd convinced herself of all along. It still held true, didn't it?

Maybe she was just feeling more connected to him emotionally because he'd taken her so intimately last night.

Just the memory of it had her mind leaping from the serious road onto the dirty one. Heat coursed through her and an ache immediately began between her legs.

Grace squeezed her thighs together and let out an unsteady breath.

Why was she so sexually drawn to Darrius? She'd asked herself that over and over. He wasn't by any means the only sexy and funny guy at the P.I.A.—hell the agency seemed to be a breeding ground for hot federal agents—but he certainly was the one who got her engines revving.

Maybe she should've just slept with him last night. Should've just taken his warning at face value and then she would've been blissfully unaware that Darrius Hilliard had already chosen his mate in life.

Could she do it? Sleep with Darrius and know it was only a fleeting, sensual affair? Or would it be better to walk away now?

The latter idea had a chill sliding through her and disappointment gathering fiercely in her heart.

No. She couldn't walk away. Hell, she'd almost slept with him anyway. She was young and she had needs. She was in her twenties. She'd be an anomaly if she didn't think about having sex.

Darrius was a pretty good fit if she was just looking to blow off some sexual frustration.

Yes, and that's all you want right now. Your life is too crazy for anything else.

So it was settled. She'd take him as her lover. Completely. Pleased, and a little aroused by her decision, Grace sat up in bed. She pushed back the covers and climbed out.

Too bad she didn't have more time this morning to make it official. Then maybe she would've invited Darrius to join her for a morning session of some hot, sweaty sex. Though that would've required she set her alarm an hour earlier.

The house was silent, and she didn't bother to slip on her robe as she walked to the kitchen to make tea. Her flannel pajama bottoms and tank top combo weren't exactly sexy, and Darrius was likely still asleep in the guestroom anyway.

But when she arrived in the kitchen she stumbled to a halt in surprise.

Darrius was obviously not asleep, because he had scrambled eggs on the stove and was currently struggling to fill her tea ball with leaves. His brows were drawn together in frustration as the leaves kept spilling over.

Leaning against the doorway, she cleared her throat.

"You're awake earlier than I thought you'd be."

He glanced over her way, surprise in his tired gaze. "I don't think I got much sleep last night."

She grimaced. "The bed too hard for you?"

Darrius set the tea ball in a mug of what she assumed was hot water before he turned back to the eggs.

"I don't think it was the bed."

He turned slightly and she saw the unmistakable bulge of his erection against his slacks. Her pulse jumped. She knew immediately why he hadn't slept. Maybe she was a little turned on this morning, but he'd given her a mind-blowing orgasm last night. And selfishly, she hadn't reciprocated.

Images ran through her head, heating her and making her want to do incredibly naughty things right now. And maybe, if she could do this quick enough, she could.

"Thank you for making breakfast." She crossed the floor to him and slid her arms around his neck.

His gaze flared with hot arousal, with hesitation, before he looked away from her. It was almost as if he wanted to avoid dealing with her—seeing her. Was he that on edge?

"And I never thanked you," she continued, her mouth so close to the corner of his full lips now. "For making me come like a room full of dynamite last night."

A shudder ripped through him and she thought he might've groaned deep in his throat.

"Grace," he rasped, his head turned just a tiny bit, so that when he spoke his lips almost seemed to brush hers.

"I thought about it, and I'm okay with this being a pleasure buddy type of thing. We'll just have fun and then when one of us is ready to get out, we call it quits." She slid her hand down his bare chest. "We could start on that fun part now."

"You don't know how fucking happy that makes me to hear you say that." He groaned. "But, sugar, we're short on time. You should sit down and eat your breakfast."

"You've got a serious problem going on down there." She nipped at his bottom lip. "You should let me take care of it."

There was no mistaking his groan this time. "We need to be at the office in less than an hour. We don't have time for what I want to do to you."

"This isn't about me this morning. This is about you. I was a selfish lover last night, but I can make it up to you. I promise it won't take long." Her heart thumped with anticipation, but wanting to give him as much pleasure as he'd given her last night, she sank to her knees in front of him.

"Oh sweet Jesus." His hands slid into her hair, but he didn't try to stop her as she quickly unzipped his fly and freed him from his pants a moment later.

She looked up at him again through her lashes, found his dark gaze blazing with fire and need.

Her mouth immediately watered at how hot and heavy he was in her hands. Grace leaned down, tracing her tongue over the tip of him, catching the drop of fluid that had already gathered.

"Shit. *Shit.*" He gasped. "The eggs are gonna get cold."

"Are you still thinking of eggs when my tongue is on you?" She made a *tsking* sound. "I must not be doing this right."

She drew her tongue over and around his length, teasing the small dent on his underside.

"*Ah shit.* You're doing it right, sugar. So whatever you do, don't fucking stop."

A smile of triumph curled her lips, before she parted them and let him slide deep into her mouth.

And then conversation died as he took control, clutching her hair as he thrust into her mouth. The slide of his shaft against her tongue sent a ripple of power and pleasure through her.

"Take me. Take me deep."

She closed her eyes as he thrust deeper into her throat, letting herself taste the slight muskiness of him. An aphrodisiac that was all male—all Darrius. It was a promise of what was to come later, when they had more time.

The way he filled her mouth only made her anticipate how

he'd feel inside her later.

He didn't warn her he was about to come, but she could feel it in the way his sac swelled in her hand and how he plunged deep toward the back of her throat.

Darrius made no move to pull out, and she wouldn't have wanted him to. She knew the choice would've been hers, had she really wanted to push him away.

But she wanted to do this. Wanted to take him as completely as he'd taken her last night.

His groan was strangled, relieved as he came. She was lost in her own world of sensation and pleasure as she took him through his climax.

Several minutes passed before he pulled free from her and she sank back onto her heels. She licked her lips, her heart racing and pulses of need throbbing in various spots of her own body.

This was for him, she reminded herself. But oh hell, calling in sick for both of them was looking so nice right about now.

No. She squelched the thought and rose to stand again.

Arching a brow, she gave him a smile that was all sex and sin. She knew it, felt the feminine power in it, and reveled in it.

"Better now, Agent Hilliard?"

He let out a shuddered breath and stared at her. His gaze was full of heat—though controlled now—and almost bemusement. As if he was trying to figure out if that had really happened or not.

"Pretty fucking amazing actually."

"Good." She gave a slow smile and then turned away.

His hand connected with her ass and she yelped, jumping slightly. He didn't move his hand from her butt as he slid up behind her and nuzzled the back of her neck.

"You are so damn sexy. Tonight, I'm going to lick you until you're screaming again, sugar."

Grace let out a squeak, everything inside her turning to molten liquid.

His tongue flickered over her earlobe, before he muttered, "And then I'm going to fuck you so hard we'll break your headboard."

Her knees almost buckled. "It's made of iron."

"Yeah, well I love a challenge." He squeezed her bottom again. "Now go get your pretty ass dressed and I'll heat up your eggs."

Grace almost ran out of the room, her pulse racing. When was the last time she'd felt lighter and happier? *Or naughtier.* My, but Mr. Darrius Hilliard, the man who was usually so light and funny, was dirty as hell in the bedroom.

Tonight, and his promises, couldn't come fast enough.

Chapter Fourteen

His email was open, some agency note about an upcoming meeting in front of him, but Darrius's mind wasn't on it. It wasn't on much, right now, except the woman sitting at her desk halfway across the room.

The day had just begun, yet he couldn't stop checking the clock to see if it was any closer to quitting time.

Last night he'd run the emotional gauntlet. He couldn't have predicted the turn things would've taken. One moment he'd had his face buried between the sweetest pair of thighs, the next he'd been waving his dirty laundry like a Fourth of July flag.

And it wasn't a trivial little disclosure—it was heavy. Had long-term implications. He'd expected Grace to ultimately turn her back on the possibility of a sexual relationship with him. He wouldn't have blamed her if she did, and had even expected it.

But she hadn't, which kind of blew his mind. It was also a confirmation that she didn't want him for anything serious. That Grace was perfectly fine with it being a temporary, sexual relationship.

Just like every other woman.

It bugged him, more than it should have. Some men would've killed for his situation. Being able to bed any woman he wanted without worrying about commitment.

Closing out the email he wasn't reading, Darrius tried to ignore the hollow feeling inside him.

He was in his early thirties, the fact that he was unmated and childless was beginning to weigh heavily. Sure, he could sleep with unmated shifter women, and human women, all he wanted. But the shifter women would soon need to settle down with unmated shifters, and marrying a human was forbidden to him.

Soon he would need to start thinking about having children. Only, it wouldn't be in a loving, mated relationship. His best bet would be to find a windowed shifter woman who was within childbearing years and form the type of relationship that was more common to humans. Attraction. Respect. Maybe a marriage, maybe not.

But he would never know what it was like to grow old with a mate. With the one destined to be at your side.

He lifted a stress ball from his desk, a Christmas gag gift because everyone knew how laid-back he was, and squeezed it in one hand.

Grace was the first woman he'd ever confided in about Jenny. Lord help him, the sympathy in her eyes had almost ripped his conscience a new one.

What would Grace think if she knew the truth? That he'd never mourned his mate's death, and struggled to feel any kind of emotion for the woman he'd known for such a short time.

With a low growl, he hurled the stress ball against the wall of his cubicle and placed his elbows on his desk, hiding his head in his hands.

He was an anomaly and didn't deserve to have anyone as his mate.

"Wake your ass up, Hilliard."

The approach of Larson had him jerking his thoughts back to work, and lifting his head to stare at his alpha.

"I'm awake. On my third cup of coffee, matter of fact." Darrius grinned and reached for his mug.

Larson stared at him. "How was your night?"

"It was all right." All right meaning amazing. And this morning had been pretty damn fantastic too.

Shit. He still couldn't quite believe it had happened. Couldn't believe that Grace had just dropped to her knees and taken him completely as if *he* were breakfast.

Dark heat gathered in him, and a wave of intense need to

be with her again. Alone. Tonight seemed too damn far away.

He never would've taken her for the type to be so sensual, though he should've. She was a fierce agent at work, and there was no reason she wouldn't have been equally fierce sexually.

"Hmm. So how was Masterson?" Larson asked.

For a moment, Darrius almost thought his alpha was asking about something else entirely. Maybe Larson had figured out that they were getting pretty hot and heavy, but then he remembered the attack at The Doornail and grew somber.

"She seems okay. I think she pushed it from her mind and tried to keep busy." *And I helped keep her distracted by going down on her until she was nearly crying.*

Last night his thoughts might've been partly occupied by Grace and the discussion about his past, but even still he'd always been alert to the possibility of another attack on her.

Someone was out to intimidate Grace, no doubt about it.

"Good. And look, whatever happens between you two, just remember that you don't need to add your name to the list of people out to hurt her."

Darrius's gut clenched at the alpha's warning, because it was something he feared as well.

"Masterson," Larson turned his head to shout. "Get over here."

What the hell? Alarm raced through him. Surely Larson wasn't about to give Grace a lecture on safe sex?

It only took a moment before Grace had abandoned her desk and arrived next to Darrius and Larson.

"Hey, what's going on?"

She didn't look at him, Darrius noticed, but kept her gaze firmly on their alpha. She was all business at the office. But then that was who Grace was—a determined, career driven female shifter. Not to mention a fucking goddess at giving head.

Don't go there.

"I called you both here, because I wanted to let you know I sent SWAT out to Wesley Parker's house this morning to execute a search warrant."

Grace's eyes lit up and she took another step forward, gripping the wall between his desk and the agent's on the other side. "Really? What did they find?"

Larson glanced at her, his brows drawn together. "Lots of interesting stuff. Some being a piece of paper with Jocelyn Feloray's name and number on it, lots of drugs, and a glass vial full of liquid and hypodermic needles."

Darrius grunted softly. "Let me guess. It wasn't insulin?"

"No, it doesn't appear our POI was a diabetic," Larson agreed with a hard smile.

Grace tilted her head. "Wait a minute, you said 'was'."

"Perceptive as always, Masterson." Larson picked up a stapler from Darrius's desk and began to take it apart. "Along with various items taken into evidence, we also found a deceased POI."

Now that certainly was a game changer. Darrius pursed his lips and absorbed the info, his mind spinning with the news.

Grace looked equally shell-shocked. "Don't tell me he died of carbon monoxide poisoning? It would be too much of a coincidence."

Larson tilted his head. "No. It looks like a drug overdose, actually."

Darrius nodded. That would've been his first guess. Their surveillance had indicated the guy was likely on something. "So you think the needles were for heroin?"

"Maybe. Though we didn't find any in the house. Which is why we're having tests run on the vials we found right now."

Darrius slid a glance to Grace and saw her staring down the hall to where the P.I.A. lab was located. The way her hands were curled into balls and she shifted her weight, he knew where she'd be heading the first chance she got.

"The body is being brought down to the shifter morgue on First Avenue for the required burning." Larson's attention shifted to Grace as well. "Would you feel comfortable viewing it, Masterson? Think there's a possibility you'd recognize the scent of your attacker from last night if you saw him?"

Agitation flashed across her face before she gave a slight shrug. “It was dark and they were masked. Plus it was clear they’d tried to hide their scent with bleach. I really doubt it.”

“Sometimes instinct alone might tell you.” Larson stood up and set down the stapler. “But I’ll leave that up to you. Any loved ones of the deceased would’ve been notified by now, so he’ll probably be cremated by tomorrow morning. Let me know if you decide to go and we’ll take you down there.”

Darrius didn’t miss the slight shiver that moved through her body, even if her expression remained neutral now.

“Yes, sir.”

“What about an autopsy?” Darrius asked.

“Being done currently, but no reason to suspect it wasn’t an overdose.” Larson gave them a sharp nod and moved away. “Good work, guys. Stay in the office today unless I give you word otherwise.”

“Will do.”

“Of course,” Grace echoed.

Their alpha strode off, leaving them alone.

“I should get back to my desk.” Grace avoided his gaze as her fingers twisted together.

“Any plans for lunch, Masterson? I was thinking we could walk down to the waterfront and grab—”

“I have a few things I need to take care of around here.” She jerked her gaze back to him, and there was a warning there. *Don’t mix business with pleasure.*

His brow quirked and irritation slid through him.

“Really?”

Going to lunch together or with any of the other agents had been common practice before. What had changed? Besides the fact she’d sucked his dick this morning.

A flush stained her cheeks and she shook her head. “Yes, really.”

“Just don’t head out on your own, Masterson. You know you’re a potential target at the moment.”

"I know. I'll be staying in." Once again she glanced away, but not before he saw something flicker in her eyes that gave him pause.

Son of a bitch, she was going to try and sneak out of here alone. He'd bet on it.

"Good." Instead of tipping his hand and letting on he knew she was feeding him bullshit, he just nodded. "Now that I think about it, I did mention to Donovan that we'd check out a new barbeque join in Pioneer Square."

"Enjoy that. I'll catch up with you later."

He watched as she turned and walked away. The black slacks she wore couldn't hide the enticing swish of her pretty little ass.

Her saying no to lunch ran deeper than not wanting others at work to get suspicious. He sensed that.

Which meant come lunchtime, he was going to be discreetly keeping tabs on her. The last thing he needed was Grace getting in any more trouble than she already was.

Darrius slipped away from his desk shortly before twelve thirty and made his way to the security room.

"Horton, how the hell are you?" He clapped hands with his friend working the room.

Horton had been around longer than Hilliard at the agency and was close to retirement. His white hair was almost gone and his dark face wrinkled when he grinned. He might've been getting up there in years, but Horton had a sharp eye and did a fine job keeping tabs on the inside of the P.I.A.

"How you doing, Hilliard?"

"Not bad," he murmured, his gaze sliding to the monitors on one side of the room. Monitors that showed every room in the building. "Do you mind if I hang out here during my lunch? Haven't seen you for a bit and figured we could catch up."

"Hell, you know I don't care. But looks like you're more interested in keeping an eye on someone than catching up."

The older man never missed a thing, did he?

"Well, I may be a little bit guilty as charged." Darrius grabbed one of the black chairs and wheeled it around. He sat down on it backward, folding his arms across the back. "I'm just making sure a friend isn't getting herself into trouble..."

He trailed off as Grace left her desk and made her way through the building. Was she going to try and sneak out? If she did, he'd be on her tail. Or he'd have another agent do it, but no way was he letting her out without protection.

"Agent Masterson, huh?" Horton made a murmur of interest. "She's a pretty thing. You two an item?"

An item. That was a quaint way of putting in.

"We're good friends," he murmured vaguely.

Grace glanced behind her as she made her way up to the floor where the P.I.A. held their lab. Hmm. Maybe she wasn't trying to slip out of the building, but was going to see Sienna instead.

Once inside the lab, the two women appeared to get into a deep conversation. Grace slipped on a pair of latex gloves and then picked up a glass vial from the metal table.

No doubt it was the same vial from the POI's house.

She held it up to the light, turned it this way and that, and then set it back down. She said something more to Sienna, who nodded, and then Grace slipped back out of the lab.

Interesting. Maybe she was just getting details on what was in it?

"Anything look suspicious?" Horton asked. "I see agents coming and going from that lab all day. Nothing strikes me as out of the ordinary."

Maybe not, but he and Grace were working on this as a team. If she suspected something, she'd better damn well share that intel.

He watched her make her way from the lab and then pluck her cell phone from her purse. A moment later she'd dialed someone and was in a heated discussion.

She paused in the hallway, shook her head fiercely and

then snarled something into her phone before shoving it back into her purse.

"Hmm. She looks a little feisty today," Horton murmured. "I've gotta say, I wouldn't have figured Agent Masterson for your type, buddy."

Him either. At least not when she'd first started at the agency. But things had changed in a way neither of them had seen coming.

His trained gaze followed her on screen as she strode down the hall back toward their department.

Good. She was going back to her desk and he wouldn't have to worry about— *Son of a bitch!* She'd slipped out a side door as quickly as it took him to blink.

"Shit, I need to go after her. I promise we'll catch up for real, Horton. Drinks in the next couple weeks." He didn't wait for the other man to reply, but had already sprinted out of the room.

He thundered down the staircase as he hoped to beat her out front. But then, maybe if he could catch up with her he could figure out what was so important that she'd blatantly disobey his order—not to mention their alpha's—that she not be left alone.

Hell, he knew she liked to prove she was independent, but this was taking it too far.

Darrius shoved open one of the exit doors in the stairs and entered an alley. He jogged around front, knowing he'd probably be just steps behind her.

Which is exactly where he wanted to be, he decided, as he spotted her a moment later.

Grace moved through the downtown Seattle lunchtime crowds at a brisk pace. Almost inhumane if one knew how to recognize the signs, and he could spot a shifter a mile off.

She took out several city blocks before making her way closer to the waterfront.

When she turned into a sleek, tall condo building he slowed his pace and narrowed his eyes.

Who was she visiting here?

He waited a moment for her to disappear into an elevator, and then entered the building after her.

Whoever Grace had snuck off to meet with, he sure as hell intended to find out.

Just before the elevator doors opened, Grace's phone began to ring.

She plucked it from her purse and saw her sister's name on the caller ID. Shit, she'd been trying to get ahold of Bree for so long, but couldn't take the call right now.

The doors slid open and she strode out. Coming at her from the left was the pretty college boy assistant.

"Miss, if you could hold on—"

"Not a chance." Grace strode into the plush condo, her gaze searching for her target.

Jocelyn Feloray stood from a desk near one of the floor-to-ceiling windows. Her brows lifted in feigned surprise. She looked cool and unruffled with her dark hair pinned up and her body in a hugging but demure green dress.

"Grace. How charming to see you so soon."

"Don't bullshit me. I told you I was coming, Jocelyn." Grace clenched her teeth, momentarily overcome by the savage hatred she had for this woman. "Someone attacked me last night. Care to explain?"

Again, there was surprise in her gaze, but this time she didn't delude herself into believing it was real.

"I'm sorry to hear that. Are you all right, my dear? You don't appear hurt."

Grace flashed a granite smile. "Such touching concern. I heal fast—but then you know how that goes, right?"

Fury flashed in the other woman's eyes, then vanished. "I suppose it's one perk you can claim to such a horrific curse."

"Being a shifter isn't any more of a curse than being an

ignorant, sadistic bitch."

"Such language." Jocelyn made a *tsking* noise and went to pour herself a drink. "Can I offer you a drink, *Agent Masterson*?"

"I'm not here to drink. And how about you outright answer my question. I've been attacked—twice now. I have a feeling you're behind it."

Jocelyn swirled her glass of amber liquid and gave her a long stare. "Grace, that makes no sense. I don't want you dead."

"You want me warned."

"What makes you so certain I'm behind this?"

"Because I'm getting close to discovering things about Thom Wilson that maybe you wouldn't want me or the P.I.A. to know."

Dark warning flickered in Jocelyn's eyes. "Thom Wilson died at his own hand, my dear. And the P.I.A. isn't capable of locating their own ass, as far as I'm concerned."

"You're so determined to take them down. To take down the entire shifter population." Unable to look at the woman she'd once trusted, Grace turned and paced the room. Her unfocused gaze scanned over the opulent furniture and décor. "I don't understand why you hate us so much."

"And you never will." There was potent venom in Jocelyn's voice, and a tinge of pain Grace knew she wasn't supposed to hear.

Thrown momentarily off balance, Grace changed tactics. "Well, here's something you *can* share with me. What kind of drugs are you whipping up now?

"Me personally? You know I don't get my hands dirty with that kind of thing."

"No, of course you don't. You sit in a multimillion-dollar condo maintaining a nice buzz while plotting how to fuck up people's lives. *Feloray Laboratories*. What kind of drugs are they creating nowadays?"

"Oh the usual stuff. Statins. Glucose reducers. Oh, we're working on this fabulous pleasure enhancer... Why? Are you interested in that last one, Grace?"

Heat stole into her face, and Grace fisted her hands so she wouldn't pluck a book from the shelf in front of her and hurl it at the woman goading her.

"Actually, no. I'm thinking about something injectable. Something you'd find in a vial."

The heavy silence had Grace turning slowly to again stare at the older woman. Her gaze was unreadable, but it lacked the antagonizing humor that had been there before.

"Feloray Laboratories is behind the creation of many life-saving drugs," she finally said coolly. "If you'd like information on them, I'm certain I can have our marketing department send you a brochure."

"I don't want your brochure." Grace strode forward, tension radiating through her body. "I'm going to warn you once. If you're hiding something—if you're in any way involved in the death of Thom Wilson, we will prove it."

"Grace, you really don't want to go down this road with me. You were lucky to survive the experiments."

"No thanks to you."

"No. *Thanks to me* you're alive.

Grace laughed humorlessly. "You know at one point I would've believed that, but that day has gone."

Jocelyn shook her head. "I'm sorry you feel that way. I truly am."

"Go to hell." Grace turned and walked away. "If I'm hurt, if any other shifters are hurt and I sense you're behind it, I'm not going to be lenient."

"I wouldn't expect anything less from you." Jocelyn's mocking laugh followed her out the door.

Chapter Fifteen

Grace moved about the kitchen, plucking chicken breasts from the fridge and spices from the cupboard. Her gaze drifted to her cell phone on the counter, but Aubree had yet to call back.

Her sister hadn't left a voicemail this afternoon and wasn't answering her phone now. Where was she? Hopefully nothing serious was wrong.

Casting a glance over at Darrius, she drew in an unsteady breath. Her hands trembled slightly and she hoped he was too busy too notice.

Busy peeling potatoes over the sink, his back was to her and he'd been unusually quiet.

Was he thinking about the same thing she was? That *tonight* had arrived, and that in less than an hour he would likely make good on his threat to try and break her headboard.

Her knees went a little weak just thinking about it. She cast him another glance from beneath her lashes and then frowned.

No. He didn't really have the look of someone who was thinking about sex. In fact, he looked almost a little pissed off.

He'd been silent and stoic from the moment she'd returned from the lunch break. Apparently he'd figured out she'd slipped out without an escort and wasn't all that happy about it.

She couldn't fault him for that, but surely he'd had enough time to get over it.

Massaging olive oil and garlic into the chicken, she cleared her throat. "Are you still angry with me?"

When he didn't reply right away, she glanced over at him and caught the slight hardening of his jaw. He tossed one peeled potato into a bowl and grabbed another, slicing the skin off with smooth, rapid strokes.

"*Should* I be angry with you?"

Yes. Maybe a little bit. Still, the terseness in his words had her swallowing against the lump of guilt in her throat.

"I suppose you have every right to be. I know I said I wouldn't go out alone—"

"Yes, you did."

"But as you can see I'm fine."

There was no reply, and she went to preheat the oven. He was angry, and he had every right to be. But she couldn't exactly have brought him along with her today.

"Yes, you're fine." He gave a low, harsh laugh. "But I'm not, because I'm pretty damn confused right now."

"Confused about what?"

"Why you went and saw Jocelyn Feloray on your lunch break."

Her heart went into triple time and she struggled to swallow against the sudden dryness in her mouth. Gripping the counter, she forced herself to stay calm. "What do you mean?"

But she knew, even before he replied, she knew he'd followed her this afternoon.

"Don't you want to know *how* I knew you were safe today? Because I followed your reckless ass." He threw another peeled potato into a bowl and then shot her a look of pure ire. "I watched you slip right into Jocelyn Feloray's condo as if you two had a quaint little tête-à-tête planned."

Oh shit. How had she not realized he'd followed her? She should've known. Should've sensed him.

How could she lie her way out of this one? Her mind struggled to find an explanation he might buy, but she came up empty.

"Jocelyn Feloray should be at the top of your shit list, Grace. She's the P.I.A.'s number one enemy right now."

"I know."

"So why would you meet with her?"

"You're right." She licked her lips, knowing she couldn't deny it. "I met with her. I...confronted her." That much was the truth.

"What the fuck do you mean, you confronted her?" Darrius tossed the peeler in the sink and turned to face her.

Her heart leapt into her throat at the savageness on his face.

"I told her I'd been attacked and asked her if she had anything to do with it." She couldn't tell him about confronting her about what might've been in the vials. That information wasn't supposed to leave the agency.

"Do you have any idea how much trouble you could be in with the agency if they knew this? You're in therapy healing from what that bitch did to you. Why the hell would you go see her?"

"Look, it's complicated."

"It shouldn't be complicated. This woman damn near killed you. How do you even know where she lives? It's not public fucking knowledge. I had to make a few phone calls to figure out who was in that damned building."

"Does it even matter? Let it go, Darrius." She set the chicken aside and washed her hands.

"This woman nearly killed you."

"You think I don't know that?"

"Then why go to her home—dammit, what the hell were you thinking?"

The truth was on her tongue, ready to come out, but she was too far buried in the lies. She was too used to hiding from the reality of what no one knew. Too terrified of the potential destruction of her life if anything was discovered.

She shook her head and met his hard stare. "You concern yourself with me, Hilliard. Far too much."

"You're goddamned right I do." He strode toward her, eyes flashing. "And I have no idea why the urge is so strong."

Heat flared in her cheeks as she backed up. The counter

hit her hips and she was literally cornered.

"Exactly, you're not my mate." Seeing the shock and flicker of pain in his eyes had her regretting the words. She shouldn't have struck with such a low blow.

"No. I'm not your mate." His words were flat. "But I won't see you hurt again, Grace. And don't think I won't tie you to the chair to keep your ass out of trouble."

Wow, and wasn't that just the image she didn't need in her head right now? Though it was the perfect way to change the subject.

She arched a brow and forced a slow smile. "Tying me up, hmm?"

His hands came down on the counter beside her and the deep, warning growl he made sent a shiver through her.

"Don't think I don't know what you're doing, and it's not going to work. You're going to tell me exactly what you're hiding. Now."

"*Now?* Oh, hell no." She lifted her hand and pressed it against his chest, trying to move him backward, but he was immobile as a granite statue. "Don't you dare try to dominate me, Darrius."

"It's in my nature, sugar." He bared his teeth and slid a glance over her body. "I'll dominate you, and I'm pretty damn sure you'll like it."

Oh sweet God in heaven. His words should've infuriated her, made her want to slap that knowing smirk off his face. But instead the flesh between her legs tingled and she squeezed her thighs together as she bit back a groan.

He lowered his head and nipped at the curve of her neck. "What aren't you telling me?"

Too much. She gave up trying to push him away, and slid her hands up his chest to curl around his shoulders.

"Just let it go," she pleaded on a whisper.

He rained kisses along her jawline, coming deliciously closer to her mouth. "I can't do that."

"You don't have a choice."

"You're wrong." His mouth brushed hers. "Promise me you're not hiding anything."

Please, please don't ask me to make that promise. Her heart ached, even as she gave a small nod.

"I promise." It was almost a physical level of hurt now. To know the level of deception she'd sunk to with him.

His gaze held hers for a moment before he gave a slow nod.

Ouch. It almost stung more that he believed her.

"Chicken," she whispered, needing to put space between them.

He nuzzled her neck again before arching a brow. "Are you calling me a chicken?"

"No, I mean I need to make the dinner."

"Hmm. I must not be doing this right if you're still thinking about dinner."

A reluctant smile tugged at her lips. "Not too original there, buddy. I believe I used that line on you this morning."

"You used more than a line on me." His heated gaze slid to her mouth.

Her heart did a backflip at the reminder. "You're awfully naughty."

"You have no idea. But you will before the night is over." He stepped back, releasing her from where she'd been pinned between him and the counter. "Go make your chicken."

"You've still got mashed potato duty." Even though her lies left a bitter taste in her throat, her pulse had begun racing again as she slid quickly past him. This time, when his hand fell on her ass in a light slap, she wasn't quite as shocked.

No, it pretty much just made her realize that dinner was going to be quite the roadblock between now and the bedroom.

Darrius carried his plate to the sink, his gaze sliding over the curves of Grace's backside.

"You don't need to do those. We can get them in the

morning."

She gave a stiff shrug, and her voice wasn't quite steady. "I prefer to do them now."

Taking the plate from her, he noticed the way her hands trembled slightly.

The tension in her shoulders and the way she averted her eyes was just another indication that she was nervous.

She had to be thinking about it. Thinking about how any minute now he'd make good on his promise and carry her off to the bedroom.

And in reality, he was damn close to doing it. Frustration and desire warred inside him, both fighting to be the dominant emotion.

He wanted to trust her, but his gut instinct told him not to. She was lying to him again. What the hell was she hiding and why couldn't she trust him enough to confide in him?

Maybe she didn't trust him enough to share her secrets, but by the end of the night she'd trust him with her body.

Darrius caught her wrist, squeezing just enough until she loosed her grip on the plate and let it fall into the sink.

"Tomorrow," he repeated firmly. "Right now you have other responsibilities."

A shiver ran through her and she shook her head. "Darrius..."

"I know you're nervous, sugar, but I'm done waiting." He cupped her hip and turned her around. "So unless you're having second thoughts..."

"I'm not." Her words were almost a whisper, while her eyes shone with a mix of heat and anxiety. "I want this."

"Good." He rubbed the pad of his thumb over her bottom lip. "I have a request for you."

"And that is?"

"I'm in control."

He waited for her immediate refusal, or the roadblock of protests. Grace was a strong woman and liked to go toe to toe with a man. She'd already indicated she didn't want to be seen as the weaker sex. What if she was the one who usually took control in the bedroom?

He sensed she might be willing to hand over the reins sexually. Grace had impeccable control over her life and maybe felt the pressure of it. She might not be willing to give up that status in everyday life, but maybe in the bedroom...

"You weren't kidding about that dominating thing," she finally muttered, but there was a flash of excitement in her eyes, and a subtle shift in her breathing that he couldn't help but notice.

He didn't answer, just waited for her to make her choice, though he suspected his instinct was right.

"Okay, you're in charge. But this stays between us."

"You know it will." Triumph seared through his blood, and he made no effort to hide the small curve of his lips.

The idea of Grace giving up control had his cock twitching beneath his slacks. He took a step backward.

"Take off your blouse."

Her eyes widened slightly and her mouth opened as if she were about to protest or question him. She closed it again and reached up to undo the first button.

Her nails were short and unadorned with paint, but watching those delicate fingers push each button free from the hole had his blood heating.

Finally she tugged the blouse open and he dropped his gaze to her chest covered by a satiny white bra.

Take this slow, he told himself and drew in a steady breath.

"And now the bra."

No hesitation this time, she just reached behind her and deftly unhooked it. After pulling it free from her body, she let it fall to the floor.

He half expected her to reach up and cover herself, but she stared straight at him. Even though she was giving him control, her chin was lifted and her eyes shone with a bit of defiance.

His lips quirked. He'd wear that down. Maybe it would be

when he spanked her amazing ass, or perhaps she'd hold out until he was going down on her and she was screaming his name again.

But for now...

He allowed himself to look over the temptation she'd just revealed.

Small, round breasts crowned with tight, berry-colored nipples had his mouth watering.

Reaching out, he cupped one in his hand. Pinching the nipple between two fingers, he tugged lightly and was rewarded by her cry of surprise.

"So pretty." He stepped close enough to her so that he could lean his head down to draw a nipple between his lips.

Grace whimpered, her hands reaching for his shoulders. "Darrius."

Wanting complete, uninhibited access to her, he took her hands and placed them on the counter behind her instead.

"Stay like that," he commanded before drawing her breast to his mouth again.

"Okay." The single word was another whisper, laden with arousal. Surrender.

He caught a nipple between his teeth, tugging lightly, while twisting the other between his fingers. The taste of her combined with the small, anxious noises she began to make went straight to his head. Not to mention his dick.

Abandoning one breast, he reached down to free himself from his pants. He wrapped his fingers around himself and stroked, bringing himself to further hardness while alternating which nipples he sucked.

Grace began to arch her back, pressing her breasts further against his mouth. At one point she almost reached for him, and then placed her hands back on the counter.

So hot. Having her like this, being submissive, was so fucking hot.

Darrius dragged his mouth from her and drew in a ragged breath.

"Take off your pants and panties, and then turn around."

This time she didn't immediately move to obey, and he looked up to see color staining her cheeks.

He arched a brow, waiting to see if she'd defy him now, but her lashes fell and she fumbled to unfasten her pants.

She eased the black slacks down her legs, and then the tiny, silky white thong he couldn't have predicted. Grace was so professional, so determined not to flaunt her feminine side, and here she was wearing a bra and panty set that looked like it belonged on a lingerie model.

She stepped out of the rest of the clothes and kicked them to the side before hesitantly meeting his stare.

"Turn around," he reminded her softly.

"Oh. Right." She nodded, a jerky movement, and her gaze glittered with excitement and arousal.

Moving quickly to obey, she turned her back to him, placing her palms flat on the counter.

Darrius let his gaze rove down the seductive trail of her spine, to the heart-shaped ass that was toned and yet fleshy enough to be sexy.

He slipped an arm around her waist and pulled her back just enough so she bent forward and her bottom stuck out.

"Good girl." As he moved his hand down her stomach, he felt it tighten and the quiver.

When he reached her mound, he took just a moment to cup it before he plunged his fingers into the slick folds below.

Grace cried out sharply, and her body clenched around his fingers.

Fuck. She was so tight. So wet.

"You're all slick." He moved his fingers in and out of her, using her breathy cries as an indicator of her pleasure. "I think you like giving up control."

She didn't answer, and he gave a soft laugh. Right before he used his free hand to lay a swat on her bottom.

"*Oh*." Her body jerked and she tried to cast him a look over her shoulder. “What was that for?”

“I don’t need a reason to smack your ass, sugar.” He landed another swat on her cheek and felt her body squeeze his fingers tighter. “Do you like it?”

“Hate it.”

Another laugh erupted from him and he shook his head. “The hell you do. I could take you right now, your body is so ready for me.”

She made a soft throaty laugh and pressed her bottom back against his erection.

“So why don’t you?”

He was damn close to doing it, but he needed to taste her again. Needed to watch her lose control—to completely surrender to him. She held back still, he could sense it. She played his game, but she still held back mentally.

Before she could react, he’d deftly turned her around again so her back was against the counter.

“Because I’m going to lick you first.”

Her answering whimper was all anticipation and fear.

“Keep your hands on the counter.” He sank to his knees in front of her, then lifted one leg and placed her foot on his shoulder.

With her body exposed and open to him, he breathed in the intoxicating scent of her. Closing his eyes, he flicked his tongue out for the first sensual taste.

“Oh God.” She gasped and he glanced up from between her legs to see her head thrown back and her eyes closed. “Maybe we don’t need to do this part,” she said raggedly.

Amusement lanced through his need. She was still trying to keep control, must’ve realized she was dangerously close to losing it. *Good.*

He found the spot on her that was guaranteed to make her lose control and went in for the kill.

But the more he tormented her and brought her closer to that ultimate surrender, the more he risked losing his own control.

His body was rock hard and it took everything within him not to stand up and take her. Lift her up, wrap her legs around his waist, and then bury himself into her sweet body. Damn, how long had he been wanting this? Wanting her?

"Darrius." She cried out his name, not once, but over and over again as her foot dug into his shoulder and her sex ground against his face.

He didn't ease up, but licked her faster. Deeper. Not sure whether he was doing this for her pleasure or his own now. The tightening of her body coincided with her sharp scream as she fell into the ultimate climax.

With lightning-quick movements, he rose to his feet and swept her into his arms before her body began to crumple to the ground.

"I've got you." He adjusted her flushed and trembling body in his arms, and she buried her face against his chest.

Were those tears at the corner of her eyes? He couldn't be certain as he carried her down the hall to her bedroom.

After kicking the door closed, he crossed the thick beige carpet to lay her down on the queen-sized bed. She rested on her back, one arm above her head and the other tracing her stomach. Her eyes were a brilliant, glacial blue that was barely visible through hooded lids.

While stripping the rest of his clothes from his body, he stared down at her. His erection had reached the painfully hard state, and his mind was reduced to a feverish mantra of how much he needed her.

Initially he'd planned to bring her into the room and take her on her hands and knees. Drive into her and just make this nothing but the sex they'd agreed it would be.

A chill of premonition ran through him, that this wasn't going to be that simple. That sex between them would *never* be that simple.

Just sex. He let the reminder slide through him as he climbed onto the bed next to her.

Reaching out, he cupped her cheek and grazed her lips

with his thumb, before dipping to take her mouth in a slow, thorough kiss.

Grace gave a soft sigh and wrapped her arms around his neck. Her lips parted and her tongue sought his.

He commandeered her mouth, demanding a response and her complete submission, but there was no doubt she'd already given it. Given herself over to whatever intense fervor drove them.

Without breaking the kiss, Darrius slipped on a condom and then stroked his hand down her thigh.

"Now," she whispered against his mouth, her legs moving restlessly on the mattress. "I can't wait anymore."

Her plea was unneeded as he parted her legs and moved between her thighs.

Catching her wrists in one of his hands, he pulled them above her head and she didn't protest. He braced his weight above her with his free hand and eased into her body.

Her lips parted on a sigh and her lids lowered even more.

The warm, wet vise of her sheath tempted his restraint and he struggled to go slow—to enjoy the slow advance to the hilt.

But when she let out a low, guttural moan, his control snapped. Answering with a possessive growl, he thrust completely into her.

Grace screamed, her back arching and her head tilting back.

Perfect. Oh fuck, the way she squeezed him. Darrius's mind blurred with hot need and he knew he couldn't be gentle. Couldn't be slow.

His wolf took over, demanding he take her hard and fast. He drove into her—again and again. The sound of their skin slapping together only heightening his frenzied need for her.

"Yes." She tugged at her restrained hands as her hips lifted to meet each thrust. Her eyes were fully closed now, and through the mask of pleasure on her face, he saw a small tinge of pain.

For a moment, sanity almost returned. Had he not

prepared her enough? He was big, but he'd sworn her body was slick and ready.

He slowed his thrust. "Grace—"

"No, oh please don't stop." She gasped and lifted her hips again, bringing him deeper. "If you stop now I may have to kill you."

His lips quirked. The reassurance that she was okay had him pushing aside all fear and hesitation as he took control again. He slammed into her again. Harder and faster, claiming her body.

But never her soul. That realization blindsided him. Made him realize how much he wanted it. Staring down at her and the complete trust and pleasure in her face, he wanted her. Not just once, he knew it wouldn't be enough.

He rolled his lips back, waited for the urge to bury his canines in to her. Thought for a moment that maybe this time would be different. It didn't happen.

He might be the man inside her sweet body now, but Grace would never be *his*.

The idea of her with another man—her future mate—sent something savage through him, and he nearly roared with the irony of it all. He couldn't claim her—he'd finally found a woman he wanted to claim, would've given anything to claim, and it was impossible. And he couldn't even remember the night he'd mated with his dead mate—she may as well have been a stranger.

Emptying the devastating thought from his head, he focused on now and this moment between them. All that mattered was pleasure, and he chased after it like a man possessed.

Grace's sharp cries were the soundtrack to their joining, spurred him to that near release.

And then it was on him, tugging at his soul as he rushed past the point of no return and detonated inside her.

Her answering cry of pleasure came moments later—her inner muscles milking the remainder of his climax from him.

Almost shaking with the intensity of what had just happened, he released her wrists and sank down onto her. His lips brushed the manic pulse in her neck. Why couldn't things be different? He clenched his jaw and barely held back a bitter sigh.

Grace slid her hands to his back, a shuddering sigh still racking her body. Her lips brushed his shoulder before she made a purr of pleasure low in her throat.

"That was incredible. And I think you damn near came close to breaking that iron headboard like you promised."

A smile tugged at his mouth, and he let it free after a moment. "You mean I didn't? I'll have to try harder next time."

"You're going to have to give me at least an hour or two." She winced and shifted her legs. "I think I need to give it a bit to recover."

He lifted his head to look down at her, arching a brow. "*It?*"

Her cheeks flushed and she gave a light laugh. "Don't make me say the word. You know exactly what *it* is."

"Hmm." Yeah he did. With a widening smile, he slid down her body toward the spot she referenced.

"Darrius, what are you doing?" Her voice squeaked, and she reached for him, but he'd already moved into place.

"Giving it an apology kiss." He brushed a series of kisses over the red, swollen lips of her sex before sliding his tongue out to find her clit.

Her hips jerked and she whimpered, her fingers scraping over his head.

He soothed the spot with gentle, wet strokes and brought her into another—though seemingly less intense—orgasm.

"You're an amazing lover, Darrius." Her words weren't quite steady as she sat up. "Which I'm sure you're quite aware of."

Was he? No swaggering jokes came to mind, and it was hard to summon a smile, because he struggled with what had just happened. Yes, he'd made love to women over the years, but never—not even with his mate—had it been at the intensity level of what he'd just shared with Grace.

"I'm going to grab us some water. Back in a few."

Somewhat reluctant to meet her gaze, he eased off the bed. He didn't want her to see the confusion in his eyes, because he'd have a hell of a time explaining it.

Chapter Sixteen

Grace watched as Darrius retreated to the bathroom. He was tall, confident and completely unabashed, and she couldn't help but think again about the absolute perfection that was his ass. Not to mention the rest of his body.

She leaned back on the pillow and stared at her ceiling, releasing a soft sigh.

What the hell had just happened? Amazing sex? Yes, okay. Without debate even. But...something was different. This hadn't just been about reaching a screaming orgasm and wanting to sing the "Hallelujah" chorus. This was feeling as if Darrius had reached in and claimed a bit of her soul when he'd taken her.

As that last thought ran through her head, she almost laughed at the absurdity of it.

You're being an idiot, Grace. Don't confuse fantastic sex for something more than it can ever be.

And yet at one point when he'd been driving into her, she'd felt it. That overwhelming desire for him to bite her. To claim her.

Ridiculous. So utterly ridiculous.

This is why you shouldn't have casual sex with a friend. Despite what you think, you're likely to get attached.

Irritated and unsettled with her thoughts, Grace slid out from beneath the sheet and strode out of the bedroom. She sought out the bathroom in the hall to pull herself together—both physically and emotionally.

She locked the door and promptly climbed into the shower, turning it on full blast. Keeping the water cold, she hoped it knocked some sense into her.

But by the time she stepped out a minute later, she was

still in a fog that seemed to be created by Darrius. Rubbing at the droplets of water that blurred her vision, she reached for the towel hanging on the door.

"Crap." She cried out as her toe connected with the garbage can, sending it and its contents sprawling onto the floor. "Ow."

"Grace?"

Darrius knocked on the door, concern tingeing his tone. "Are you all right?"

"I'm fine." She tried to quickly scoop the contents back into the bin.

"You, uh, wanna open the door?"

What, was this an insecurity thing? Giving up, Grace set the bin down and went to open the door.

"I'm fine."

His gaze slid over her, lingering on her wet hair before sweeping down her body and back to her eyes.

"You didn't hang around for the water."

She swallowed hard, and couldn't help but drop her gaze from the scrutiny in his. The way he seemed to be reading every little motion she made, weighing every word she spoke.

Had he been as affected by what had just happened as she was? No, of course not. Darrius was used to having sex that meant nothing. Ouch. It hurt to think that, and she'd never be callous enough to say the words, but they stung in her heart.

"I wasn't thirsty. I, um, just wanted to shower."

"Understandable." He shifted in the doorway. "In fact, you mind if I catch one real quick?"

"By all means." She ducked under his arm and moved down the hallway. "I'm going to get dressed."

He didn't immediately close the door and she could almost feel his gaze burning into her back. But then, as she ducked into her bedroom, she heard the bathroom door click shut.

For some reason her pulse was all out of whack and shyness had taken hold. Why? She never got shy after sex, usually she just got the hell out of there. Sex with other men had never been all that great, and the aftermath had always been awkward. So she'd left.

But the sex had been mind-blowing this time, and Darrius was at her house, so running wasn't exactly an option.

Or maybe it was—if she counted her garage as running. She could head out back and spend some alone time playing with glass. Actually, hell yeah that sounded like a decent idea.

Grace quickly threw on clothes and then made her way to the front door, grateful Darrius was still in the shower. Then it turned off.

She had the front door open when he stepped into the hallway.

"Where are you going?"

Wincing, she turned to glance back at him. Then promptly wished she hadn't. He had a towel slung over his hips and that was the only thing covering up his dark, wet, muscled skin.

"The garage. I have to do a few pieces tonight."

Incredulity flickered in his eyes. "Not without me you don't."

"You can't be serious. You're staying at my house. My being a hundred yards away is hardly risky."

"It was at the pub."

How did she explain this? That she needed time to process what had happened between them? That she did her best thinking alone and while out working with glass?

Feeling almost deflated, and helpless at how her life kept spinning out of control, she gave a weary shrug.

"Never mind." But now she regretted not taking a long bath instead of a quick shower. It would've given her a tiny bit of privacy for a little while. "I'll just skip it."

She started to shut the front door, but it thrust back open.

Grace blinked in shock, her jaw falling at the sight of the woman who'd just stepped foot inside her house. She'd never come here. Why now? Son of a bitch, this couldn't be good.

Darrius was beside her in an instant, placing himself

between her and Jocelyn Feloray as the woman strode inside.

"How the hell did you get past all the security?" Darrius ground out, taking a threatening step forward.

"It's not all that hard if you put your mind to it." Jocelyn smirked. "Or if the homeowner doesn't activate her alarm system."

She hadn't turned on the alarms? The traps? Hell, she *must've* been distracted.

"You have a hell of a lot of nerve showing up here. Get out," Darrius ordered. "Consider this asking nicely, because you have about five seconds before I escort your sorry ass from this property."

"Well, isn't this adorable. Are you two sleeping together?" Jocelyn's gaze swept over Darrius's nearly nude body, and appreciation shone in her eyes. "I can't say I blame you, Grace. He looks like a nice toy. Maybe I should switch to dark meat."

Oh the hideous cow. "Stop it," she seethed and took a step forward. "What are you doing here?"

Darrius caught her arm, hauling her back with a low growl. "Go in the other room, Grace. I'll take care of this."

It wasn't that easy, and never would be. Something was wrong. Grace knew, even though Jocelyn was trying to keep things light and degrading, there was something dark beneath her mood. An indication something was deeply troubling her.

"Look," Grace hedged quietly, "maybe I should just talk to her really quick."

Sweat beaded on the back of her neck. She needed to get him out of here for a moment—she needed a moment alone with Jocelyn. Convincing him she would be safe would be a hell of a challenge though. *Shit.*

"No. I'll take care of this. In fact I wouldn't mind having a one-on-one chat with the bitch myself." He barred his teeth in a hard smile.

"Aren't you sweet. You think you know me, do you?" Jocelyn gave an equally hard smile. "Yes, Darrius, why don't we have a *talk*. I'm sure we'd have a lot to tell each other."

Grace's stomach dropped to her toes. "*Don't.*"

"I want to rip your throat out." Darrius took another step forward. "See you rotting in hell for everything you've done to hurt her."

"Me? Hurt her?" Jocelyn arched a brow and then looked directly at Grace again. "Well now, that's just silly. Why on earth would I hurt her?"

Grace shook her head, the blood rushing through her veins even as everything seemed to slow down. Oh God, she couldn't stop it. It was going to come out.

"Jocelyn, *please*—"

"I've raised Grace since she was a child, why on earth would I hurt her?"

The words seemed drawn-out, distorted even, and Grace couldn't drag in a breath as everything went silent. The smile on Jocelyn's face was pure satisfaction, and it only grew when Darrius released her arm and jerked back.

She kept her gaze lowered, shame and misery lancing through her as she felt the condemnation in his gaze.

"Grace?"

Her name was a harsh rasp on his tongue, and all she could do was shake her head again.

She'd never wanted him to know. Never wanted anyone in the P.I.A. to know.

"Jocelyn Feloray is the aunt that raised you? Tell me it isn't true."

She wanted to more than anything.

"Answer me, dammit. This fucking bitch shares your *blood*?"

"Yes," she whispered, curling her hands into fists.

"And you never thought it might be relevant to let me know? To let *anyone* in the P.I.A. know?" he ground out.

No. If anything, she'd tried like hell to keep that part of her life buried and a secret.

"Dammit, look at me," he snarled.

Grace lifted her chin and met his gaze, trying not to flinch at the rage and dismay in his eyes.

"I tried to protect you all this time. I felt anguish for what you'd gone through." He gave a slow shake of his head. "And all this time you've probably been working with her."

Shock ripped through, momentarily robbing her of a response. And then it tumbled out. "No. Never. You've got the wrong idea."

He shook his head and strode past her. "I don't think I do. Fuck this. Fuck you."

The pain that lanced through her nearly brought Grace to her knees. But pride and the fact that Jocelyn stood watching in glee made her hold herself together. Just barely.

"Where are you going?" she asked, hating how husky her voice was and the desperation in it.

He paused at the door, shooting her another loathing glance. "I'm going out. I figure that yeah, maybe I will give you both that time to talk alone. Besides, it's not looking like you need my protection as much as I thought."

Before she could reply, he'd strode out the door. She heard the sounds of his body shifting and could envision him racing out into the darkness of the woods.

Turning to face the woman she hated to acknowledge as family, she shook her head. "That was despicable. You know I never wanted them to realize who I was."

Jocelyn closed the door and gave a slight shrug. "You shouldn't be ashamed of your roots."

"Why not? You sure as hell are." Her little jab that Jocelyn Feloray was half-shifter didn't go unnoticed. The other woman's face tightened with disgust and her eyes narrowed, showing the fine lines she tried so hard to hide.

"Of course I'm ashamed. It's a disease I would rid the earth of if possible."

"Even if that meant eliminating yourself?"

Jocelyn didn't even hesitate. "Even then."

"You're so absolutely insane," Grace whispered. How had

she ever made it the first twenty or so years of her life without realizing how bat shit crazy her aunt was? How blatant her hatred for the shapeshifter population had become.

Grace's mother and Jocelyn had been twins, and both half-shifter. As far as Grace's memories went, she couldn't recall her mother despising that side of her when she'd been alive.

"I need a drink." Jocelyn sighed. "Do you have any vodka? Champagne? Wine? Anything, really?"

"No." She turned and walked into the kitchen, wishing like hell she *did* keep alcohol in the house because she could sure as hell use something right now. "You'll have to make do with water."

"I suppose."

"Why are you here, Jocelyn? Why show up at my house tonight? Besides attempting to ruin my reputation." It had been her parents' house, one of the things they'd left her and Aubree in their will. The first item Grace had eagerly claimed when she'd turned eighteen. "You just don't come out here."

"No, I don't. But I'm wondering if Aubree's here, or has been here recently?"

Grace froze as she handed Jocelyn a bottle of water from the fridge. Unease slid through her.

"No, she's not here. She's been at school, hasn't she?" She crossed the room to her purse that sat on the table and fished around for her phone. "Have you checked the dorms?"

"I've checked everywhere I know to check. The school contacted me to let me know she hasn't been seen in two days and wanted to confirm that I'd taken her out on an extended weekend."

Grace's stomach bottomed out as she searched her phone for new messages, but there was nothing. Fear began to coil its debilitating tendons around her insides and each breath she drew in, she reminded herself to be calm.

"Let me try calling her again." She hit the button to dial her sister's number, but had little faith she'd answer this time.

Come on, Aubree, where are you?

Betrayed.

Darrius lunged through the forest in his wolf form, barely hindered by the night that surrounded him. The betrayal he felt right now was like a poison in his gut, burning acid-like on his tongue.

She'd lied. She'd fucking lied to his face when he'd asked her what she was hiding. Nothing? Hell, she was hiding everything. Every goddamn thing.

Jocelyn Feloray—the woman who'd made it a personal goal apparently to bring down the shapeshifter community and the P.I.A. in particular—was Grace's aunt.

Grace had told him some things, had mentioned that her parents had been killed and she'd been raised by her aunt and uncle, but she'd never indicated who that aunt was.

A howl of rage erupted from inside him, and he quickened his pace. His volatile presence sent nocturnal animals scurrying away in surprise.

There were evil souls in this world, and Jocelyn ranked right up there with the worst of them.

The realization that had been playing in the back of his mind sank in. If Jocelyn was Grace's aunt, that meant she likely had shifter blood. The woman was part shifter—and her goal in life was to exterminate them?

What the hell?

Christ, he didn't even know what to do with this information. He couldn't keep it from the agency. Could he? It would ultimately come out—was amazing it hadn't already.

Grace hadn't wanted anyone to know. With good reason. How involved was she with her aunt's plans? It all made a little more sense now—why Grace would've signed up for the experiments. Were her goals as nefarious as her aunt's? Was she a plant within the P.I.A. for Jocelyn?

And yet she'd nearly lost her life during the experiments.

None of it made sense.

He tried to pinpoint what part made him most angry, and the discovery left him oddly deflated.

Darrius slowed his run and paused at the edge of an incline. His gaze swept the small valley of trees below, but he wasn't really seeing them.

She hadn't trusted him enough, that's what stung. He'd pleaded with her to confide the truth—because, dammit, he'd sensed she was hiding something big.

He just hadn't suspected *this.*

The anger left him, seeping from his body with the sheen of sweat that now covered it.

Dammit. What a mess. What was even more screwed up was that he still trusted her. Now that the fury had abated—the shock of her betrayal diluted—he knew without a doubt that Grace wasn't in cahoots with her aunt.

Those attacks on her life hadn't been random, and they sure as hell hadn't been staged. He'd seen the blood and bruising. The aftermath that had left fear in her eyes and a vulnerability Grace Masterson didn't show many people.

And you just left her alone.

With another low growl, Darrius turned and charged through the trees, heading back to her house. No matter her reasons for hiding the truth, he'd been an idiot to run out on her.

When he arrived back at her house—after carefully maneuvering through the alarms that were once again on—he noticed the lights were still on but there was a heavy silence.

He strode in the door, his gaze sweeping the interior. "Grace?"

Footsteps sounded, and then she moved out of the kitchen to meet him in the hallway. Her brows were drawn together and her eyes round with uncertainty.

"Darrius—"

"Is she gone?"

Grace gave a slight nod.

With a ragged breath, he strode forward and dragged her

into his arms. Her palms slid to his chest and she made a startled sound that he quickly caught with his mouth.

His tongue stroked deep, finding hers and lashing at it, almost punishing her for his earlier anger, and his constant need for her. She molded into him, sliding her hands up his chest to his shoulders. Her nails bit lightly into his skin as she clung to him and kissed him back.

He tore his mouth from hers a moment later and pressed his forehead against hers.

"No more lies," he rasped. "Do you understand?"

"Yes," she whispered brokenly. "I'm so sorry."

"I am too. I shouldn't have run out on you. No matter how angry I was."

"Honestly, I don't blame you."

He stepped back, putting just enough distance between them that he could watch her. There was the spark of wariness in her eyes, but the fear underneath sent a frisson of unease through him.

"What's going on, Grace?"

"Aubree is missing." She hesitated. "I think. That's why Jocelyn was here tonight, to ask if I'd seen her."

Darrius swore softly under his breath. "When was the last time you saw her?"

"A couple nights ago—when you first met her."

"Any texts? Phone calls?"

"I missed a phone call from her this afternoon, but she didn't leave a message. I've tried to call her several times since but she's not answering." She shook her head. "I just assumed she was busy with her classes. I know she has some big tests coming up."

"We'll find her. We can track her." And they could. The P.I.A. did this kind of thing all the time. "Did Jocelyn file a missing person report with the P.I.A. or human police force?"

"No, she wanted to talk to me first. I don't sense she's in danger, and I really think I would. I have before. She hates her school, hates Jocelyn, she's ready to be eighteen and on her own. Or with me. Maybe she just took off somewhere for a few days…"

But why wouldn't she answer her sister's calls then? Something wasn't right.

"Remember how the tires on her car were slashed? I thought whoever did it was targeting me, but what if they weren't. What if—"

"No what-ifs. Not yet. Call Jocelyn back and tell her we're handling this. Let's give it a day or two before we make it official. If we need to, we'll call Larson and let him know what's going on and recruit more help. But we'll find her."

"I know. I trust you, Darrius."

Did she? He couldn't help but arch a brow and give a low, slightly bitter laugh. "But you obviously didn't trust me enough with who you are."

"That's not it…" Unhappiness flashed in her eyes and she folded her arms across her chest. "It's just not something I publically acknowledge. I am *nothing* like my aunt—I can barely tolerate her."

"Then why don't you tell me the real reason you volunteered for the experiments?"

She visibly swallowed and there was anguish and regret in her eyes. "Essentially I was blackmailed. She threatened to put Aubree in them if I didn't volunteer. My sister isn't quite eighteen and unfortunately my aunt has complete custody. She would've used her chronic pain from her disability as an excuse."

Of course. It made complete sense from everything he knew about Grace that she wouldn't hesitate to sacrifice herself for her sister's safety.

"Those of us in the experiments went through hell, and to think that she might've had to go through that… She's not as tough, Darrius. I don't know if she would've come out alive."

It was almost too incredible to believe.

"What the hell kind of aunt would do that to her own niece?" Darrius ground out. "Why does she hate shifters so much? Hell, isn't she one?"

"She's half. And I have no idea."

Wait a minute. "Was your mother only half as well?"

A flush darkened her cheeks. "Yes."

"So that makes you and Aubree—"

"We're not full-blooded shifters. We're three-fourths, but it's always been enough for us to have most of the same capabilities." She glanced away. "Some things we just have to work a little harder at. It's another thing I don't share openly, because I'd rather not have that flaw on my record."

Interesting. He'd never sensed she wasn't full. Any disadvantage Grace had at having diluted wolf blood she hid damn well. The P.I.A. would've known, because she would've had to have disclosed her shifter status when she applied. A blood test would've confirmed it.

Three-fourth shifters weren't discriminated against, though. Not the way that those with only half-shifter blood had been. It was only with the recent discovery of the drug that could give halves the ability to shift that had balanced things out more—had there been more acceptance.

Someone like Sienna, or Jocelyn's aunt, might not have even realized they were shifters before unless they'd been told.

"Did your aunt ever take the drug she created? The one that ended up giving halves the ability to shift?"

Grace's laugh was loud and full of harsh amusement. "Never. She'd rather die first. I know she hates that side of her."

Hmm. Someday they'd figure it out. Learn why that bitch hated the side of her that most of the shapeshifter population saw as a gift.

"Thank you for coming back tonight." She stepped closer to him again. "I would've understood if you chose to leave."

"I couldn't." Hell, he'd been mad, but leaving her would've been impossible. Something connected them that confused the shit out of him, but it was potent and couldn't be ignored. He was more protective of her than he could remember being with his mate. There wasn't a sacrifice he wouldn't make to keep her safe. It made no sense, but he couldn't deny it.

"Give me a moment to get ready, and then maybe we can go drive around?" Grace suggested. "Check some local spots I know she frequents?"

"Smart. Let me throw on some clothes."

Her lips quirked. "Probably a good plan."

When she moved to pass him, he caught her hand and stopped her, drawing her close for another slow, and hopefully reassuring kiss.

"We'll find her."

She nodded and squeezed his hand before slipping away from him and into the bathroom a moment later.

Darrius returned to her room to throw on some clothes. He'd just pulled on his pants when he heard her soft footsteps.

"That was quick..." He trailed off, not as much distracted by the expression of disbelief on her face, but the item she held in her hand. His heart accelerated into a quick thump. "Uh, sugar, what is that?"

"A pregnancy test."

He waited a beat, felt his heart lurch into his throat. "Okay."

"I just found it on the floor... I'd knocked over the garbage earlier, but somehow missed that this had fallen out behind the toilet."

"Something you want to tell me?"

"No. God no, it's not mine!" She shook her head and gave a small frenzied laugh.

Darrius took a step forward, unable to ignore the relief that she might've been carrying another man's child. The idea of another man impregnating her had a growl of rage building inside him. But why? Grace was not his mate and never would be. Someday, this very well may be her reality. At some point she'd be rejoicing at the fact she'd gotten pregnant.

But not today. It wasn't her test, she'd just admitted it. He quickly restrained the raging wolf inside him that threatened to surface.

“What’s the result?” he rasped. “Can you read it?”

“It’s positive. Crap, it’s positive.” The longer she held the test, the more the color seemed to leech from Grace’s face. She looked up at him again, and her eyes glazed with shock. “I think Aubree’s pregnant.”

Chapter Seventeen

Grace leaned her head back against the couch and closed her eyes, trying to stop the nausea and spinning.

She'd left countless messages on her sister's voicemail and Darrius had driven her around town for the last two hours. Now it was creeping up on midnight, but they still had no idea where Aubree was.

Pregnant. Her little sister, not even eighteen yet, was pregnant. There was no other explanation of who that test could possibly belong to.

It all kind of made sense now. The way her sister had been behaving the last week—the way she'd rushed out of the bathroom looking a little stunned. Had that been when she'd taken the test?

"Why didn't you confide in me, Bree?" she whispered, opening her eyes again.

"I brought you some tea."

Darrius entered her line of vision and deposited the teacup on the coffee table. The delicate china looked almost silly in his large hands.

But the gesture, so patient, kind and without expectation, brought tears to her eyes.

"Thank you." She leaned forward to pick it up with unsteady hands, and took a sip of the hot liquid.

"I don't suppose you've heard from her?"

She gave a slight shake of her head and set the tea back down with a sigh.

"Was Aubree involved with anyone that you can remember? Dating?"

"No, not at all." She frowned, another memory tugging at

her mind. "Although, we did have an interesting conversation recently where she said something about guys being stupid. Or something like that."

"Trouble in manlandia."

"No, I mean, I didn't think she was dating. She told me she wasn't. This makes no sense." Frustration gnawed at her gut, and she picked up her phone again to check for a text message or call that maybe she might've missed.

It was silly, because of course nothing had come in.

"We'll find her."

"What if she doesn't want to be found? I've already driven all over Seattle and half the suburbs. I've contacted the few friends she has, but they aren't close. And none of them have seen or heard from her."

Darrius sat down on the couch next to her and slid an arm around her shoulders.

"Sugar, trust me on this. Your sister is a teenager with not a hell of a lot of resources or money. It's only a matter of time."

The comfort from his presence was immediate. Grace snuggled closer to him, placing her hand on his chest and breathing in a slow breath.

But what if they couldn't? What if Aubree wasn't just a scared, pregnant teenager in hiding? What if she were actually in trouble?

"We should get some sleep." The reluctance in his tone indicated he wasn't thrilled by the suggestion either.

"You're right. I don't know how I'll sleep, but we should try." She eased away from him, but kept her phone clutched in her hand.

She continued to clutch it when they settled into bed a few minutes later. With the comfort and peace of having his arms around her, and sleep dragging at her exhausted body, a part of her brain still waited for it to ring.

The sound of wood snapping outside had her eyes blinking

open and Darrius sitting upright in bed.

Dawn hinted it was near by the fading darkness through her curtains.

"What—"

"I've got this. Stay in bed." Darrius was up and across the room before she could reply.

Stay in bed? Her heart pounded as she tossed back the comforter. Did Darrius know nothing about her?

She grabbed a robe and tied it around her, then ran into the living room. The sight awaiting her almost brought her to her knees.

Aubree rushed forward with a sob, flinging herself into Grace's arms.

"I'm sorry," her sister cried. "I know you've been so worried."

Relief and emotion slammed into her over and over, making tears fill her eyes and her cling to Aubree's waiflike body.

"It's okay. Oh, sweetie, why didn't you call? Text? Anything to let me know you were okay."

"I didn't know you were looking for me. I should've. The moment I left school, I should've known Jocelyn would find out and go to you." Aubree drew in a ragged breath, heavy with tears. "I threw away my phone. I knew she could and would track it. Track me."

Grace drew back enough to take in the tear-stained face of her sister and the hint of fear in the back of her eyes.

"Bree, was that your pregnancy test?"

Fresh tears flooded Aubree's eyes, before rolling in fat drops down her face.

"Yes."

Heavy disbelief washed over Grace again, but she struggled to hide it. She wasn't going to ask how it was possible, she knew how babies were created. But her sister was so responsible, so shy with people and especially men. And yet now it appeared she'd not only engaged in a sexual relationship, but she was pregnant.

"Aubree, why don't you sit. I've got a blanket." Darrius's words were gentle as he took her arm and guided her to the couch.

Her sister didn't protest, but curled up on the couch and drew the fuzzy blanket around her.

"I'll give you two ladies some time to talk. Go make some breakfast for us all."

Grace sank down onto the couch next to her sister, but met his gaze over the back of the couch.

Thank you, she mouthed, knowing her eyes also reflected the depth of her gratitude.

He gave a small nod, his own gaze troubled, before he disappeared into the kitchen.

Grace turned her attention back to Aubree and tugged part of the furry blanket up and over her legs. The scenario wasn't all that unfamiliar. In fact it could've been any Saturday morning when they were growing up. They'd always sat on the couch together, sharing a blanket while watching TV and talking.

Despite their age difference, they'd always been close friends. Closer than any friends they'd met in school or otherwise. It wasn't until recently and joining the P.I.A. that Grace been able to say she had loyal, true friends.

"Can you talk about it, Bree? Can you tell me who the father is?"

Her sister scrunched her eyes closed, her face pinching with misery.

"You don't know him. He's just a guy I made the mistake of trusting. Of falling for."

Someone from school. "Is he like us?"

"Yes, he's a half-blooded shifter."

Not that it mattered as much this day and age, but Grace gave a small nod.

"Did he mark you?"

"No. Oh hell no."

Maybe it was better that way. It certainly sounded better that way.

Gently, she asked, "Have you told him you're pregnant?"

"I can't. I don't want him to know. I don't want Jocelyn to know." Aubree opened her eyes and the sheer panic there momentarily took Grace aback.

"Bree," she began gently, floundering for what to say. Could've never begun to imagine herself in this situation. "He has a right to know. And it's going to be really difficult to hide a pregnancy from Jocelyn, from your school. Or... I didn't even ask. Do you intend to have the baby?"

"Of course." Aubree almost seemed shocked as she slid her hand to her belly, pressing against it through the fleece blanket. "For me, there is no other option."

Grace's throat ached with unshed tears and she nodded. Her sister's future had changed on a dime—nothing about her life would be normal. But she couldn't afford to think about that now.

"Why don't you want to tell the father?"

"He's not a decent person, Grace. I don't trust him and can't believe I ever did before. I was stupid. I fell hard for a much too handsome guy who said all the right things." Anger flashed across her face now. "I'll do everything in my power to make sure he never finds out."

"All right. I'll help you in any way I can. How are you going to keep this from Jocelyn though?"

"I don't know. Crud." Aubree's brows drew together and she shook her head. "I don't trust her either. There's no saying what she might get in her head to do to me and the baby if she knew I was pregnant. I wouldn't put anything past her with all the sick little experiments she does—"

"Wait, which experiments?" Grace fumbled for her sister's hands, her heart suddenly pounding. Surely her sister couldn't have been aware of what had happened just two months ago.

But the shock on Aubree's face and then guilt sent a slow, awful sense of premonition through her.

"Bree?"

"I…you were never supposed to know." Misery laced her sister's soft words. "She promised me the tests would help me and that if I did it willingly she wouldn't try and force you to do them."

The noise that erupted from Grace's throat was almost animallike. "No. Dammit, *no*. Aubree. Tell me you weren't given those injections."

Aubree shook her head. "Wait, you know about them?"

"Of course I know," Grace rasped, pressing her hands to her head and digging her nails into her temple. "I can't believe this. I cannot fucking believe she'd do this. And you never told me?"

"I didn't want to tell you." Tears of pain reflected in her sister's eyes. "I didn't want to worry you. And it's better this way, I'm okay, and at least you didn't have to go through them—"

"But I did," Grace rasped. "She blackmailed me into doing them, Bree. Told me she wouldn't force you to do them if I did."

"Oh no…"

Grace knew the almost childlike disappointment and dismay on her sister's face was the complete opposite of the rage brewing inside her own soul.

Fuck it. She was done with Jocelyn Feloray. The woman had gone too far this time—much too far. It was a good thing their aunt wasn't standing under the same roof right now, or she might not leave alive.

"I hate that you went through that too, Grace. But please don't be upset for me, I don't remember a lot of the bad parts, honestly." Aubree shrugged. "Which I suppose is a blessing, and Drew pulled me out before I started showing complications from the drug."

Grace narrowed her eyes. "Drew?"

Aubree's cheeks flushed and she lowered her eyes. "He's a worker at the lab, helped out with the transport of the shifter volunteers, I think."

Holy shit. Maybe Aubree hadn't been seduced by some horny teenager, but a grown-ass man.

"And let me guess. He's also your baby's father?"

Her sister gave a slight shrug. "He took me away from those horrible tests and kept me safe at his apartment. I was so ridiculously grateful...when he told me I was pretty and wanted to kiss me, all I could think of was how lucky I was."

"Misplaced hero worship," Grace said grimly. "And apparently an asshole who took advantage of it."

She wanted to kill them all. Have her own vigilante justice on the pieces of shit of this world—family or not.

What the hell was wrong with people? Just like Grace, her sister had been blackmailed by her own aunt. And some shady fucktard had seduced a teenager and got her pregnant.

"I hope you're hungry." Darrius returned to the living room, a couple of steaming plates in his hand. "Pancakes. Eggs. Tea."

"No coffee?" Aubree asked hopefully.

"I think you should skip it now," Grace murmured, accepting a plate and balancing it on her lap. "We need to have you see a doctor about this pregnancy."

"Crud. I'd rather not."

"Not an option. No niece or nephew of mine is being born without proper care." Holy hell, just saying those words was still shocking.

Grace stared at the food on her plate and knew it would be a challenge to eat anything.

"While you both are eating, I figured I'd head out and take care of a few things." Darrius turned away and grabbed his keys off the desk.

The hairs on the back of Grace's neck rose. "Care to elaborate on that?"

He gave a hard smile. "No, actually, I don't."

The knock at the door saved her from any response.

Darrius pulled it open and motioned for Sienna and Donovan to come inside.

Grace set her plate down and shook her head. “What—”

“Darrius promised us breakfast.” Sienna smiled and strode across the room, giving Grace a big hug. “Hey, sweetie.”

“Apparently my security system is a piece of shit.”

“I wouldn’t say that.” Donovan plucked one of her wooden needles from the back of his arm. “Damn impressive actually. So...food?”

“I’m sorry, but are you here for breakfast, or babysitting?” Grace glanced pointedly at Darrius and then Donovan.

Donovan gave a slight shrug. “We take care of our own, Masterson. And the hell if I’m going to turn down a free meal.”

She had a bad feeling about this. A really bad feeling, actually. The hard glint in Darrius’s eyes and his death grip on the keys in his hands had her stepping forward.

“Wait—”

Donovan caught her arm, halted her advance. “Just let him go, Masterson.”

Her pulse quickened and she shook her head when Darrius met her gaze. He gave a small smile, a quick wink, and then he was gone.

Darrius drove through the back roads of North Bend as if the speed limit was simply a suggestion and the tires on his truck had wings.

Traffic was almost nonexistent at this hour, and the pink fingers of dawn were only now sliding up over Mount Si.

The rage inside him only grew with each mile he put between him and Grace’s home.

Generally in life he tried to give people the benefit of the doubt. Tried to assume not everyone was an asshole—which was actually kind of a challenge in his field.

But Jocelyn Feloray had just been promoted to Queen Bitch in his eyes. And she was going to start being accountable for her actions.

He pulled up alongside the luxury condo he now knew was her residence a few minutes later.

The front doors were locked, but it didn't take him long to find a way in, or to override the security code in the private elevator that went to the penthouse.

When the doors slid open, the lush hallway was silent. He made no move to silence his footsteps and just strode purposefully in through the penthouse's doors.

The electronic blinds were drawn, leaving the opulent living room in near darkness, but his gaze was already sliding over the condo in search of the bedroom. No doubt that's where the viperous bitch was.

Instinct slammed a cold warning into him a second before a hard body nearly knocked him down. Darrius regained his balance and swung his fist into the jaw of the man coming in for another attack.

His punch connected with a promising crunch that sent the younger man to his knees. But he was quickly back up, hurtling himself at Darrius and wrapping beefy arms around his face in an attempt to bring him down.

Who the hell was this asshole attacking with all the subtlety of a bull in a china shop? He was young and had a pretty face that was now going to be marked up from the punch Darrius had just thrown.

Darrius brought his elbow down on the back of the man's neck, and was rewarded when he slumped to the ground.

"Very nice, Agent Hilliard." Jocelyn strode out of the bedroom, a red silk robe tied around a tiny waist. "I must say I'm impressed. Though I'm not sure I appreciate you leaving marks on my toy."

"They'll fade." The young man was a shifter, he could smell the wolf blood in him. "I'm surprised you'd let a shapeshifter even touch you."

"Only because he does it so well. I reduce him to a penis and it works out quite well. I just try to block out *what* he is."

"Why? It's partly what you are too."

"Hmm. And I try so hard to forget that." Jocelyn moved past him and into a sparkling, state-of-the-art-looking kitchen. "Can I get you something to drink? Mimosa? Bloody Mary?"

"You're lucky I don't end you, Jocelyn. Right here, right now."

"End me?" She arched a brow as she poured vodka into a tall glass. "As in kill me? How utterly dramatic."

"Just about as dramatic as trying to ruin the lives of your nieces." He walked slowly into the kitchen, glancing around.

"My nieces were never in danger."

"Grace almost died."

Jocelyn added the Bloody Mary mix to her vodka. "There were complications with the drug I couldn't have predicted."

"Bullshit, Jocelyn." He gave a harsh laugh. "You're so damn lucky we don't have a leg to stand on for a lawsuit. But right now I'm pretty close to ignoring the human justice system anyway."

"Is that a threat, Agent Hilliard?"

"You're damn right it is."

Jocelyn took a sip of her drink and then narrowed her eyes. "I don't respond well to threats. You realize I could have you arrested. Breaking and entering. Assault. All that delightful business."

Darrius strode forward until he was just inches away from her. Up close, he could see the resemblance between the three women. All were beautiful and had the same crystalline blue eyes and small upturned nose.

All three were petite, though Jocelyn and Aubree had more delicate frames. Grace was small, but had curves and muscle from the demanding, athletic lifestyle being a P.I.A. agent required.

And then there were the eyes—the windows to the soul. All three women's eyes told a different story. Aubree's held an innocence and fragility of being so young and vulnerable. Grace's a hard defiance and confidence. But Jocelyn's gaze always shined with a calculation that was pure evil.

"I think I would actually enjoy it if you called the human cops on me, Jocelyn." He tilted his head and bared his teeth. "And I'll be sure to let them know how you imprisoned and condoned the seduction of a minor."

All amusement disappeared from Jocelyn's gaze. "What the hell did you just say?"

"I wonder how that would go down in the media. The high and mighty owner of Feloray Laboratories blackmails her teenage niece into an experiment during which she's seduced and impregnated by your employee."

The glass fell from Jocelyn's hands, shattering on the floor and spreading red over the ground. It almost looked like blood, the dark red against sparkling black tile.

"Aubree is pregnant?"

Fuck, had Jocelyn not known? Unease slid through him at the thought of having tipped a hand that shouldn't have been shown. He tried to remember parts of the conversation he'd overheard from Grace and Aubree at breakfast. Had Aubree said something about not wanting Jocelyn to know? Or was his mind creating that?

Shit. *Shit*, he'd been so caught up with his own emotions he hadn't even stopped to think what he was saying.

With a growl of fury, partly at himself and the monster in front of him, he strode forward.

Jocelyn backed up, eyes wide, until she hit the counter.

"You don't touch them. You don't come near them," he rasped. "Do you understand? If you so much as try, I will personally destroy you and your company."

Her lower lip trembled and she shook her head. The blood had left her face and her skin had an unhealthy paleness to it.

"Do you fucking understand me?" he screamed.

"Yes." Her voice was husky now, her eyes not meeting his, but instead on her little boy toy still unconscious in the other room. "You've made your point, Agent Hilliard. Now if you wouldn't mind taking your charming caveman tactics out of here and let me get on with my morning? Some of us have work to do today."

He didn't trust her, but knowing he'd already fucked up by both coming here and threatening her, he turned and made his way out of the door. As he left, he just barely resisted the temptation of kicking the little shit who'd attacked him.

Time to instigate the rest of the plan.

"You're back sooner than I thought." Sienna opened the door to him and gestured him inside. "Aubree is asleep and Grace is showering. She's determined to go into work."

"I figured she would be." Darrius strode inside the small house and slid his gaze to Donovan, who was currently on Grace's computer in the corner of the room. "But I called in for a sick day. Can you keep an eye on her at the office today, Donovan?"

"You know I will. We all will." Donavan spun his chair around and folded his arms across his chest. "What have you got in mind?"

"I'm taking Aubree to my parents' house. They're going to keep her safe."

"Jocelyn will never allow it."

He hadn't heard Grace's approach, but glanced back to see her drying her hair with a towel as she shot him a frown.

"She will," he said with grim confidence. After he'd threatened her 'til she'd probably peed herself, he had a feeling Jocelyn would stay away.

"She has full custody of Bree. We tried, but the courts wouldn't even let her come and stay with me."

He offered a stiff shrug. "Trust me, Grace, she's going to look the other way on this."

Uncertainty flashed across her face before she gave a small nod. "And your parents, how do they feel about harboring a pregnant teenager?"

"I've already spoken with them and they're waiting for us now." Not caring that Sienna and Donovan were there—because fuck it, he was tired of hiding it—he crossed to Grace and pulled her into his arms. "They raised four kids, sugar. I'm sure they'll do fine."

She didn't pull away, or even glance at the other couple in the room. Instead she just gave a soft sigh and pressed her cheek to his shoulder.

"Thank you. I'm worried about her. And she's determined to not say anything to both the father of the baby and Jocelyn."

Darrius closed his eyes and took the punch of guilt to the stomach. "Yeah, about that..."

"Oh God, Darrius, you didn't."

"I wasn't thinking. It didn't occur to me that she didn't know, or that Aubree didn't want her to know." He slid a damp strand of hair between his fingers. "Which is another reason I'm taking full responsibility and keeping her with people I trust."

Grace shook her head, unease on her face. "Shit, I don't know—"

"I'll have my youngest brother drive her to school and pick her up." He grinned. "He's bigger than me and plays basketball for the UW. She'll be safe."

"I guess we don't have a choice."

"Trust me on this."

"I do." She finally nodded and stepped away. "I have no idea how Aubree will react—"

"I'll take care of it. Why don't you head into work with Sienna and Donovan?"

"We're ready when you are," Sienna murmured, her bright tone not completely natural with the mood in the room.

"You're not coming to work today?" Grace's gaze flickered to him in surprise.

"I took it off to get Aubree settled."

"Oh, Darrius..."

Seeing the gratitude and hesitation in her eyes, he reassured her the only way he knew how. He pulled her closer and took her mouth in a gentle, reassuring kiss that ultimately had her sighing and Donovan clearing his throat.

"Well, I guess the word discretion has been eliminated from both of your guys' library," Donovan drawled. "You've got ten minutes, Masterson. Then we're leaving."

Grace nodded, not even the least bit flushed as she moved away from Warrick and back to her room.

"Thanks." Darrius shoved his hands into his back pocket and jerked his chin at the other man. "I appreciate this."

"We're happy to do it." Sienna grinned and moved toward the kitchen, but nudged him in the side. "And I think you two are adorable together. You should bite her soon, before some other wolf does. She'd be a great mate."

Somehow he didn't flinch and just managed a slight smile. Donovan, however, grimaced and shook his head.

"Sorry about that. I never told her anything, bro."

"I know. And I appreciate you keeping my business quiet." Darrius slapped his friend on the back and went to wake up Aubree.

Any man lucky enough to have Grace as a mate wouldn't have any idea how good he had it. Unfortunately, Darrius would never be that man.

Chapter Eighteen

"You holding up okay?"

When there was no immediate answer, Darrius cast a glance over at the silent girl in the passenger seat. The truck almost swallowed up her slight frame, and she stared straight ahead with wide eyes and a slightly turned down mouth.

A lost soul.

"I'll be fine." She slid her hands to her belly, still flat beneath the jeans and clingy red T-shirt, and didn't look at him. "Thank you for helping me."

"Not a big deal."

"But it is," she said softly. "You don't know me. You've only known my sister for less than a year. And now you're taking me to your family. That's kind of a big deal."

This girl might be quiet and shy—so unlike her sister—but one thing they had in common was their candor. They didn't hesitate to speak what was on their mind.

"I care about your sister and there's not a helluva lot I wouldn't do for her right now." He paused. "And that transfers over to those she cares about."

"Do you love her?"

Holy hell. Darrius nearly swerved off the road as sweat broke out on the back of his neck.

"I know it's none of my business." Her words were infused with a shyness and curiosity that was appropriate for her age. "You don't have to pretend you're not sleeping together, because I can see it in the way you guys are with each other. I think... I think it's really cool."

Ah shit, this was not the conversation he wanted to be having with a teenager. Grace's sister especially.

"I care about Grace. Quite a bit," he admitted honestly, but then hedged with the, "it's a little early to know whether it's love."

"You're probably right. Or sometimes you think you're in love, but it's just... I dunno, a crush? Lust?" She sighed. "And the guy turns out to be a smarmy bastard who should be living in a sewer."

Maybe he wasn't supposed to laugh, but Darrius let out a soft one anyway.

"First loves are always the hardest."

"So you know from experience then?" She turned in her seat to look at him, curiosity burning bright in her eyes.

Darrius shifted, uncomfortable with this turn of conversation. He wasn't about to divulge that he'd been mated, but the story of his first love should've been Jenny.

They'd mated, for heaven's sake. And yet...the only emotion he could remember was lust. And really the desire for his mate had only been from that night. After they were joined, he could barely bring himself to touch her. His emotions for her should've been love and protectiveness, and yet they'd been resignation and resentment.

He'd failed her, and in a huge way.

"It's what I've always heard," he finally replied. "You're young, Aubree. You'll find the right mate when it's your time."

She gave a soft grunt. "Thanks, but I'll pass. I'll do just fine raising this kid on my own. Men just complicate things."

His lips quirked and he didn't reply. He'd bet his soul a guy would come along someday and make her eat her words.

When they arrived at his parents' house, his parents were ready for them.

Darrius helped Aubree from the truck and carried the small bag of clothes she had—which wasn't much since she'd had to flee the dorms at her school pretty fast.

"Mom, Dad, this is Aubree. Grace's little sister."

They'd only met Grace once over the summer, when he'd dragged a handful of fellow agents over for a Labor Day barbeque. No one could've predicted that a few weeks later Grace would be in thresholds of hell.

"Well hello, aren't you just the prettiest thing?" His mom rushed forward to give Aubree a hug. "I'm Olivia and this is my husband Rodrick."

Aubree flashed them a grateful smile. "Nice to meet you both. Thanks for taking me in. It really means a lot."

"Not a problem," his dad replied.

"Where's Terrance?" Darrius asked.

"Lifting weights in the garage." His mother gave him a hug. "Why don't you go grab him and I'll show Aubree her room and around the house."

"Appreciate that, Mom. Hey, Dad." He grinned and hugged the older man. "I'll go find T, thanks again."

His brother didn't even glance over when Darrius entered the garage, just kept his focus on the two-hundred-pound weights he was pressing.

Finally, after five more minutes of grunting, he set the weights back on their holder with a clang and stood up.

Terrance strode over, wiping the back of his arm across his forehead to remove the sweat. "So I hear you've got me a babysitting gig?"

"I'll owe you."

"Hell yeah, you will. But I don't mind." He shook Darrius's hand. "You know there isn't a lot I won't do for my big brother."

"You should consider that offer to become an agent after college."

"We'll see. Depends on if I go pro."

Basketball. His brother's life revolved around the sport—hell, it was hard not to when he was locally and internationally revered by the media and courted by numerous schools. And yet he'd chosen to stay local at the University of Washington.

But the NBA wasn't the only one trying to recruit Terrance. The P.I.A. saw his potential as well.

"So where is this sixteen and pregnant chick?"

Darrius scowled and jammed a finger in his brother's chest. "Watch your damn mouth. She's been through a lot and is vulnerable as hell right now. And she'll be eighteen before the baby's born."

He wasn't about to spill the details of how Aubree had gotten into her situation—hell, he only knew a handful from what he'd overheard this morning while making breakfast. But they weren't his business, and they sure weren't his brother's.

"I'm just fucking with you, D." Terrance sobered, looking even a bit ashamed now. "The parents and I will take good care of her, you can count on me."

Darrius nodded, not doubting it for a minute. "I know you will."

He went back into the house, Terrance following behind him, and spotted Aubree and his mother out in the backyard.

They waved and made their way back inside.

"Aubree, this is my little brother Terrance. He'll be keeping an eye on you for a while."

"Little?" She glanced at both men, eyes twinkling as she gave a lopsided smile. "Well, I guess if we're talking chronologically. Nice to meet you, Terrance. And like I told your parents, I really do appreciate this. I promise I won't be a bother."

"You're not a bother, sweat pea." Their mom stepped in with an admonishing look at the two brothers and grabbed Aubree's arm. "Come on, I'll help you unpack."

Darrius waited for some smartass reply from his brother, and turned to find the younger man seeming at a loss for words. His jaw hung slightly, and his eyes were round and appreciative as they followed every step Aubree made out of the room.

"No."

Terrance glanced at him, guilt flashing across his face. "What?"

"Don't even think about it."

"Thinking what, big bro? I was just—"

"You were just nothing. Exactly." Darrius smacked him in the back of the head.

"It's a natural reaction. Dammit, you didn't tell me she was beautiful."

"Runs in the family." Darrius shook his head and walked to the door. "I'm going to run and pick up some stuff from Aubree's dorm. I'll be back later."

"Don't get into any trouble."

"Yeah, I think I'll offer the same advice." Darrius grinned and left the house.

"The autopsy results on Thom Wilson came in this morning."

Grace glanced from her computer as Larson appeared next to her cubicle.

"And?"

"Died of asphyxiation due to carbon monoxide poisoning."

She nodded, disappointment gathering thick in her throat. The morning so far had basically sucked to high hell, and this news wasn't helping.

But she should've expected it, because it's what everyone had said all along.

"All right. So basically you guys were spot-on."

"Well, hold on a second. There was something else interesting we found." Larson leaned back against the cubicle wall and shrugged. "An injection site on his body."

"Heroin use?"

"Can't be certain, we're still running tests on what was in that vial." Larson stroked his jaw. "But you know the injection spot was kind of bizarre."

She arched a brow, trying not to get too excited. "Oh?"

"Between the toes."

Her breath caught and the excitement took hold. "Wow, that can't be normal."

"Not really. No."

What came to mind when she thought of an injection between the toes was a case a while ago where a shifter woman had tried to kill her mate by injecting him between the toes with a high amount on insulin to make it look like an accidental death.

What possible reason could anyone have for such an absurd injection site?

Larson's pursed lips and narrowed gaze were a pretty clear indication he thought something was off as well.

"What's your gut saying, Masterson?"

"That even though most signs point to suicide, I think we should dig a little deeper."

"Agreed."

"Permission to keep researching?"

"Permission granted."

She loved that he trusted and respected her enough to put this back in her hands.

"And, Masterson, I've requested that the autopsy being done on our POI check for injection marks in the same spot."

"You're amazing," she breathed. "Thank you. Hey, did we ever get his cell phone records for the weeks prior to Thom's death?"

"Sure did, and there's quite a few calls to a personal cell phone registered to Jocelyn Feloray."

"I knew it," she whispered. "Do you think I can get clearance to visit Thom's widow today? Ask a few more questions?"

"I don't see why not."

"Fantastic." She stood up and began gathering her things. "I'll give her a call and see if she's available."

"But bring Yorioka since Hilliard called in sick. I don't want you going out alone."

Yorioka. Crap. Somehow in the last couple of days she'd almost forgotten about the new agent on their team.

Her high at being given a green light to keep investigating diminished some, but she gave a small nod. Of course she was still on orders to be protected, and going out alone would've been impossible.

Once Larson had left her alone again, she made a few notes on her purse-sized notepad and then glanced at her phone. She resisted the urge to call Darrius again and check on Aubree. He'd called her about an hour ago, reassuring her that her sister was fine and settling in.

And she trusted him—trusted his family that she barely knew. All of them had the biggest hearts.

Her throat tightened with gratitude for the man who'd come to mean so much to her in such a short amount of time. He was selfless and sacrificed far more than he should've—today it happened to be his work life.

Trying not to think about how much she missed him here, Grace pushed aside her emotions and went to find Yorioka.

"How are you feeling?"

The silence in the company car had been so thick, Yorioka's sudden words had made her jump.

Grace glanced away from the road and over at the other agent. The woman looked severe as ever with her shiny black hair pulled back and a gray suit that looked so starched it could break in half.

"What do you mean?"

"Well, after getting your ass kicked at the pub the other night." Yorioka's deadpan expression cracked a bit as her lips curled. "I wanted to make sure you're okay."

Grace gave a harsh laugh. "No you don't. Just don't even bother, Yorioka. You couldn't give two shits about me."

Yorioka gave a small frown. "You're a fellow agent, so regardless about what I may think about you professionally, of course I'm concerned for your well-being."

Resisting a snort of disbelief, Grace didn't bother

responding. Instead her mind had flittered back to the attack that had happened two days ago, but felt like a lifetime.

Reliving the attack in the bathroom sent a cold shiver down her spine. It had been so brutal, so deliberate, and entirely about intimidation.

She tried to remember details about the attacker. Could Larson have been right about the male attacker potentially being their now dead POI?

She hadn't visited him in the morgue—couldn't bring herself to and had known there wouldn't be a point. Their scents had been disguised

But...oh God, how had she forgotten this bit? The female's voice had seemed familiar. But from where?

Grace froze, not daring to breathe for a moment, and cast another glance at Agent Yorioka.

She struggled with the memory of the night—tried to remember if the other woman had been at the table still when Grace had gone to use the bathroom.

Was she just being paranoid? Yorioka was a fellow agent. Maybe she didn't like her, but animosity wasn't a motive to threaten her. And to threaten her off the Wilson case?

Unless the Wilson case threat was just a guise—she'd thought it awfully flimsy anyway. Maybe the attack had been a way to scare her away from the agency. Maybe the motive had been to keep her from returning to work, not just the case. Or maybe Jocelyn had another inside agent. It wouldn't be the first time.

When they arrived at Thom Wilson's house, she couldn't push aside the sense of distrust toward Yorioka, but did her best to disguise it.

Thom's widow was just as sweet and helpful as before, and showed Grace to his personal computer when she asked.

"What are you looking for?" Yorioka leaned down to glance over her shoulder. "We've already checked emails. There's nothing to link him to Feloray Laboratories."

"That's fine. I'm not looking for that." And she wasn't. She clicked on the sent items in his email and scrolled through the topics.

Nothing looked overtly suspicious, but her attention did snag on an email he sent himself with a curious subject line.

Grandma's Lasagna recipe.

Premonition tingled through her as she kept the cursor hovering over the email.

"Lasagna? Seriously?" Yorioka shook her head and walked away. "Waste of fucking time coming here today."

No it wasn't. Relieved that the other woman had walked away, Grace opened the email and exhilaration raced through her.

What was in the email wasn't even close to a recipe. But then she'd anticipated that the moment she'd seen the subject line.

During their time locked up in the experiments they'd talked about everything under the sun. Including Thom's grandma's lasagna. While delirious from hunger and bad drugs, they'd talked about food and what a real bed would feel like again. He'd talked especially long about his grandma's lasagna recipe that was so amazing, and how someday he'd email it to her if they survived.

Grace opened the email, knowing with one-hundred-percent certainty the body of the email wouldn't contain a recipe.

What she stared at was probably some kind of final journal entry Thom had sent himself. Maybe he'd sensed something might happen to him, and had known if it did Grace would be one of the people investigating.

The email was mostly incoherent rambling, but he mentioned being depressed and trying to overcome it without medication. Her heart sank a bit, knowing that it didn't do well as proof that he hadn't killed himself.

He then went on to mention an elderly uncle named Curt who had retired from the P.I.A., and how on his deathbed the man had confessed to using the memory-wiping machine for sinister purposes—both on shifter women and children. Thom had ended the email by labeling Jocelyn a murderess and said he'd make sure she paid for her crimes.

Murderess? Grace frowned, drumming her fingers on the desk. She hadn't outright killed any of the volunteers. None had even died from side effects to the drugs.

But maybe he'd had something on her, maybe this Curt—whoever he was—had legitimate information that had cost Thom his life.

Grace forwarded the email to herself, wanting to study it in more detail later.

"So is the recipe to die for?"

Yorioka's sarcastic question announced her return, and Grace quickly minimized the screen.

To die for. Interesting choice in words.

"It's nothing special," she murmured succinctly. And now she'd just lied to a fellow agent. Why didn't she tell Yorioka about what was really in the email?

Because you don't trust her.

And the drive back to the agency made her realize that even more.

She snuck another glance at the other agent and found the woman watching her.

Ignoring the trickle of disquiet that slid through her blood, Grace turned her attention back to the road.

Yes. Until she was certain she could trust Yorioka, she was going to be careful with the information she divulged.

"So you think it means something?" Darrius set down the email Grace had handed him a moment ago and rubbed his jaw.

He had his own thoughts about what he'd just read, but he was curious about Grace's.

"I think it could potentially mean everything," she said,

animation dancing in her voice as she pulled out a chair and sat down beside him at the kitchen table. "I want to find out more about Curt Lancaster."

"Not a bad idea. What were Yorioka's impressions on this email?"

Grace's eyes became shuttered and her mouth tightened. "I didn't show her."

And yet he was aware the agent had been with Grace most of today. "Really?"

"Really. I don't trust her, Darrius."

"She's a member of your team."

"I'm aware of that. When I was attacked on Wednesday, do you know for certain she was at the table?"

Darrius blinked, stunned by the not-so-subtle implication Grace was throwing out about Agent Yorioka.

"I don't know. I think she and Alicia might've all gone out to smoke. What the hell are you implying?"

She shook her head and looked away. "Nothing. Forget I said anything."

"Uh, a little hard to do."

"All I'm saying is that one of the people who attacked me was a woman. And Yorioka's made it pretty damn clear she doesn't care for me."

"Right. Which would make her pretty damn stupid if she did try and attack you," he pointed out tersely. "What would her motivation even be?"

"I don't know." Grace pulled her hair down from a ponytail and shook it out, threading her fingers through the strands. "Like I said, forget it."

Mentally dumping her asinine accusations wasn't too hard, as she began to unbutton her shirt.

His pulse jumped. "What are you doing?"

"Undressing. I'd like to have sex now, if you don't mind."

Chapter Nineteen

Holy shit. Darrius's cock lurched against his jeans, and the air hissed out from between his teeth.

"Are you deliberately trying to shock me tonight? You're not holding back any punches."

"I'm not trying to shock you." She shrugged out of her blouse and then unhooked her bra. "I just want you, have been thinking about you all day, and I think sex will be great stress relief."

"You're using me for stress relief?" He didn't know whether to be offended or relieved, but was a little distracted by the sensual way her small breasts curved upward and were crowned with those mouth-watering nipples.

Grace moved around the table and sat down in his lap, wrapping her arms around his neck.

"Don't look so pissy. You're good at sex. Really good at it. I enjoy having it with you and I know doing it now—or fairly soon—will take my mind off of things."

His ego swelled a bit over the *good at it* comment and he curled his fingers into the strands of her hair, tugging her head back slightly.

"Good at it, hmm?" He kissed the pulse beating lightly in her neck and felt it quicken beneath his lips.

Maybe she did need the distraction. She'd already called her sister twice tonight, and seemed reassured of her safety, but apparently her mind wouldn't shut down. Whether it was Aubree or work, she seemed pretty high-strung.

The idea of taking her again sent a surge of lust through him, and he moved his other hand up to cup her bare breast. The nipple hardened further in his palm and he murmured appreciatively.

"So you're okay with this, Grace? With us and just casual sex?" Where had that question come from? Why the hell was he even bringing it up again?

Because he didn't want to hurt her. Didn't want her to become attached... *Fuck*. Like he was.

His heart beat a little harder and he clenched his jaw. He cared about her, more than he should've. More than he had any right to.

Because someday she would leave him. Someday, hell, it could happen tomorrow even. But it *would* happen. Grace would find her mate and then she'd be done with Darrius.

The pain, the utter jealously over a man he didn't even know yet, swelled inside him and nearly blinded him in a haze of red.

"Don't worry. Casual sex is perfect." She cupped his face, drew her thumbs down his jaw and then pressed a soft kiss to his lips. "It's all I have time for right now. You don't need to worry about me."

Her words only stoked the fire of frustration in him, while at the same time brought the flames of need higher. He wanted her. Now. And he didn't want her to be so damn cavalier in her attitude about sex with him. He wanted her driven mad with the same need that rode him like a demon.

Tightening his fingers in her hair, he tugged her neck back as a low growl escaped from his throat.

Grace made a whimper of surprise, but didn't protest as he kissed the pulse in her neck again. His tongue flicked over the delicate skin, and the need to bite her was almost tangible.

Fuck. But there was nothing. No dropping of his canines—nothing that would ever give him the chance to claim the one woman who should've been his.

But he could fuck her. He could take her until she couldn't see straight and was screaming his name. Until his image was burned into her mind and soul.

Or was that just wishful thinking?

His chest tightened. He shoved aside the encumbering thoughts and tried to focus on the lust that lingered beneath.

Moving his mouth lower, he lifted her slightly so the roundness of her breast brushed his lips.

He caught the stiff peak of her nipple in his mouth and drew on it, listening and responding to her cry of pleasure. Using his teeth, he grazed the flesh and was rewarded with a low moan and her nails digging into his shoulders.

Using his free hand, he unfastened her pants and delved his fingers inside and beneath the panties.

While sucking on her nipple, he worked a finger inside her, maneuvering it in and out of her hot, wet channel.

Grace's breathing grew heavier and she started to move against his hand.

He added a second finger, stretching her and preparing her for him, because he knew he wasn't going to last very much longer before it wasn't his fingers, but his dick inside her.

She fumbled to unbutton his shirt, and then smoothed the palms of her hands down his chest.

"Darrius," she whispered. "I don't think I can wait any longer."

Needing so much more—and especially needing the clothes off—Darrius adjusted her in his arms and stood up. He strode through the house to her bedroom and set her back down on her feet.

She immediately pushed his shirt from his body and then reached for the button on his pants.

"In a hurry, sugar?" he rasped, catching her hand.

Red faintly stained her cheeks, but other than that she didn't show the slightest bit of embarrassment. "I can't seem to go slow with you. I'm not going to apologize."

"I don't mind," he murmured. "But I might want to take my time with you this time."

She let out a small groan and she freed him from his pants. But then it was his turn to groan as she began to stroke him into rock-hard readiness.

Part of him wanted to take her slow—to force her to feel and acknowledge the complex emotions running through her. Because, hell, he couldn't be the only one feeling a little messed up inside about what was between them.

When she made to sink to her knees, he caught her elbow and gave a hard shake of his head. He wanted to slow things down, and if she took him in her mouth it would be over before it began.

"I want you on the bed. Naked and on your hands and knees."

Her breasts rose with the sharp breath she drew in, but she immediately moved to comply. She shirked her pants and thong with quick ease before climbing onto the bed and assuming the position he'd required.

"You're such a good little order-taker," he murmured as he finished taking off his clothes.

"Mmm. Don't get used to this." The laughter was held back, but thick in her voice. "I'm having fun right now, but watch out because one of these days I might take over and be Miss Bossy Pants."

"Now that just might be interesting." Naked, he climbed onto the bed beside her and trailed two fingers down the curve of her spine.

"So beautiful." He pressed a kiss at the small dent just above her bottom and she shivered slightly. "So trusting."

"You made it hard not to trust you, so blame yourself." There was wariness in her words now.

He lowered his head to press a kiss against the curve of one ass cheek. She had the sexiest bottom.

"Oh, I'm not protesting, sugar." He slid his hand down between her cheeks to find the damp folds of her sex. "It's actually pretty damn humbling to have your trust."

He slipped a finger inside her again, then moved it up to circle her clit.

"*Yes.*" Her body shuddered and she pressed back against his hand.

He kept stroking her, teasing her flesh until her cries grew higher and her body finally convulsed into a small orgasm.

"I want to wait, but I can't."

"Then don't." She reached behind her and touched his erection again. "I want you inside me now."

He moved away and pulled open her bedside drawer where he'd stashed a box of condoms and quickly put one on.

Grace hadn't moved, and the way she was positioned sent another surge of need through him. She'd lowered her upper body and turned her face against the pillow, and her bottom was raised and ready for him.

Along with the need, there was another emotion. One that had his throat tight and his heart pounding a little harder. He hadn't thrown that trust comment out lightly.

Somehow he'd earned Grace's complete trust, not only with her body, but with her life and family.

"I swear if you wait any longer, I may just push you down and do all the work." Her words were still drowsy from her orgasm.

"You really are okay with this," Darrius said quietly. "Just being sex between us."

She didn't lift her head, but gave a slight shrug. "You need to stop worrying about me. I've said I am okay with it."

Then he would have to be too, because really, what choice did he have?

Darrius moved behind her, slid his hands to the small curve of her hips, and then eased into her body.

Her gasp of pleasure ripped through his soul, and he feasted on it. He used her pleasure, the only thing she could have from him, and found his own.

Each stroke Darrius made into her was like a caress to not only the physical need in her body, but the need in her heart.

You don't need to worry about me, she'd told him. And it had all been a lie. To herself, mostly. Because it wasn't Darrius's problem. She'd agreed to strings-free sex with him, had sworn she'd be okay with it.

Darrius moved harder inside her, and her head jerked against the pillow with each thrust. The position brought him deeper than ever before, and he was already a lot to take.

But the discomfort was tiny compared to the pleasure. The position also offered her privacy for her thoughts. So that maybe he wouldn't see the array of emotions on her face.

She didn't blame Darrius. It was her fault that her heart was breaking a little bit now. Her fault for being so damn weak and falling for a man she could never belong to—who could never love her or claim her.

She almost cried out at the nearly physical pain of the realization, but she bit her lip and smothered it.

"Time to make good on that promise, sugar."

Before she realized what was happening, Darrius had moved out of her and onto his back on the mattress.

Then he was lifting her astride him, with the soft command of, "I want to look at you while you ride me."

He hadn't even finished his sentence before she was moving on him and seeking her pleasure.

On top also felt amazing, but it left her vulnerable. She could feel his stare as she rode him. Could almost hear his brain struggling to work through the pleasure.

Did she look like a lovesick idiot? Or hopefully just someone in the throes of pleasure.

She risked a glance down at him, watching him through hooded eyes. Beneath the haze of lust in his eyes was something darker—almost tormented. Sad.

He felt something. She knew it in her heart. They could throw the words "casual sex" about all they wanted, but he felt something too.

Maybe she couldn't have Darrius as a lifemate. Maybe she had no fucking say who her mate was and who would ultimately claim her—which was pretty common in their community. The men chose.

But she knew—dammit in her heart she knew—that

Darrius should've been hers. And no matter what happened down the road, no matter who she ultimately ended up mated with, she'd know that her heart had been given to another man. To Darrius Hilliard.

Unable to stop the tiny cry of torment this time, she instead buried it by pressing her mouth against his neck. She kissed the pulse there and moved up to the rough stubble of Darrius's jawline.

He made a low, almost feverish growl as he thrust harder up into her. Deeper. Wrapping his hand around her hair, he pushed her head lower again—guiding her mouth back to his throat.

She opened her mouth, flicking her tongue over the pulse. She tried to keep up with him, to keep riding him, but her mind and her body were no longer her own.

She could only take him and follow the blind need driving her. Sucking the pulse harder, she closed her mouth lightly and let her teeth graze over it.

"*Yes.*" Darrius slammed harder into her. Fast now. Taking over what little control she'd tried to maintain.

Whimpering at the mix of pleasure and pain, Grace didn't think, just instinctively caught the skin in a light nip.

Light seemed to rocket through her and the world tilted. She was no longer on top of Darrius, but flat on her back on the mattress. He was on top now, his hips forcing her legs wide as he slammed into her.

His mouth crashed into hers, dominating and taking everything she had to offer. She gave it all back and more. When he lifted his lips she cried out with disappointment.

But her cry sharpened when pain rocketed through her. She tried to focus, to glance down, and lost her breath at what she was looking at. Darrius's mouth at her neck—his teeth on her skin. Almost piercing it.

Not possible.

The thought raced through her head before it was gone and replaced with a pleasure so intense her mind went white.

When she came to, Darrius was shaking her gently, his face hovering over hers.

"What happened?" she whispered and reached up to touch her neck. "I think I had some weird, superimposed dream or something."

Darrius's eyes, round with shock and concern, lowered to her neck. He shook his head.

"It wasn't a dream."

"What?" She traced her fingers over her neck and felt the slight indention of bite marks near her pulse. "I don't... How. *How?*"

"I don't know."

"You marked me?" she whispered.

"I... Fuck. I think I somehow did. The last thing I remember is you kissing my neck. Almost biting me...and then...I lost it."

If Darrius's dark skin could've gone white, she knew it would've. He looked so damn shocked. Almost sickened by what had happened.

Oh God. What seemed like just minutes ago, she'd been wishing this were possible. Had wanted it more than anything. But it hadn't been a possibility. *It hadn't.*

Yet Darrius had just claimed her. And he looked as if he wanted to go throw up.

"How is this happening?" she whispered. "You were already mated."

Panic seared through her at the complete loss of control. How her future had just been decided for her and she couldn't have possibly seen it coming.

She had the childlike inclination to scream at him to undo it. To take it back, but somewhere in her frenzied mind she knew it wasn't possible.

Despite neither of them thinking it was possible, Darrius had mated with her. And despite all the protests she'd made, the words she flung to try and deny it, her soul knew.

She felt different. Somewhat warm inside, and almost mentally and spiritually connected to the man next to her. She belonged to him now. Was his completely. For better or for worse, like it or not.

Did she like it? Wasn't this what she'd wanted?

"I need..." She shook her head and slid out of bed. "I need you to give me a moment."

She went to the bathroom and stared at the mirror—at the marks that were fading, but their meaning did not.

Eyes wide, she touched the two red circles and let out a strangled groan.

"I've been claimed," she whispered.

She should've been elated. Not even an hour ago she would've given anything for Darrius to claim her as his mate, but had it only been because she'd thought he couldn't?

You always want what you can't have. The cliché raced through her mind, but she had to wonder if there was an element of truth to it.

Never in her wonkiest daydreams could she have predicted she'd be mated so young. It hadn't even been on her five-year plan...maybe ten year.

Grace climbed into the shower and made quick time washing her hair and body. When she finished, she walked back into the bedroom to get some clothes.

To her relief, Darrius wasn't in the bed any longer, and she could hear the shower in the hall bathroom running.

After dressing quickly, Grace grabbed her keys and headed out the front door. She had to move fast, because Darrius would be pissed to realize she'd left without someone to watch her.

She climbed into her Eclipse and put on her Bluetooth. By the time she turned onto the highway she'd called her sister.

"Grace? Hey, it's getting late. What's up?"

"Just checking on you, sweetie. How are you?" She knew her voice sounded bright, maybe a little brittle, but hoped Bree wouldn't notice.

"Fine." Her sister laughed. "Getting my butt kicked by Terrance at some snowboarding on the Wii though."

"She's actually pretty good," a voice called in the background.

Grace couldn't help a small smile. "Hey, I'm thinking of coming by and taking you for an ice cream run."

"But it's almost nine and like forty degrees out."

"I know, but I miss you. And we didn't have enough time to catch up this morning."

That and she desperately needed to talk to someone. Despite the age difference, her sister had always been her closest friend and confidant. Ice creams runs had ben somewhat of a tradition between them. It was almost code for *girl talk time.*

"Ice cream sounds great. You'll pick me up?"

"Give me half an hour to drive over, then yeah."

"Hang on, Grace."

There was some muted discussion back and forth between Aubree and Terrance, before Aubree came back on the line.

"I don't suppose Darrius is with you?"

"No." Grace's heart skipped and she swallowed hard. "He was in the shower when I left."

"Okay, well then Terrance is insisting on coming with us."

"Fine." Crap. She'd just have to figure out how to ditch him for a bit. "See you in a bit, Bree."

"Sounds good."

Grace disconnected the call and slowed down for a yellow light.

The hairs on the back of her head lifted, and she started to turn her head but stilled as she felt the prick of a needle at her neck.

"You don't mind if I drive, do you?" an indistinguishable male voice rasped. "It's tight as hell in the backseat."

She tried to shove the needle away, but it pierced her skin and she felt the burn of the medication enter her flesh.

Shit. How had she not sensed him back there? Checked to make sure she was alone? Even people who didn't work for the

P.I.A. were usually paranoid enough to check the backseat of their car before climbing in.

Almost immediately her vision began to blur and she lost the ability to control her muscles. She was vaguely aware of a dark form climbing into the front seat.

He put the car in park and then hauled her out of the driver's seat and moved her into the passenger side, before climbing behind the wheel.

"There we go." He reached out and touched her cheek. "You made this so easy for me. I thought I was going to have to break into your house and knock out your boyfriend, but then I realized you were going to make it easy on me."

Had he been watching her through the window? *Shit.*

"Don't you just look beautiful with drool on your face, but then, I've seen you like this before."

Realization slowly sank in. It was him. The same man who'd attacked her at the Doornail and who she'd suspected had been involved with the experiments.

Even with her body paralyzed and her slumped over position, she could watch him.

He pulled the black knit hat off his head and she squinted, trying to distinguish his features in the darkness.

All it took was passing under one streetlight to figure it out.

The pretty boy who worked for her aunt. Andy? He'd made that comment about her being familiar, and she'd messed with him by suggesting they'd met at a club. Because he'd been so damn skeevy.

But the familiarity had come from him working in the lab during her imprisonment. He'd been a full part of her torment—she knew that now without a doubt.

Anger built hot inside her—volatile and unfortunately useless.

He glanced over at her and his smile flashed white in the darkness.

"Ah, look at that. I think you're starting to remember me. Remember how I said I'd always find you? Well, you made it a lot easier when you showed up at your aunt's."

Hell yeah, she remembered him, and this wouldn't bode well for him later.

"You know what's hot?" he asked lightly, turning onto the interstate. "Fucking your aunt and thinking of your sister."

Her sister? This bastard knew Bree? Wait... Her heart began to thump harder and inside she was shaking her head furiously.

Andy. Drew. *Andrew.* One and the same. She should've put the pieces together, because it all seemed so obvious now.

"She was a sweet little virgin, nice piece of ass, and I think a little bit in love with me after a while. But I had to let her go."

She was going to kill this son of a bitch, without a doubt.

"Because I was screwing Jocelyn, and it just didn't seem right doing them both. She's amazing, you know. Jocelyn? Pretty damn goal-driven. A powerful, beautiful woman," he said softly, his tone almost wistful as he cast her a sideways glance. "It must run in the family. You're all pretty hot."

He reached out and touched her thigh. "I almost had you too. During the experiments. You were so out of it, you couldn't have known your head from your ass. I was on the verge of taking you..." His lips twisted, his expression hardened. "Then you nearly ripped out my throat."

And she'd do it again before the night was through. She knew without a doubt this bastard would die.

"But I learned something this morning. See, your boyfriend came over and broke into Jocelyn's apartment. Kicked my ass a little bit, which trust me, I'm not proud to admit. So later I'll have to kill him for that."

Good fucking luck—one of us will kill you first.

"But while I was playing at being unconscious on the floor, I learned something." Andrew gave an incredulous laugh. "I'm going to be a daddy."

He knew. *Oh God.*

"So how about we go get your sister, just like you planned."

Grace tried to protest, make some kind of vehement reply,

but all that came out was a bare whisper of a groan.

"No need to tell me where she's staying. I followed your boyfriend over earlier." He reached behind him into the small backseat and grabbed a Glock.

Fear overrode the fury at the sight of the gun, but not for her, for Aubree. Grace couldn't help her right now—she couldn't even help herself with whatever drug had paralyzed her system.

And that became abundantly clear when they pulled up outside Hilliard's parents' house. Andrew didn't get out of the car, but just waited. Terrance and Aubree came outside a moment later—Terrance had a cell phone to his ear.

Maybe he was talking to Darrius. Oh please, please let him be talking to Darrius.

The windows were tinted, and she knew they couldn't see inside. Inside her head she screamed at them to run. In her version of things, she sat up and waved them back. But she was trapped inside herself, and they were sitting ducks.

Terrance pulled open the door. "Hey, Grace—"

Grace had the briefest moment to take in the horror on Aubree's face and the sudden rage on Terrance's before Andrew pulled the trigger.

Chapter Twenty

"She's coming there? Are you sure?" Darrius asked grimly, adjusting the cell phone against his ear as he jogged out to his truck.

"Yeah, D. She just called Aubree." The wariness in Terrance's voice made it clear he hadn't been too happy about Grace coming out alone either.

A snarl of frustration erupted past his lips, and Darrius shook his head and started his vehicle.

"Don't let her go anywhere. When she gets to the house, you bring her inside. Got it?"

"I got it. Shit, bro, what happened between you two? Why'd she run?"

That was a damn good question. Though he had a pretty good idea of the answer.

Despite every belief that it couldn't happen, he'd marked her tonight. Had claimed Grace as his mate and decided her future for her.

She had to be livid. How many times had she stated she wasn't looking for serious?

And you somehow bit her anyway.

Their mental connection was new and fragile, and he hadn't tried to lock on her mind yet or pull up her emotions. He wasn't sure that ability would've kicked in so soon, or if he wanted to see what was going on in her head.

"Oh, hey, they're pulling up right now, D."

"Great. I'm just a minute away from the highway and then I'll be there in like fifteen."

"Sounds good. Hey, Grace—"

A gunshot snapped through the phone line—Darrius knew

that sound without question—and he almost went dumb with shock. His foot slipped off the accelerator and the truck lost speed rapidly.

Screaming. There was a woman screaming. Grace? Aubree? There was no sound of his brother though. And then there was silence.

Instinct kicked back in. Darrius slammed his foot back onto the accelerator and the truck lurched forward. He steered it onto the interstate a few minutes later and then pushed close to one hundred all the way to his parents' just over ten minutes later.

The front yard was silent and empty, but as Darrius made his way to the door he saw the dark stains of blood on the grass.

His blood turned to ice, but he tried to keep his head on as he pushed inside the front door.

"Darrius." His mother rushed him, tears in her eyes. "He's hurt pretty bad."

He looked beyond her to the couch and where his brother lay clutching his bloodied chest. His eyes flickered open and he winced.

"I'm sorry. I tried to stop them, D..." His words trailed off into a liquid-filled cough.

"It's not your fault." Darrius strode across the room and fell to his knees before his brother. "You're going to be okay, Terrance."

"I've called the shifter emergency aid number. Paramedics should be here soon," Dad said quietly.

Nodding, Darrius tried to decipher where the bullet had entered and how close to his brother's heart it had come. Apparently not a direct hit, because that would've killed him. Quick healing shifter blood or not.

"You're going to be okay," he said again, with more conviction this time. "Can you tell me who took them?"

"Some big blond dude." Terrance drew in another slow breath. "Probably around my age. Shot me the minute I opened the door to Grace's car."

The only person that came to mind was Jocelyn's assistant—the pretty boy whose ass he'd kicked this morning. Shit. Nothing worse than a guy with a bruised ego and a motive.

Figuring out that motive was the key though.

"Thanks, little bro." Darrius squeezed Terrance's hand lightly, hoping to reassure. He glanced at his parents hovering nearby. "Keep pressure on his wound, Mom."

His mom nodded, eyes wide with fear, but kept the towel pressed to her son's chest.

Darrius pulled out his cell phone again and called Larson.

"We've got a problem, sir."

"Besides that it's ten at night and I was just about to climb into bed with my fiancée?" Larson drawled. "What's up, Hilliard?"

"Masterson and her sister have been forcibly taken by one of Jocelyn Feloray's cronies."

"Son of a bitch. Now that's not good, not good at all, actually." The alpha's tone sobered. "Call in the rest of the team and have them meet us at the office ASAP."

"Will do."

"Do you have any idea where they are?"

Darrius hesitated. "I installed a GPS tracking device on Masterson's car—just in case some shit like this went down, or if she got into any more trouble. I've got the receiving unit in my desk at work."

"Smart thinking on the tracking device."

"Larson…I need to tell you who Grace is."

"No need. I'm fully aware Jocelyn Feloray is her aunt."

Shocked into silence, Darrius struggled to find a suitable reply.

"I know everything about everyone in my pack, and especially someone I trust on my P.I.A. team. It doesn't detract from the fact that Grace is an excellent agent and I trust her completely."

Shit. Larson had had more faith in Grace than Darrius. Shame swept through him and he struggled to swallow against the lump in his throat.

"We'll get them back, Darrius."

"I know." Instinct told him they'd find Grace and her sister, but the what-if factor was wreaking havoc on his emotional state.

"Good. Now get your shit together and I'll see you at the office."

By the time Darrius arrived at the downtown office, the rest of his team was there and waiting.

Yorioka, Larson and Donovan were all dressed in black, ready for a rescue op, and just as alert as a midday shift.

Donovan handed him a cup of coffee. "How are you hanging in there, Hilliard?"

"I've been better." He didn't smile, didn't bother trying for his upbeat persona. "I appreciate you all coming in tonight."

"Hell, Masterson is one of our own. Why wouldn't we?" Yorioka shook her head, her lips compressed.

Right. One of their own. Of course it was logical thinking on their part—they were looking to rescue their comrade. He was looking to rescue his mate.

His mate.

The idea was still so fucking unbelievable it almost brought him to his knees. But it had been there in the red marks on her neck and the way he occasionally got a sense of her emotions. It was quick, like a scent on a breeze that came and went before you could realize it.

But from the glimpses of her emotions he'd caught, he knew she was murderously angry. Angry, and yet terrified as well.

Grace belonged to him now. And some asshole had made the mistake of taking her—a mistake that would cost him his life.

“Thought you were supposed to be watching her?” Donovan muttered. “How’d someone manage to grab Masterson and her sister if she was under your protection?”

Darrius bit back a snarl of frustration. He’d been asking himself the same question for the last hour, and the answer was because Grace had fled the house not even fifteen minutes after he’d marked her.

Hell, he couldn’t have predicted that. But he should’ve. She had probably panicked. Gotten depressed. Who knew what had been going through her head when she’d snuck out while he’d been showering.

“She left my protection without notifying me,” he finally replied. “And apparently that’s all it took.”

“Do we know where Grace and her sister are, Hilliard?” Larson asked.

“I have their location,” Yorioka volunteered, striding forward with the small handheld receiving unit that would tell them where the two were. “Hang on and let me read this.”

How had Yorioka known where he kept the receiving unit? Darrius cast her a sharp glance and opened his mouth to ask, and then told himself Larson had likely mentioned it to her.

When Grace had voiced her earlier concerns about Yorioka, he’d brushed them off. Now there wasn’t anyone he wouldn’t consider a traitor.

“Looks like they’re traveling west…weird.” She shook her head, her brows drawing together. “It’s putting them in the middle of Puget Sound.”

Remembering she wasn’t native to the Pacific Northwest, Darrius filled her in. “They’re likely on a ferryboat.”

Donovan grunted. “That’d be my guess.”

“Let me see the unit.” Darrius strode forward and easily took the unit from Yorioka’s hands. “Looks like the Edmonds to Kingston run.”

Larson gave a terse nod. “All right, we’ll take two vehicles to the peninsula. Donovan and Hilliard, I want you both to bring the van and Yorioka and I will follow you in the sedan.”

As everyone moved out, Darrius approached their alpha.

"Hey. I'm sorry I interrupted your evening—"

"Forget it." Larson waved his hand in dismissal, his gaze darkening with irritation. "Things weren't exactly going as planned anyway. Let's get out of here."

"You're pretty damn quiet. Just worried?" Donovan, who was driving the van, glanced over at Darrius.

They'd caught the last ferry over to Kingston and were currently waiting to disembark.

"Yeah." Worried as all hell definitely took over as the dominant emotion, but he was also confused. A little elated, and a lot guilty. Shit, his emotions ran the gauntlet.

Grace hadn't asked to be mated, and yet he'd claimed her without her consent. Without even discussing it—because he hadn't thought it fucking possible.

But none of this would even be relevant if they didn't rescue Grace and Aubree. Shit, just the idea of anything going wrong made his stomach heave and cold sweat break out on his neck.

Jocelyn's lover had made a huge fucking mistake by taking the two girls tonight. Had Jocelyn forced him to?

He'd pay for what he did, that much Darrius did know. Clenching his jaw, Darrius forced himself to stay calm and draw in a slow breath.

"You look like you're ready to rip someone's head off," Donovan muttered and shook his head. "You need to be careful, Hilliard. It's pretty clear you both are sleeping together, but keep your hearts out of it."

A little late for that. Darrius didn't reply. He couldn't bring himself to admit he'd marked Grace tonight, because he didn't fully understand it himself yet.

But he'd figure out how this had happened. Once he had Grace safely back, he'd be doing some digging on his supposed first mate.

"So where are they heading now?" Donovan asked as he drove the van off the ferryboat.

Darrius glanced down. "It shows Port Angeles. You know the way?"

"I've been there a few times." Donovan tapped his hands on the steering wheel. "I like the peninsula. It's nice. Got trees and shit."

Darrius couldn't even crack a smile at his friend's somewhat derisory, yet amusing, description of nature.

Donovan glanced in the rearview mirror. "Looks like Yorioka and Larson are still behind us."

A thought slid through Darrius's mind. "You ever have any reason not to trust Yorioka?"

"What the fuck? No. Yorioka is cool. Where'd that question come from?"

"Grace was a little uneasy about her."

"Hmm. I can see that. Yorioka isn't exactly giving off the warm and fuzzies to Masterson. But she doesn't trust her."

"That's pretty much what I said." Darrius closed his eyes for a moment.

Where are you, Grace. Can you sense me?

He tried to lock on her mind again, but the sensation was so new. It was like trying to lock a butterfly in the crosshair of a rifle. He'd have her thoughts one second, and then they'd be gone.

And trying to see through her eyes at what she was looking at wasn't giving up much, because the bastard had obviously tied her up or something, and her current view was mostly the darkness of the floor and dashboard—not out the window.

This shit was hard. Had he ever been able to do this with Jenny? Had he ever tried? Connecting mentally with Grace would mean he had a better chance at rescuing her quicker.

If he could only—

The view through Grace's eyes changed. The dashboard disappeared and then it seemed as if she were being moved out of the vehicle because he saw the night sky and streetlights. It was almost as if she were unconscious, because she didn't move. But her mind was alert, he'd heard her occasional thoughts, which left the possibility of her being hurt. Or paralyzed.

His heart pounded and he tried not to think about the second possibility. He just let himself continue to see through Grace's eyes.

But if Grace was aware of him in her head, she didn't show any sign of it.

"They're changing cars."

"What?"

Donovan's sharp response made Darrius realize he'd said the words aloud.

"Who's changed cars, Hilliard?"

Darrius didn't answer, couldn't reply as he tried not to break the connection between him and Grace.

"Hang on."

I can see you, sugar. Where is he taking you?

And then he saw the sign. Literally as the car's headlights reflected upon it.

"Hurricane Ridge." He opened his eyes again and glanced at Donovan.

There was comprehension in his friend's eyes, and disbelief. "I don't fucking believe it. You're in her head. You mated with her."

Of course Donovan would realize it. He had to have realized it the moment Darrius had gone silent and started spouting off details as if the tracking device were on Grace herself.

"Yes."

Donovan's brows shot sky high. "How in the *hell* did that happen?"

"Besides the obvious?" Darrius gave a stiff shrug. "I have no fucking idea."

"I thought you already mated once."

"I did. Hell, I just don't know, Donovan. This is all a

complete mind fuck to me too, but can we just focus on finding Grace and her sister?"

"Yeah, of course." Donovan grunted. "Grace is your damn mate now, it makes a helluva lot more sense why you look ready to go on a murderous rampage."

And he likely would if he got the chance.

"I'm happy for you, Darrius. Sienna was right—you're good for each other."

Maybe. But did Grace even want him? Want a mate at this time in her life? The way she'd run after he'd claimed her sure wasn't a good sign.

"So Hurricane Ridge you say?"

Darrius nodded. "If you trust me, yeah."

"Put a call in to Larson and tell him the change in plans. I trust you. And I trust your connection." He paused. "I've been in your shoes, Hilliard. Pretty similar situation with Sienna, which you remember. That connection between us saved her life."

Darrius couldn't resist a small smile, and saying, "I think she saved her own life, actually."

"Hell yeah she did." Pride flickered across Donovan's face. "My woman can kick some serious ass when need be."

So can mine. But why wasn't she moving? There had to be a reason she wasn't fighting back...

Chapter Twenty-One

Whatever he'd injected into her must have been starting to wear off.

Grace tried not to show any indication she was getting feeling back, but the tingling that was rocking her nerves right now was painful. She'd first noticed it when they'd switched cars and Andrew had carried her, and then Aubree to a bigger SUV.

Was Aubree recovering just as well? She wished she could give herself away and turn her head to the backseat where he'd placed her.

Her sister hadn't gone easily with Andrew. The moment he'd shot Terrance and grabbed her, she'd fought like a crazed animal. Scratching his face and managing to nearly get away to Terrance's parents, who were trying to get to her.

Until Andrew had sunk the same needle into her neck and it had all been over. Aubree had collapsed into his waiting arms, and he'd forced her into the backseat.

Why had he taken them? The question had spun endlessly in her mind like a hamster on a wheel. It just didn't make sense, and unfortunately she couldn't speak and ask him what the hell he was thinking.

Was Jocelyn behind this? How could she not be? The only thing Andrew had tipped his hat at was letting on that he knew about Aubree's pregnancy, but he hadn't spoken to either of them since giving them the injections.

At least he'd propped her up somewhat this time, and she could see out the window. After seeing the sign, she had a fair idea where they were going and it sent waves of nausea through her.

Hurricane Ridge.

A lovely vista nestled in the Olympic Mountains. Tourists loved it and locals loved to ski it in the winter. But to her it would always be the place her parents had died.

She'd never gone back. Even though she loved hiking and exploring the Pacific Northwest, Hurricane Ridge was the one popular destination she avoided.

And as they continued to climb in elevation and wind through the dark, two-lane mountain road, her panic rose. She struggled to keep her breathing even while inside she was screaming.

As they climbed higher the headlights started to reflect snow on the road. But Andrew must've been prepared for it, because the tires on the SUV were studded.

All too soon Andrew pulled into a parking spot and turned off the car.

"How are you gals doing?"

When he turned to face her, a wide grin on his face, Grace just barely resisted the urge to slam her fist into it.

"The drug should be wearing off by now. You can talk."

She didn't reply, refusing to play his little game. Was Darrius aware they were missing? Surely Terrance and his parents had called someone at the P.I.A.

A thought slammed into her, and she struggled to breathe. She was mated with Darrius. That meant something. Huge. She'd always heard that once you were mated there was some kind of mental connection that could be developed.

Was it working? Had Darrius been able to hear her thoughts? Would he know where she was?

She closed her eyes—desperate to locate him in her head.

Darrius. She sent out a mental beacon, searching her mind for any trace he might be there.

And then she felt it. A warm light slid through her mind before she heard her name on his lips. Then his voice came soft and steady in her head, telling her to be calm. To wait for them and that help was on the way.

"Don't want to talk? Fine. We'll see how long that lasts." Andrew jerked her from the car.

Her delicate connection with Darrius was severed as she was flung to the ground. She landed on her hands and knees, the rocks and ice stinging as they bit into her palms. She sucked in the icy mountain air and tried to orientate herself.

The moon was out and it reflected off the snow, giving her more visibility than she could've hoped for. They were at the visitor center—which was dark and obviously closed. How had they even gotten up here? Weren't there security points at the bottom of the road? At this time of night the park would've been closed.

"It was you," she accused, glaring at him. "It was always you. Trying to run me down in the street, slashing Aubree's tires, the bar attack?"

He grinned. "Borrowed the van from my mom—we've got a big family. Figured you wouldn't recognize me as easily."

"But you always recognized *me*. Like that day I showed up at Jocelyn's condo and you'd asked if we'd met? You knew."

"Yeah, I knew. You made some bad joke about screwing me in a nightclub bathroom. Which would've been kind of hot." He bit his lip and gave a suggestive nod. "I've never forgotten you. Or your sister."

Andrew turned and returned to the car, and her sister made a pained whimper as he plucked her from the backseat.

"Damn, I do believe I've missed you, beautiful." He pulled her against him and pressed a hard kiss to her lips.

A growl of rage rose from Grace's throat and she started to rise, but her sister didn't need her defense. Not yet anyway. Aubree slapped the smirk off of Andrew's face and pulled away.

All she needed was a second and she could shift and tear his throat out. Her nails started to lengthen and she felt the wolf in her rise to the surface. And then she saw the gun in his hand, and even though he was watching Grace, it was trained on her sister.

Grace stood up, careful not to make any sudden moves.

"Why did you take us?"

He gave her a bland glance. "Aubree was an afterthought, I admit. Once I heard she was pregnant I realized the right thing to do would be to mate with her."

"I'd rather mate with a cow!" Aubree screamed.

Andrew gave a small laugh and cast a fond look her sister's way. "You're going to be so much fun to tame."

It would never happen. Never. Grace would see him dead if he so much as leaned toward her neck.

"But, Grace, you've been in the works for almost a week now. Ever since I figured it out."

"Figured what out?"

"What happened here fifteen years ago." He gestured widely at the hills around them. "Come on, some of it has to still be there in that sharp little brain of yours."

Icy shivers of premonition trailed down Grace's spine. Fifteen years ago her parents had been killed here. How could that possibly be of any interest to him?

"What are you talking about?"

"I suppose I'm getting ahead of myself. Let me back up a little." He paced in the snowy parking lot, his feet crunching on the ground. "So I'm sure by now you've realized that Thom Wilson was given some kind of drug that convinced him to off himself, right?"

Rage slammed into her, hard and violently, blinding her with red, and she automatically lunged forward with a growl. But he was next to her in an instant, pressing the gun to her head.

"Keep your inner bitch restrained. Or I'll personally silence it."

And he would, she didn't doubt him for a second. The light from the moon reflected off his eyes and the glassiness to them and dilated pupils made her wonder if he was on something.

He sure wasn't acting rationally. She might've tried to take him down anyway, but if something happened to her it would mean she was leaving Aubree alone with him. It was a risk she couldn't take.

Come on, Darrius, get here fast. She sent out the mental plea but kept her hard gaze on Andrew.

"You know, let's go for a walk." He caught her arm and walked to Aubree, grabbing her as well. "Follow me, ladies."

Grace followed, for now. He was so young and cocky. Stupid. He'd let his guard down and when he did, she'd be ready to make him regret it.

"What did Thom Wilson do that was so awful? Why kill only him and not the rest of the survivors of the experiments?"

"It actually had nothing to do with the experiments. Thom came to see us—or he came to see Jocelyn, but I was there. He was going to blackmail her with some dirt he'd dug up on her. I couldn't let him do that. Somehow she'd become my world."

"Oh, how fucking touching. Really. Excuse me while I puke," she ground out, not bothering to veil her sarcasm. "What kind of dirt did Thom have on her?"

"That she was a murderer."

It was the same thing Thom had said in his email, but what did it mean? And if Andrew was confessing all this to her, obviously he wasn't going to allow her to leave alive today. Or he intended to memory-wipe her.

The realization sent panic through her, but she fought it. She had to stay calm for Aubree. She kept her expression blank as they trudged up the snowy trail in the semi-darkness.

"Don't you see? I couldn't let Thom Wilson stay alive. Jocelyn was all upset, though she never confessed to the murders."

What murders?

"So I hired some junkie who would've done anything for a fix. Once he managed to give Thom that injection, all he had to do was tell him to park the car in the garage, get in it and turn on the engine."

"And he died from carbon monoxide poisoning. How do you live with yourself?" She gave him a look of disgust. "He had a family."

Andrew's smile vanished. "Look, it's not like I didn't feel guilty about it. But he was threatening Jocelyn and I couldn't let that happen."

"She was your meal ticket."

"Dammit, I cared for her! And you know how she thanks me? That bitch fired me—kicked me out of her life and condo like I was fucking nothing. After everything I'd done for her."

"She probably didn't like the idea of you seducing her teenage niece."

"I wasn't her assistant then, she barely knew who I was. Feloray Laboratories had me working in that hellhole building where the experiments were being held."

It didn't matter, none of his shitty excuses nullified what he'd done. The life he'd taken. "And I suppose you killed Wesley Parker as well?"

"Wesley?"

"The druggie you hired." Their POI who'd just been found dead.

"Oh him. I gotta say, that was awesome. I got hella lucky when that dumbshit overdosed legitimately."

"You're a fucking heartless bastard."

"Me? No, you've got it wrong. Don't you get it yet?" Andrew grabbed her shirt, halting her progress. "Your aunt is the heartless one. She's probably killed, or had killed, more people than some dictators. She's also guilty of the death of your parents."

Her heart nearly stopped, and then started a slow erratic thud again. The accusation was ludicrous and completely implausible.

Wasn't it?

"I was there, asshole," she rasped. "I know she didn't kill them."

"Do you really know that? Yes, you were there. And did it ever occur to you that maybe you saw too much?" He stepped forward, his face just inches away from hers. "That maybe you had your memory wiped because of it."

Another part of Thom's letter flickered in her head. Memory wipes on shifter women and children. Could Andrew be on to something? Had something sinister happened that day?

Grace stumbled, nearly falling into the snow that was almost above her knees now. The lodge wasn't even in their line of vision anymore, and she couldn't be certain they were even technically on the path.

"See, I took notes when Thom came to visit and I've done a little research of my own. The man who wiped your memory when you were a kid worked for the P.I.A. and was in bed with your aunt—literally. Apparently it always haunted him and was a deathbed confession to Thom."

Wiped your memory when you were a kid. No. It couldn't be possible. She shook her head, but even as she did there were flashes of her childhood. The constant resentment toward her aunt and the sadness and anger she'd struggled with. Her aunt had always told her she was just a moody child and hormonal teen—had often encouraged her to go on medication.

But had it been a lingering undertone of a memory she couldn't remember? Had Jocelyn killed her parents?

"Grace, what is he talking about?" Aubree glanced between them, arms folded across her chest and her teeth chattering.

Grace was abruptly brought back to the present, and the very serious threat of hypothermia. They weren't dressed for these conditions. The whole idea that Andrew had kidnapped them both and dragged them out into the mountains was surreal to say the least.

"Andrew, we need to get Aubree back inside the car. She's pregnant, for heaven's sake."

"In good fucking time, Grace," he yelled, and then dug something out of his pocket that looked like a recording device.

What did he want her to say? This whole night was such a clusterfuck. Being abducted by their aunt's knock-off Abercrombie-and-Fitch-model lover. They wouldn't be in this situation if she hadn't run from Darrius tonight. If she hadn't panicked.

Instead of questioning their mating, she should've celebrated it. Celebrated that somehow he'd managed to claim her, even though he'd supposedly already taken a mate once.

But she hadn't. She'd run instead—probably leaving him with anger and self-doubt.

Darrius was her lover. Her mate. And she couldn't regret that. She only hoped he could see into her heart right now. Hear her thoughts.

I'm so sorry, Darrius. If anything happens, please know I don't regret anything.

"Aubree, you move a muscle and your sister dies. Grace, I want you to look around." Andrew's harsh order interrupted her message to her mate. "Surely you'd remember the spot your parents died."

The words knocked the breath from her, and she found herself obeying him. Turning, she let her gaze slide over the darkness and where the cliff seemed to drop off.

Despite it being nightfall, the moon, snow, and her wolf sense gave her enough ability to see things. She remembered parts of that day. Remembered fields of blue flowers…

Flowers like the ones she now created every time she worked with glass in her garage. Flowers like the tattoo she'd gotten on the back of her neck at eighteen.

Her heart started to thump faster. She closed her eyes, trying to remember. Something was there, buried deep into her conscience, but she couldn't pull it up. But instinctively she knew there was something she should be remembering.

Emotions were just below the surface of her memory. Terror. Shock. And horror. So much horror.

"You're remembering something. This is good, Grace. Real good. Now tell me exactly what happened that day…"

"Hilliard, are you in position?"

"Affirmative. I can confirm visual on the two hostages," Darrius replied into the tiny mic along his jawline. He was hunkered down behind a tree, never letting his gaze slip from the three people near the edge of the cliff.

Donovan had come around on the north end of the group and was also positioned to take out their tango. Larson and Yorioka were out in the woods as well, preparing to try and rescue Aubree.

They were set up for a standard op, but nothing about the situation was standard. The victims were Darrius's mate and her pregnant sister.

"What do you remember?"

The way Andrew leaned in too close to Grace to ask the question had Darrius itching to pull the trigger on his Glock.

"Don't do it, Hilliard." Donovan must've sensed his fury.

"I've got a clear shot," he muttered.

"Yeah, me too, but we can't take it. Killing a shifter gets you in deep shit."

There was no arguing that. Donovan had nearly been kicked out of the P.I.A. for killing a shifter who had gone after Sienna.

"I'm thinking I can just slow him down by shooting him in the leg."

"Grace is too close, you don't want to risk it."

"Larson, have you gotten close enough to grab the sister?" Darrius asked.

"Making my way in. But I don't trust this guy, he's jumpy. Like he's drugged or something."

"I asked what the hell you remember?" Andrew demanded again.

"Things I wish I didn't." Grace's words were quiet. Haunted. And with obvious reluctance.

"You remember her killing your parents after an argument?"

"Yes. They didn't fall over that cliff—she pushed them."

"That's right. That's exactly what I heard happened." His voice rose with excitement, but he suddenly froze and grabbed

Grace, jerking her to him and pressing the gun against her temple.

"I know you're there. Come out," he yelled.

"Nobody move," Larson snarled in a harsh whisper. "Stand your ground until I give an order otherwise."

But there was a rustling noise as someone began to emerge from the trees.

Darrius held his breath, wondering which agent had been stupid enough to defy their alpha. But it wasn't an agent who stepped from the woods.

Chapter Twenty-Two

Unlike any of the other people here, Jocelyn was dressed for the cold. A long, fur-lined jacket that looked as if it belonged on a red carpet event in Aspen, rather than the middle of the night in the Olympic Mountains.

"You've got to be kidding me. I don't believe this shit," Darrius muttered.

"I've got a clear shot of Jocelyn if you want me to take it," Donovan mentioned a little too casually. "You don't have any idea how much I want to take this bitch out."

Darrius smiled humorlessly. Oh, he had a pretty good idea.

"Stand down," Larson finally spoke. "And cut the goddamn chatter."

"I guess it was too much to hope you were more than just a pretty face, Andy." Jocelyn strode into the middle of the group.

"I loved you, Jocelyn."

She rolled her eyes. "You loved my bank account."

"I—"

"You fucked up. Abducting my nieces proved just how stupid you really are. You don't touch my family." The last words were said with slow deliberation.

His disbelieving laugh snapped through the trees. "Are you fucking kidding me? You're not going to actually pretend you care for them. You *murdered* their parents."

Darrius watched Jocelyn, a little more than curious to see her reaction. Was there truth to it? But besides a slight tightening of her jaw, there was none.

"You're acting irrationally, Andy. You really should lay off the drugs."

"You fucking whore, you're the one supplying them!"

"Is there no end to your evil, Jocelyn?" Grace spoke finally, her voice quiet and yet threaded with accusation. "You probably ordered Thom murdered and my attack when I got too close to the truth."

"Actually, no. I've told you that from the beginning. I had absolutely nothing to do with Thom's death. Apparently that was my ambitious little assistant." She sighed and turned a brittle stare at her assistant. "I must say I'm learning all sorts of unpleasant things today. Andy, you've been quite busy. Seducing minors, murdering middle-aged men… "

Andrew's eyes rounded and he looked ready to blow. "I killed him for you. You should be kissing my ass."

"Ready yourselves," Larson warned.

Darrius heeded the order, leveling his gun at Andrew. He flicked a glance at Aubree. She must've known this was her chance, because she was inching toward the woods and away from her abductor.

Jocelyn laughed, thrusting her hands into the pockets of her fur jacket. "You killed him because you're an idiot."

"Screw you all. You're just as guilty of murder as I am, Jocelyn. If I go down, you go down." He jerked Grace harder against him, rough enough that it must've hurt because she flinched.

You're going to die, boy. Darrius allowed his finger to graze lightly over the trigger, but before he could move or Larson could give the order to fire, a savage snarl ripped through the air and there was a blur of black.

"Now who in the hell is that?" Donovan muttered in disbelief.

Shock reflected in Andrew's eyes as well, before the wolf was upon him. Grace pulled free and slammed her elbow into his face, helping in his descent to the snowy ground.

"Apprehend the tangos!" Larson commanded.

Larson and Donovan surrounded Jocelyn, who seemed to have no intention of leaving and seemed almost amused by the turn of events. Certainly not surprised.

Darrius, however, had only one goal, and when he finally reached her side, he swore he'd never leave it again.

"You found me." Grace bit back a sob of relief and flung herself into Darrius's arms as he strode purposefully toward her.

Being pulled into his hard embrace gave her the reassurance and security she'd so desperately needed. She wanted to just melt into him and stay there until she had the energy to move. But then she remembered…

"*Aubree.*" She struggled free of him, remembering the danger her sister might be in.

Darrius pulled his gun out and turned and followed her gaze. They both watched as the wolf who'd attacked Andrew began to shift back to human. Aubree's features took form before she took a step away from Andrew and collapsed.

"She shifted," Darrius muttered in disbelief.

Aubree might've taken him down in wolf form, but in human she was half Andrew's size. And Andrew knew it. In an instant he'd knocked her down, and pinned her on her stomach. He grabbed her hair, tugging her head back and exposing her neck.

"You want to ruin my life, Jocelyn? Watch me ruin hers."

When his canines flashed in the moonlight, Grace leapt forward with a shriek of fury.

Before Darrius could shoot, or Grace could shift, there was another blur of movement as Yorioka rushed forward in wolf form. In an instant, she'd knocked Andrew off Aubree and pinned him to the ground.

When he growled in dismay and swung his gun toward Yorioka, Darrius pulled the trigger and Andrew slumped back into the snow.

Grace rushed to her sister, who was far too still and lying in the snow. "Oh God, Bree. Are you okay?" She gently lifted her to her feet and took in her sister's far too pale face that was wracked with pain.

"No. I feel..." Aubree wavered on her feet, "...like shit."

Darrius was beside them in a moment, sweeping Aubree into his arms right before she apparently passed out from the pain. "I didn't think she could shift."

"She can, she just never has since childhood. It's entirely too painful." Grace's throat tightened and she pushed back a dark strand of hair that had fallen in her sister's eyes. "It must've been instinctive. She was protecting me. Do you think she'll be okay?"

"She'll be fine. I'm going to take her to the van."

"Thank you." Grace nodded, her throat tight with emotion. She wanted to follow them, but first there was something she needed to do.

Yorioka was busy securing a bleeding, but apparently not fatally injured, Andrew, and barely glanced up at Grace's approach. How had she ever doubted this woman's loyalty? Ever considered Yorioka might've been a threat to her? She'd just risked her life for Aubree's.

"Thank you," Grace said softly. "You saved her from a lifetime of misery in being mated to a complete asshole."

"Asshole?" Andrew snarled. "You fucking bitches are so—"

Yorioka pressed his face back into the snow to shut him up.

"No problem. I wouldn't wish him on anyone." The other agent stood up and met Grace's gaze. "How are you doing?"

"I've been better—" she glanced at her aunt, "—but I'm doing okay."

"Understandable. Look, I'm sorry, Masterson. You know, for judging you so harshly."

"I don't blame you, and honestly, I might've done the same. Besides, I wasn't all sunshine and roses with you either." Not at all. Up until this evening she'd been convinced Yorioka had been one of the two people who'd attacked her.

Grace frowned. Which...if it hadn't been Yorioka, then who had it been?

"We got off to a rough start," Yorioka continued, breaking

into Grace's thoughts. "I didn't know what you'd been through. Didn't know the type of evil you had the misfortune of being related to."

Misfortune of being related to? Grace's heart froze a beat. "You...you know?"

"We all do." Yorioka gave a small nod. "Larson filled us in before the rescue op. Seems like he's always known, I guess, and didn't want anyone to judge you by who your family is."

Larson had always known? But he'd never let on. Grace glanced over at their alpha, who seemed to be in a heated discussion with Jocelyn.

"If you'll excuse me for a minute...?"

"No worries." Yorioka squeezed her shoulder. "And, hey, I mean it, Masterson, I've got your back. And am sorry if I ever let you think otherwise."

"Thank you, Yorioka. And likewise." Grace turned and made her way over to Larson and her aunt. Straightening her spine, she met Jocelyn's gaze. "You've gone too far."

"Whatever do you mean? Clearly, I had nothing to do with this." Jocelyn gave a light shrug, but there was a sparkle of amusement in her eye. "I can't be responsible for a crazed employee who steals my drugs and uses them for his own nefarious purposes."

"And yet it seems to happen a lot with you, Ms. Feloray." Larson folded his arms across his chest and stared her down. "It's always somebody else responsible, leaving you to go free. And yet I doubt with a clear conscience."

The amusement died in Jocelyn's stare, and something that looked like a dark warning replaced it. "My conscience should be the least of your worries, Agent Larson."

Larson took another intimidating step toward her. "Know this. I'm making it a personal fucking goal to bring down you and your disgusting laboratories."

"It's nice to have goals, Agent Larson."

It was like some bad western movie stare down. Neither looked away. And then Larson shook his head, but didn't break eye contact with Grace's aunt.

"Agent Masterson, you are from this point forward forbidden from having any contact with your aunt if you want to remain with our pack or the P.I.A."

Grace blinked in shock, opening her mouth to reply, but Jocelyn cut her off.

"What did you say?" There was panic in her aunt's voice now. Alarm. "You can't do that."

"I can do whatever the hell I want. I'm her goddamn alpha. Do you or do you not accept my terms, Masterson?"

"I accept," Grace replied without hesitation.

"And, Jocelyn, I want you to sign away all rights for Aubree as well. Grace will be her legal custodian until the date her sister turns eighteen."

"You've lost your mind if you think I'll agree to that."

"You'll agree, or I'll have the local police begin investigating why one of your drugs was found in Thom Wilson's blood."

Rage flashed in her eyes and she compressed her lips. "I had nothing to do with it. We both know how this will work—Andrew was behind all that."

"It's a controversial drug created by your company. It's not going to look good for you."

"Do it and you'll risk exposing the shifter population."

His smile hardened. "And expose the fact that you're half bitch and your lab's creating drugs that can control a man's mind enough to make him kill himself if told to. That'll make the stock rise, don't you think?"

Even in the dark, Grace could see the blood drain from her aunt's face.

"So what's it going to be, Jocelyn?"

Her aunt's hands closed into fists and she gave a deceptively light shrug. "Well, Agent Larson, it appears you have a deal."

"I thought we might. Come on, Masterson, let's get out of here."

"Wait." Grace pulled back when he reached for her arm. "I have one last question for her."

Jocelyn's mouth twisted into a bitter smile. "And what might that be, dearest niece?"

"Did you kill my parents?"

Her aunt didn't reply, just stared at her for a moment, before she turned and walked away.

"You falling back asleep?"

At Darrius's drowsy question, Grace gave a small shrug. "Maybe a little bit."

They were both exhausted. Both from the previous night and the long and slow lovemaking when they'd woken up this morning.

Larson had given everyone the day off, insisting they needed the sleep and he had personal business to attend to.

Languid and still feeling amazingly connected to Darrius, she snuggled deeper beneath the arm around her and pressed a kiss to his chest.

"Mmm. I love it when you do that." His eyes drifted shut. "I didn't mention it yet, but I'm leaving town in a few hours. I'm hoping to make it back by tomorrow night."

Grace frowned. "Sounds ominous. Where are you off to?"

"I'm flying to Boston to meet with the elders."

That had her sitting upright. "Why? Are you in trouble?"

Usually being called before the elders was a sign you'd done something wrong, or were being rewarded for doing something very right.

"Hell no, sugar. What would I have done? I've requested time in their presence and their help in discovering why I was able to mate again. They're bringing in a Reader to read my past and hopefully give some answers."

Readers. The few psychics within the shifter community were rare and extremely accurate. They hadn't discussed the mating—at all really. They hadn't had the chance last night after driving back from the peninsula, and this morning instinct had simply led them to speak without words.

"Darrius, if you have any regrets—"

"I have none. I just need to know what's going on."

Understandable. He probably still loved his dead first mate, and wanted to know how to move on. Or maybe that was her just being optimistic.

"Don't worry about it." He smoothed his hand down her back and she lay back down, her head on his chest.

She pushed aside the tiny stab of sadness that had taken root. The thought of any other woman with Darrius made her a little murderous, but she knew if they were to have any future together she needed to accept his past.

"Did you know when the team arrived, Grace? That we were in the trees?"

She hesitated. "I felt you nearby, but my mind was so clouded with panic and fear for Aubree, I couldn't seem to make that connection."

"We only just mated, it makes sense." He paused. "So you really remembered what happened to your parents?"

Grace squeezed her eyes closed and drew in a ragged breath. "No. I wish I did, more than anything. I just started to tell him what I thought he wanted to hear."

"Smart thinking. Look, you were young, you've probably blocked it—"

"No. I don't think everything Andrew rambled on about was crap. It makes too much sense that I might've had my memory wiped after that day. I remember the beginning of the hike with my family, and then nothing until I woke up in my aunt and uncle's house. Which must've been several days later."

Darrius's fingers paused in the midst of tracing down her spine. "So you really think Jocelyn murdered your parents?"

"I asked her, but she didn't answer. But I saw this look in her eyes. A sadness and guilt before she turned and walked away. Something happened that day, and unless she confesses,

I don't think I'll ever know what could've motivated her to do it."

"I wouldn't count on her confessing."

"I won't. I just wish I knew." Grace folded her arms beneath her head and rested her cheek on them. "Wish there was a way to make her pay for what she's done."

He closed strong fingers over her shoulder blades and began a massage. The overly taut muscles in her body eased and she let out a soft moan.

"Grace, even if there were a trial in shifter courts, it would never have held up. It's all hearsay from Andrew. There're no public records of the memory wipes—we've checked. And the one witness—the man who did the wipes—is dead."

"Even though the memories of that day have been stolen from me, in my heart I believe what Andrew said. I know she killed my parents."

"I believe it too." Darrius paused. "At least you don't have to have any contact with her anymore thanks to Larson. Are you sure you're okay with that?"

"Absolutely. In fact I'm grateful to him. It was easier having him take the decision from my hands and being forced to make the choice."

He kneaded her shoulders deeper. "He must have some serious dirt on her."

"It's not hard to find."

"But apparently not the kind of dirt that will ever let us convict her."

"She's tricky." Sighing, Grace rolled over so she could look up at him. "Jocelyn always manages to have legal ways out. Someone else to take the blame."

"It's how she's climbed so high in her industry."

"If she's that high, she'll fall. Someday, that bitch'll fall. And I'm going to laugh as she tries to pick up the pieces."

It was a nice image, but she wondered if it would ever happen. Jocelyn Feloray had always seemed untouchable.

"I heard the P.I.A. is sending someone over to talk to Thom's widow—explain what really happened."

"Yeah, I know it will bring her comfort. Some peace." Grace murmured. "Which speaking of, I think I did solve one mystery, though. About myself."

"What's that?"

"Those glass flowers I make? I think it's from a memory I somehow retained. I don't remember much from that day, but while we were up there last night it flashed through my head. Being with my parents on the ridge and sitting in a field of those blue flowers. The mountains over there are covered with them in the summer."

"That's hauntingly beautiful. Think you'll stop making them now? Is it too emotional?"

"No, it actually motivates me to make more of them. Brings me peace. I think my mom loved those flowers, was probably picking them by the handful that day..."

"You should keep making them."

She nodded to acknowledge his comment, but closed her eyes as her heart clenched with grief. It had been years since she'd grieved for them, because she'd been too young. But last night had ripped off the scab of their death. Ripped it off and poured acid in the wound.

"I cleared the air with Yorioka," she confessed, trying to think of lighter thoughts.

"Good. I knew you guys would finally come around. So you don't think she's out to get you anymore?" he teased, dropping a kiss on the curve of her neck where he'd marked her.

"No, I'm over that. But it made me wonder who attacked me in the bathroom at the Doornail. There was definitely a woman there."

Darrius grunted. "That's a damn good question. Maybe Andrew hired some random chick to help? He did hire that druggie to kill Thom."

"Maybe. I suppose I could always visit him tomorrow at the P.I.A. jail and ask. I can deal with his crazy to try and figure it out."

"If you do, make sure there's another guard around. I don't

want you alone with him." Darrius traced a finger down her cheek. "Speaking of tomorrow, I should shower soon. I have a flight to catch in three hours."

She nodded and started to slide away, but his arms came down on either side of her head and then he caught her mouth in another slow kiss.

"But before that shower, I'm thinking...one more time?"

Grace let her gaze slide down his body to his growing erection, felt that answering heat gather between her legs, and gave a quick nod.

"Yes." She slid down his body, already ready to taste him. "One more time for sure."

Chapter Twenty-Three

Being away from Grace had been hell.

Darrius had felt the twenty-four-hour separation in every inch of his body. His mind and soul had craved her. And now he knew why.

He'd never officially been mated to Jenny. The thought was still roaring through his mind with the excitement of a lottery win, when the call to the phone on the agency plane came in.

"I hope you got some good news, bro," Donovan began, "because I sure as hell don't."

"The Elders handed me my life back. I'd call that amazing news." Darrius stared out the window as the plane flew over Seattle in its descent into the private P.I.A. airfield. "What's your bad news? It's got to be pretty bad if you're calling me on the agency plane."

"You must've just taken off from Boston when shit hit the fan. Because the elders are all over this." Donovan gave a wary sigh. "Andrew was found dead in his holding cell."

Darrius stilled. "No way. Suicide again?"

"No. Murdered. Violently. Tore up to pieces, bro."

"Holy shit. Who do they think did it?"

"I'm getting there, but now I'm getting to the bad news. Alicia and several members of her pack were found slaughtered not even an hour later."

Darrius sucked in a breath, disbelief roaring through him. "Who the hell did it?"

"Fuck." Donovan cursed and then gave an almost manic laugh. "They're saying it was Larson, man."

"No. I don't believe it."

"You think I want to? But there were witnesses. I was one

of them. The P.I.A. got a tip that the alpha wanted to speak with us. Yorioka and I went out there, and when we arrived the whole place looked like a slaughterhouse. I fucking watched Larson rip Alicia's throat out."

Jesus. It couldn't be true. "Alicia's dad—the alpha—did he survive?"

"No. The alpha was dead. Larson took out half the pack it sounds like."

Son of a bitch. This was bad. "Where is he now?"

"On the run, I guess. No one has seen him since he took off after we tried to corner him. The elders have put out a huge bounty on him. He pretty much signed his own death warrant, Hilliard. They can't let this slaughter slide due to lack of numbers in our species. They're going to want his blood."

Darrius paused, vaguely aware of the plane descending to the runway. "You think he did it?"

"How do I deny what I saw? It just doesn't make any sense. The man I saw today—he wasn't our alpha."

"You think he was drugged when he did it?"

"Hell, I don't know. Maybe? It'd be the only reason I could see him losing it like this."

Jocelyn.

"We'll figure this out. We'll clear him if he's innocent, Donovan."

"Shit. I need a fucking beer. Something."

"Yeah you do. You need to go and be with Sienna, take some time to calm down." He shook his head. "And, Donovan, you know we'll find Larson first."

"I sure as fuck hope so." Donovan sighed. "Thanks, bro. When you get off that plane go enjoy your woman and call me later."

"I will." Darrius ended the call and found his hands shaking a little.

What the hell was going on? How had their alpha's life gone to hell in a handbasket so quickly? The whole idea was insane. And yet Donovan had witnessed it.

The plane landed and began to slow on the runway, and that's when he saw her. As impossible as it seemed, all thoughts of their alpha disappeared and Grace became his focus.

Even though it was pouring down rain, she stood outside the small terminal and with no jacket or umbrella.

When he was cleared to leave, Darrius barely let his feet touch each stair. He just ran. Ran to his mate and the woman he loved.

"Darrius!" She charged at him as well, nearly colliding into his chest, she had so much momentum.

He caught her with a small *oomph* and slid his hands into her drenched hair.

"I've missed you," he muttered and pulled her head back just enough so he could easily claim her mouth.

She let out a moan and kissed him back hungrily, as if they'd been apart weeks rather than less than twenty-four hours.

When he lifted his head, his breathing was ragged and his heart had yet to slow from its rapid pace.

Grace buried her face against his shoulder. "I've missed you too. Darrius…so much has happened—"

"I know about Larson and the murders."

She lifted her head and there was distress in her eyes. "It just doesn't make any sense."

"No, it doesn't. And I promise you that we'll get to the bottom of what happened." He caught her arm and steered her toward the small terminal. "Come on, let's get out of the rain."

He led her under the overhang of the building, where they were out of the rain and hidden from the windows of the terminal.

"How is Aubree?"

Grace cracked a slight smile and pushed a wet strand of hair behind her ear. "She's good. She and your brother have been inseparable, both claiming a couch in the den while your mother fusses over them as they heal."

"Good. They could use some fussing over. Especially Aubree, it sounds like. We can visit them tonight."

She gave a sheepish grin and glanced out at the tarmac. "I figured we would and already committed to dinner with everyone."

"See, you're already fitting in perfectly with me and my family, sugar."

Her mouth tightened and he saw the flash of unhappiness in her eyes. It sent a chill of unease through him.

"I know you're about to tell me what the Reader said." Her words were soft and she didn't quite meet his gaze. "But first let me just say that whatever you learned, Darrius, I'm okay with that. I understand and will really make an effort to accept that I'll always be your second mate. That you may never feel that way about me that you did her—"

"She was never my mate."

Her lips stayed parted and her eyes grew round with disbelief. She didn't utter a word.

"Not technically," he continued. "Jenny and I met at a club. I remember being attracted to her and dancing with her, and that was it. The Reader told me Jennie was pregnant with a married human man's child before we 'mated'. And that she needed a shifter mate quickly to avoid suspicion and punishment for getting pregnant with a human's child."

"But you marked her, didn't you?"

"Not in the way I needed to, I guess. When I woke up the next day, my teeth marks were on her neck. But my heart didn't make the choice to claim her; there was no awareness in it. So maybe she was able to make me bite her, I don't know how, but it was null. I just never realized it until I was able to claim you."

Her eyes filled with tears and she shook her head. "Darrius..."

"It wasn't that I couldn't claim a woman, it was just that the right one hadn't come along. I have *never* felt the way about another woman the way I feel about you." He slid his hands around her small waist and pulled her closer again, so that her body was flush against his. “Even before we mated, Grace, I was more possessive and protective of you than I ever was of Jenny. She was a fraud and maybe I should’ve realized it earlier.”

“How could you? I would’ve assumed the same thing.”

“Maybe. But now we’re exactly where we’re meant to be. As fate intended. You’re mine, Grace, and I will love you and protect you as long as there is breath in this body.”

Tears spilled from her eyes and she nodded, cupping his face and tracing her fingers over his jaw.

“And I will do the same. I love you so much.” She stood on her tiptoes and pressed her mouth to his

“I want everything with you. I want a wedding, kids, the whole deal.”

“Yes.” Her gaze was wistful before it clouded and her lashes fluttered down. “I want all that more than you realize, but…we should wait on a wedding. It wouldn’t feel right with what’s going on.”

“With Larson?”

She nodded.

“Agreed.” He kissed her again, slowly, tenderly, a clear promise that they would marry someday when the time was right. “But for now, are you ready to head over to my parents’ and see everyone? Maybe officially announce we’re mated?”

“I like that idea.” She gave him a slow smile and traced her thumb over his mouth. “Though I might make a suggestion we stop by your apartment first… it’s on the way.”

“Is that so?” He nipped at her finger, liking the way she was thinking.

“Mmm.” She gave a breathy laugh. “I think a quick reminder of your duties to me as a mate could be in order.”

“Oh, sugar, I like those kind of reminders.” He slid his hand down to swat her bottom. “In fact, the sooner I can start proving my worth, the better.”

Her squeal of delight as they ran to her car was just the cherry on the top of his mounting happiness…

Oh, the big bad wolf…look at him run.

Jocelyn lifted her martini and took a sip, satisfaction coursing through her as smoothly as the vodka. She closed out of the email and set her laptop on the bed beside her.

That chilling message had gone out to the entire shifter community, not only in the United States, but all over the world.

Wanted for murder.

The email had been the equivalent of an old west Wanted poster—and Agent Larson's picture was plastered all over it.

Everyone in the shifter community was in a tizzy that such an upstanding citizen—a highly respected alpha—could be responsible for such a heinous, horrific slaughter of innocent people.

Though some were more innocent than others… Jocelyn took another sip of her martini and smiled. Perhaps Agent Larson had been driven over the edge after he'd learned the truth about his fiancée.

Alicia had come to Jocelyn months ago offering an alliance and help in any way possible to help find a cure for the shifter gene. Even though she was the daughter of an alpha, she'd never been able to merge her wolf side with her socialite side. In the end she'd chosen to fight for humanity, and the price, it seemed, was her life. She'd been an invaluable ally. It really was too bad she was dead now—leaving the earth looking as if she'd come out the business end of a meat grinder.

But who could've expected that Alicia would go behind her back and pair up with Andrew? The two had assaulted her niece in a bathroom, and that simply couldn't be tolerated.

You didn't mess with family. Jocelyn lifted her gaze to the framed picture on the far end of her dresser. Her sister Mitsy and husband Teddy—the parents of Grace and Aubree.

Jocelyn experienced a pinch of regret, but she pushed it aside. She'd made her choices in life, and she would have to live with them. Her family was either dead or had now shunned her.

She was alone. Again. This time thanks to Agent Larson's command.

Bitterness and hatred swirled through her blood, making a toxic thirst for revenge. And she *would* have it someday.

She'd realized after the experiments that she'd been aiming too high in trying to eradicate the shifter gene. The task was too massive—too expensive, at the very least. She needed to start small and grow. Eradicate the fucking mutants with slow thoroughness. Her plan had gone into action weeks ago and the consequences were already being felt.

Yes, the best way to eliminate the shifters was to start with the people who protected them. The P.I.A.

And Agent Larson would be the first to fall.

She took another drink of martini and closed her eyes. "Run, wolf... *Run*."

About the Author

Shelli is a *New York Times* Bestselling Author who read her first romance novel when she snatched it off her mother's bookshelf at the age of eleven. One taste and she was forever hooked. It wasn't until many years later that she decided to pursue writing stories of her own. By then she'd acknowledged the voices in her head didn't make her crazy, they made her a writer.

Shelli currently lives in the Pacific Northwest with her daughter. She writes various genres of romance, is a compulsive volunteer, and has been known to spontaneously burst into song. You can visit her at www.shellistevens.com and join her newsletter at www.shellistevens.com/contact.

He's going to show this wedding crasher just how dirty the outdoors can be.

Seducing Allie

© 2011 Shelli Stevens

Seattle Steam, Book 3

Allison Siegel is out to stop a wedding. With one of her best childhood friends about to marry a gold-digger, who wouldn't at least try to stage an intervention? Apparently, her *other* childhood bestie, Clint.

The minute Allie grew out of her sneakers and into her curves, Clint's hormones went ballistic. But she had eyes only for Ken, so Clint made himself scarce, even after the relationship fizzled. Now she's back, looking better than ever—and hell-bent on sabotaging Ken's wedding. So Clint knows he needs to do whatever it takes to head her off at the pass.

Kidnapped! Allison can't believe it. Now she's stuck in the Montana backwoods fending off nature's friends, and fighting a losing battle to resist Clint—the sexiest forest ranger on the planet.

Clint has big plans for Allie. Not only will he convince a city girl that she needs to embrace her inner nature freak, but he's going to prove there's sparks flying in more places than just the campfire.

Warning: This book contains a city girl out of her element, a forest ranger determined to keep her there, and a campfire seduction hot enough to melt more than just marshmallows.

Strike a match, light the candle…and fall into the spell.

Shadow of the Wolf

© 2012 Dana Marie Bell

Heart's Desire, Book 1

Christopher Beckett is from an ancient line of wizards, but with one aspect that sets him apart. His wolf. Right now that wolf is howling for a mate. Knowing it's only a matter of time before the wolf's needs override everything else in his life, Chris casts the spell all the Becketts have used to call their mates to them.

His wish list is short: She must be of a lineage at least as old as his own. And she must accept his wolf. When his mate appears, he realizes his list should have been one item longer.

Alannah Evans, a powerful witch of the Evans Coven, has no problem with Chris's wolf. It's the wizard part that sticks in her magical craw. Witches and wizards have always been at odds, so by rights, she and Chris shouldn't be striking sparks of attraction this bright. But Chris will not be denied, and gradually she finds herself trusting him—then falling into the fire of desire.

When it becomes clear an old enemy has targeted them both for death, Chris charges into a duel that could cost him his life. Or worse: Lana.

Warning: Product contains explicit sex, graphic language, magic, mayhem, and a wet, naked wolf shifter bearing hot chocolate. Mmm…chocolate.